Merry
Kissmas
to You

Merry Kissmas to You

JENNI JENNINGS

SCHOLASTIC

Published in the UK by Scholastic, 2021
Euston House, 24 Eversholt Street, London, NW1 1DB
Scholastic Ireland, 89E Lagan Road, Dublin Industrial Estate,
Glasnevin, Dublin, D11 HP5F

Text © Jenni Jennings, 2021

The right of Jenni Jennings to be identified
as the author of this work has been asserted by her under the
Copyright, Designs and Patents Act 1988.

ISBN 978 07023 1415 5

A CIP catalogue record for this book is available from the British
Library.

Printed by CPI Group (UK) Ltd, Croydon, CR0 4YY
Paper made from wood grown in sustainable forests and other con-
trolled sources.

1 3 5 7 9 10 8 6 4 2

www.scholastic.co.uk

For my nieces, Lily, Amelia, Amber and Daisy.
You are marvelous humans and I love you! x

Chapter 1

Tuesday 1st December

Robert

Milly and Sam came into view at the bottom of Millers Field high street, their heads bobbing as they hurried up the lazy snake of the hill, past restaurants and shops with twinkling fairy lights and Christmas displays in their windows. It was eight a.m. on a chilly Tuesday morning, but the light was so muted it could easily have passed for dusk. Still, it was the first of December, and even clouds like grey boulders weren't going to dampen Robert's Christmas spirit.

Robert Barlow stood beside the twenty-foot-high community Christmas tree in the middle of the high street, stamping his feet and hugging his arms round himself against the cold as he waited for his best friends to reach him. Some people thought it was strange for a guy to have two girls as best friends, but Robert liked getting the female perspective on things, plus they never judged him when he talked about feelings. A shiver rippled through his body; the only feelings he was experiencing right now were cold ones. He glanced up towards the Old Windmill sat at the top of the hill, as though surveying the town below, its static sails stark white against the moody sky; it looked like a painting.

Milly and Sam were late; not unlike the community tree, which was supposed to have arrived over a week ago – the school newspaper had run a *thrilling* expose on the scandal. Robert had noticed that Sam and Milly seemed less pumped about Christmas this year – usually a time when the three of them fully embraced their Christmas-nerd spirit – and so he had arranged to meet them here before school to try and kick-start their festive joy. After all, what better way to get the Yuletide juices flowing than being in the presence of an enormous Christmas tree!

Boxes of donated decorations had already begun to arrive, ready for the small army of Christmas elves who would turn up on Friday and try to make sense of the mishmash of festive ornaments, in advance of the big lights turn-on at Saturday's late-night shopping event. The tree would look like a thousand unicorns had vomited glitter all over it, but that was what made it unique; no other town could boast a tree that so embodied a 1970s disco diva.

Up and down the street, shopkeepers bustled out with A-boards displaying today's specials, calling greetings to each other, and the air was thick with the scent of bacon and coffee. Most of the shops had been showcasing Christmas displays for weeks already, but now that December was here, the festive vibe would ramp up significantly.

By the time Sam and Milly finally arrived, Robert's own festive vibe had begun to experience a slow puncture. He began to doubt himself; sure, his motives were good, but was a big tree really going to boost his friends' Yuletide mood? Maybe this was a rubbish idea. Milly especially had some pretty huge worries to deal with; he didn't want to be a "cheer up it might never happen" guy.

"You're late!" he said, with mock annoyance as he blew on his hands. "I've been freezing my *baubles* off here." He wondered if they'd pick up on his shoehorning a Christmas reference into a sentence.

"Woah," said Sam, grinning. "The first festive swear of December."

Robert's mood instantly reinflated. "You know the rules," he said. "From now until January first, the only swears allowed will be festive swears. So be prepared to jingle off and kiss my holly berries!"

"It's my fault we're late," said Milly, laying a carrier bag of tinsel against the trunk of the towering Norwegian spruce, like an offering. "I couldn't get Jasper out of bed this morning and Tara wanted some weird plait thing done to her hair that required a YouTube tutorial. Why do thirteen-year-old boys' bedrooms smell like gerbil cages?" She looked at Robert.

"Don't look at me!" said Robert. "My natural body scent is Lynx Dark Temptation," and he waggled his eyebrows mischievously.

Sam rolled her eyes. "How ironic that you're the pastiest white boy I know," she said, giving his rosy cheek a playful tap.

Robert frowned and pulled a comical sad face. Sam turned to Milly.

"Where was your dad?" she asked.

"He didn't get up in time. He was probably up late job-hunting."

Robert and Sam exchanged a glance but said nothing. Milly's dad had been made redundant nine months ago, and despite being at home every day, from what Milly said, it seemed like he was more absent now than he ever had been when he'd worked in the city.

4

Robert had known Milly for ever; their parents had been friends since before they were born. Milly's dad was affectionately known as the King of Christmas, due to his excess of seasonal goodwill and ostentatious festive front garden decorations. It had been said that the national grid had to boost power levels when Noel Parker busted out the Parker family yuletide display. But things being what they were, it looked like the King of Christmas – K.O.C. for short – was likely to sit this Christmas out.

Sam dumped the large cardboard box she'd been carrying down on the ground. The contents of the box jingled. "I hope they like black glitter," she said, peeling back the lid to reveal a jumble of tree decorations.

"Oh, yeah," Robert mused, bending to sift through the black baubles. "I remember your mum's style aesthetic last year was proper gothic-vamp chic."

"Sometimes I'm astonished that *I'm* the gay one," said Sam.

"What's your mum's *style aesthetic* this year?" asked Milly.

"Electric blue and cerise," Sam replied.

Milly raised her eyebrows and said: "Traditional."

"Now," said Robert, "I suggest that we bust out our festive wardrobes early this year, really give ourselves time to feel the jolly season." He studied his friends; Sam looked like she could be persuaded, but Milly's expression was distinctively bah humbug. "I am leading by example." He unzipped his jacket to reveal a navy-blue knitted sweater with a snowman on the front, complete with 3D scarf. "Whoop whoop! Sleigh bells ring, *are you* listening?"

Robert was a musician; he played bass guitar in a band and had a gift for cramming a Christmas song phrase into any conversation.

"It's like you enjoy the abuse," said Milly.

Robert knew she was referring to the teasing he would get at school, but he had a very high tolerance for bants.

"Oh, come on," said Sam, nudging Milly. "It's not that bad. All right, Commander Jolly Holly, I'll dig out my stuff tonight."

Robert grinned. Sometimes he wondered if it was normal for a seventeen-year-old boy to be this excited about Christmas. And then he thought, *You bet your candy canes, it is!*

"So, what do you think about this year's tree?" he asked. "Sniff that sprucey scent in. Oh, Christmas tree, oh, Christmas tree, how lovely are your branches!" he recited, grinning.

Milly gave a pantomime groan, but Sam grabbed Robert into a hug. "Ooh, you're just so *Elf*, I love it!"

Robert felt his cheeks get hot. He was pretty much over

the excruciating crush he'd nursed for Sam through the summer, but the memory of it was still vivid enough to make him blush when she got too close. Sam – to his knowledge – hadn't had the faintest idea that she'd ever been anything more to him than a bestie. For a while, when he'd had it really bad, he'd wanted to tell Sam – as if somehow she would realize she wasn't gay at all and would fall madly in love with him – but Milly had talked him out of it, and now he had come out the other side he was glad. It would only have made things awkward if she'd have known. He had a history of falling for unattainable women; it was his curse.

A bell tinged from the row of shops behind them and Cassia – queen of mean and generally fricking everything – stepped out of a little Italian deli holding a coffee in one hand and swinging a petrol-blue satchel in the other. A delicate robin hair clip nestled in her salon-perfect curls. Robert saw Milly tug self-consciously at her scarf. The mean-minions scuttled out behind Cassia, like a flock of wood pigeons.

"Good morning, losers," Cassia trilled. Her flock tittered. "Milky –" Cassia's *hilarious* nickname for Milly – "you look even paler than usual. Are you ill?" For all anyone knew, Cassia's natural skin tone might be exactly the same as Milly's, but it was impossible to tell after years of spray tanning had rendered her the colour of a baked bean.

Milly rounded her shoulders and tried to look smaller.

"It's the sight of you," said Sam sweetly. "You make her sick."

"I'm feeling a bit queasy myself," added Robert, feigning retching noises. It was a familiar routine; Cassia would make snide remarks towards Milly, because Milly was shy and rubbish at confrontation, and he and Sam would close ranks around her. It would take more than Cassia's sour face to unnerve Robert; he was one of ten children, so nothing short of a zombie apocalypse was liable to bother him, and even that probably wouldn't compare to the terror of the Barlow family at the all-you-can-eat buffet.

"Pathetic," snorted Cassia. She crossed over the road, the mean-minions at her heels. Miranda, who had joined Millers Field for the sixth form when her family had moved over from Canada, stumbled out of the deli, trying to balance her eco-bamboo travel cup and stuff her purse back into her oversized rucksack at the same time. She tripped on the uneven pavement and sloshed coffee on to the shoes of a passing businessman.

"Watch out!" he snapped, shaking the steaming liquid off his shoe. "Stupid cow!"

"Hey, easy!" said Robert. "She didn't do it on purpose."

But the man was already stomping off along the

road. Miranda's cheeks and neck were blotched with embarrassment. Robert stepped forward and took Miranda's travel mug, so that she could finish wrestling her large rucksack back on to her shoulders.

"Don't worry about him," said Robert. "He's just an a-hole!" He cupped his free hand around his mouth and shouted this last part down the street. The man didn't turn, just shook his head and carried on walking.

Miranda smiled. "Thanks, but you don't need to fight my battles."

"People shouldn't get away with behaving like that," said Robert.

"I'm Japanese Canadian," Miranda replied, as though explaining something to a small child. "You think I haven't been dealing with aggression like that my whole life? Trust me, that was tame."

"That doesn't make it OK," said Robert.

"No, but I've learned to choose when to fight back and when to leave quietly."

"I don't get it. He called you a stupid cow and you want to leave quietly?"

"Robert, I love you, but you don't get it because you're white," Sam chimed in. "The same rules don't apply if you're a person of colour. If you accidentally stand on someone's foot on the bus, *you'll* get tutted at. If *I* do it, there's a good chance someone on that bus is gonna tell me to go back to where I came from, even though I've never even been to India and nor has my mum. But it doesn't matter; you put a foot wrong, someone's going to use the colour of your skin against you."

Miranda nodded in fierce agreement and added: "So when some random guy shouts at me for throwing coffee on his shoe and *doesn't* insult me for being Asian, I'm going to quit while I'm ahead, thank you very much."

There was a moment of quiet and then Miranda joked: "And I don't even like coffee! I only bought it because Cassia said hot chocolate is immature." She rolled her eyes.

Milly, Robert and Sam all blurted: "What?!" at the same time in horrified disbelief – drinking hot chocolate throughout the season to be jolly was an integral part of the Christmas code of conduct – but their shock was cut short by Cassia's voice snapping out across the street.

"Miranda!" A flock of starlings rose up out of the bony trees, screeching in protest.

Miranda looked apologetically between Sam, Robert and Milly. Robert handed back the mug.

"Thanks," she said. "Sorry," and dashed across the road, dodging between the cars.

"We should really try to emancipate Miranda," said Sam.

"I'm not sure we'll need to," said Milly, watching Cassia shoot a death stare back at Miranda as she trotted up behind the rest of the mean-minions.

"How did she even end up with the mean-minions?" Sam asked. "I feel we should have made more of an effort when she first arrived; you know, got in there before Cassia got her manicured claws into her."

"I heard her mum's a buyer for Zara," said Robert. "I think Cassia was hoping for discounts."

"Figures," said Milly.

Robert's phone pinged and he quickly checked it. It was a like on a photograph he'd put up this morning of the Barlow family Christmas tree. The decorations looked as though they'd been hurled at the tree – which, in fairness, a lot of them had been – and it was a shocking mishmash of clashing colours with a serious lack of symmetry on every level. The like was from @secretgeek. Robert quickly tried to hide his smile and his phone, but it was too late, Milly had already clocked it.

"A like from @secretgeek, huh!"

"Ooh!" said Sam. "Let me see, let me see!"

Robert lifted his hand with the phone in up away from her, but Sam swung on his arm and Robert surrendered.

"So are you hoping for some Mrs Grinch encore photos this year? 'Tis the season to be pervy!" Milly teased.

"It's not pervy," Robert sulked.

"It is a little bit pervy," Sam chimed in.

"I appreciate her for her art!" said Robert.

"Yeah, right," Sam teased.

Milly affected a singsong voice: "@secretgeek, *oh my god that is awesome! You rock!*"

Sam joined in: "@secretgeek, *you're so talented you blow my mind!*"

"Eggnog off!" Robert laughed.

"Aww, don't be angry, my little Who of Whoville," pouted Sam, pulling him into a sideways hug. "We love you even though you fancy a chick with green skin and whiskers."

@secretgeek was a girl Robert had befriended on Instagram. Well, first of all he'd seen her at a comic book convention he'd attended with his brother Nemo last Christmas; she was dressed as Mrs Grinch, complete with green face and snout nose – Robert had confessed to Sam and Milly that he thought she was hot, and he had never lived it down. That day, most people were dressed as Thor or members of the Suicide Squad, but there she was, in the middle of all the superheroes – Mrs Grinch, like a beacon of Christmas in a sea of six-packs and ripped fishnet tights.

She was giving out business cards with her Instagram account on, and the rest, as they say, is history. She was an artist, and most of her posts were of her sketches and paintings of famous women from history in superhero form, like Suffragette Girl and Marie Curie Radioactive Woman, which were just insanely good. They'd PMed a lot over the last year, but for all he knew she could live in Antarctica. She never posted pictures of herself except for that one of her dressed as Mrs Grinch. Robert sighed inwardly - another unrequited love situation. Sometimes he felt like fate was on a mission to kick him right in the family jingle bells.

Milly

"So, Milly's talking about not going to the Christmas ball," said Sam.

Milly raised her eyes to the sky. *Here we go*, she thought.

"What?" Robert exploded. "Why not? This is our last big party of high school!" At Millers Field High, the Christmas ball doubled as the prom. In terms of milestones, it was up there with first kisses and getting your first bra.

"In case you hadn't noticed, we haven't had that many

parties at high school. We are not the sort of people who get invited to parties," said Milly.

"All the more reason to make this one count," Sam chimed in. "And as my mum keeps telling me, *This is a rite of passage, babes!*"

Milly snorted into her mittens. Sam was an excellent mimic.

"Although, of course, my mum got pregnant with me at her prom, so maybe don't follow her down that particular passage."

Milly and Robert pulled "Eek" faces.

The sixth form Christmas ball – technically the Magical Snow Ball by order of Cassia, who had commandeered leadership of the organizing committee – was only seventeen days away, and as it stood, none of them had dates. Usually that wouldn't have bothered Milly; historically, they would go to school events as a threesome. But there was something about this being their last year that made it feel like a bigger deal, like she'd be letting down her future self when she looked back and remembered she was Milly-no-dates.

"I've got nothing to wear," countered Milly. "I can't exactly ask my parents to fork out for a prom dress right now. And, you know, I'm not really that bothered."

As lies went, this was a whopper. Milly wished she wasn't bothered, but the truth was, though it went against her every feminist impulse, she yearned to have her moment in the spotlight. Despite herself, she fantasized about walking into a room in a dress fit for Emma Watson as Belle, to the sound of jaws hitting the floor all around the dance floor. Just once she wanted to feel like the swan instead of the tall, gawky gosling with clown feet.

"Mills, don't even," said Sam. "Not with us. We both know you are secretly uber-bothered about going to the ball."

"But we won't tell anyone," Robert added in a pantomime whisper.

"Maybe we could go anti-ball and wear onesies instead," said Sam.

"Christmas onesies!" added Robert.

This was just the kind of thing Sam would do; Milly knew she was dying to wear the prom dress she'd bought on a day trip to London with her mum, but she'd pass it over to wear a onesie if it made Milly happy.

"Or you can borrow one of my mum's dresses," Sam went on. Sam's mum was like the love child of *Made in Chelsea* and *TOWIE*. The spare room in their tiny terrace opposite the park had been turned into a walk-in wardrobe, with rotating shoe rack and handbag hub.

"Sam, your mum is five foot one, I really don't think her clothes are going to fit me."

"I'd say you could borrow one of my mum's dresses, but she's been mostly pregnant for like twenty years, so you know ..." said Robert.

"OK," Sam relented. "We can work on the dress thing. But that's no reason not to go."

Milly sighed and an extra-large cloud puffed white into the cold air. "I've got no one to ask."

"Oh no you don't!" said Sam. "You're straight, you've got nothing to complain about! You've got a whole sea of boys you can ask to be your date. It's slim pickings in the gay pool, let me tell you."

"It's not that bad, Sam," said Robert. "You could ask Sophie H, she's gay."

"She eats like a hamster," said Sam.

"So don't ask her out for dinner," Milly suggested helpfully.

"And anyway, just because she's gay, doesn't mean I've got to fancy her. That's like me saying you should ask out Stefan Peters because he's straight."

Milly grimaced. Stefan Peters had become notorious for sending girls unsolicited pictures of his body parts. "OK," she said, wincing. "Point taken."

"Come on," said Robert. "I think my trainers are starting to freeze to the tarmac and I can't afford another late mark."

They left the high street and cut down an alleyway, through a small wood, and then picked their way gingerly across the little wooden bridge – slippery with ice – over the stream running down from the Old Windmill Café – where Milly worked as a waitress – before emerging out at the corner on to Mile Road. The gothic building which housed the sixth form of Millers Field High loomed large in the distance, its grey brick mirroring the slate sky.

"I'm not finding Christmas so easy to love this year," Milly sighed, linking arms with Sam and Robert.

The pavement was glittery with frost this morning, and the friends' breath plumed out in front of them in clouds of white against the cold grey morning.

"Are you thinking the King of Christmas is just dragging his heels this year, or are we talking a total no-show?" asked Robert.

"Baubled if I know," Milly replied. "At the moment he's full 'head in the sand' mode."

Normally her dad was in full festive swing by now. When he'd first lost his job, having him around all the time had felt like a holiday; he made pancakes for breakfast and Mum joked that she wished it had happened years ago. They were all sure he would find another job before the redundancy money ran out. He hadn't. More and more these days, when her mum was on an early shift at the hospital, it was left to Milly to get her younger siblings ready for school, while her dad stayed in bed.

Robert gave her a sympathetic shoulder barge. "He'll come round," he said. "He's probably just struggling to find his festive mojo this year, with the job sitch and everything. Which is all the more reason for you to carry the Parker family Christmas spirit with you until he finds it ... starting with the Christmas ball!"

"Smooth, Bertram, real smooth," said Sam.

Robert ignored Sam's use of his familial nickname and said: "You have to go. The Indigo Tigers are playing a set. I need my groupies there to cheer me on and stop people throwing rotten fruit at us." All Robert's years of practising in the garage had finally paid off when he'd auditioned for the Indigo Tigers the summer before last and been taken on as their bass player.

"Oh my god, you got Cassia to agree!" Milly exclaimed.

"Yep. You know –" he made a show of running a hand through his dark wavy hair and cocking his head – "I think when it comes down to it, she respects me as a fellow artiste." Milly sniggered. "We're playing in between the DJ and the Glee Club, so you could say we're the main attraction."

"What a line-up," said Sam. "Don't worry, I'll be there;

ain't nobody gonna throw fruit at my boy, except me. Hey, we can do an Insta live stream!"

Robert smiled, and from the corner of her eye, Milly could see his cheeks flush from more than just the biting wind. Milly couldn't blame Robert for having fallen for Sam; who wouldn't be in love with Sam? She was smart and funny, and she never apologized for who she was, unlike Milly, who apologized for everything she was and all the things she wasn't as well.

"Whatever you decide, Milly, we'll have your back," said Sam, resting her head on Milly's shoulder.

"Abso-bauble-lutely," Robert agreed.

The three of them hurried, arms linked, along the busy road towards another day in the jungle otherwise known as high school.

Chapter 2

Sam

PSHE Lessons - short for Personal, Social, Health and Economic education, or in Sam's opinion: Personal Social Hell and Embarrassment - were held on Tuesdays and Fridays in tutor groups and took up the whole afternoon. Despite the often cringeworthy lesson content, Sam liked PSHE; she, Robert and Milly had all chosen different A levels, so these were the only classes they had together.

Ms Tibbott leaned against her desk and waited for the post-lunch hubbub to quieten down. Everyone liked Ms Tibbott; she was kind, and with her long, flowery dresses and hair piled up in a bun that looked set to topple at any moment, she always looked like she'd just stumbled in from a festival.

"So," she began, and the last whispers ceased. "I've got

an exciting announcement today. With this being your final Christmas at Millers Field, I thought we'd mix things up a bit in our PSHE space. From now until Christmas, I have arranged placements for all of you to help within specific areas of the community. You'll start them this Friday."

Sam felt her attention sharpen. She liked to get involved with things; she thrived on the feeling of being an instigator of change.

"Aww, miss," piped up Toby. "You're not going to have us out litter-picking again, are you?"

"No, not this time. Although litter-picking is a worthy pursuit." Ms Tibbott began to move around the room, handing out named envelopes to each student. "I have tried to play to all of your strengths and, where possible, even picked things for you that tie in with the career paths you've chosen to pursue. And for those of you yet to fill out your uni applications, these will look great on your personal statements. I want you to bear in mind that these are all for good causes, so I don't want to hear any moaning."

There was a *yip* of joy from across the room as Miranda read her assignment, immediately followed by a scowl from Cassia. Miranda had been unable to master the mean-minion glower, to Cassia's eternal consternation. Sam found their dynamic amusing to watch.

"Urgh, choir!" Cassia groaned exaggeratedly, letting her envelope slip to the floor. "Just kill me now!"

"Cassia, you have a lovely singing voice," said Ms Tibbott.

"*The Voice!*" Sam coughed. Across the room, Nadia let out a squeak of laughter and clapped her hands over her mouth. Sam scowled at Nadia but couldn't suppress her inward smile; *still some work needed there*, she told herself. Ms Tibbott shot Sam a look and Sam looked down at her notebook. Cassia had made a huge deal about being chosen for *The Voice*, only to find herself evicted before Battle Rounds stage. She claimed to have been unfairly dismissed from the competition after snogging one of the handsome co-producers. It may have been true, but Sam felt it more likely that Cassia just didn't make the grade and had said it to save face.

"Singing for old people!" Cassia scoffed as she read the details of her placement.

"You will be joining the Glee Club and choir and spreading Christmas musical joy around care and nursing homes," said Ms Tibbott. She wafted her arms in the air and performed a couple of impromptu dance steps, presumably to emphasize the Christmas musical joy.

"Great!" said Cassia, her voice nasal with contempt. "Singing for old people, who smell like wee and probably won't remember we've even been there."

"You'll be old one day," said Robert.

Cassia sneered at him. Sam's heart gave a little squeeze for her friend. Outwardly Robert might appear to let things bounce off him like Teflon, but she knew better. Robert's nan had moved in with his family last year when she'd been diagnosed with dementia. Sam had watched Robert struggle to come to terms with his nan not always remembering who he was or mistaking him for her long-deceased brother.

"Cassia," said Ms Tibbott. "I won't have unkindness in my classroom. Perhaps this placement will imbue you with some of the humility you seem to lack."

Cassia narrowed her eyes at Ms Tibbott's back as she glided over to Robert and laid his envelope down on the table.

"This should suit you down to the ground," she said.

Robert opened the envelope. "Oh great!" he said, his voice dripping with sarcasm as he turned his letter to show Sam and Milly.

"I thought you'd be pleased, working with pre-schoolers at the community centre. You're gonna find it hard to be a primary school teacher if you don't like working with kids," Sam observed.

"It's not the kids, the kids are fine. Look who I'll be working with!" Robert pointed to the names Miranda and Trinity at the bottom of the page.

Sam laughed and then smothered it when she saw Robert's expression.

"As MMs go, they're not the worst," said Milly.

"Although Trinity will probably have all the kids entered into a beauty pageant by the end of the week," said Sam.

They looked over to see Trinity applying lip gloss in the reflection of Miranda's glasses. Robert groaned.

"Do you think we ought to call them mean-minions?" Sam asked. "Is it a bit, you know, objectifying?"

"The thing is," said Robert. "They *are* mean."

"And they behave like minions," added Milly.

"We'll pick this up again later," said Sam. Though she had to agree with both their statements, her feminist senses were tingling; in a world that judged female presidents and prime ministers by their shoes, she didn't want to be part of the problem.

Sam's placement was with a local charity who put together Christmas gift hampers for refugee families.

"I know you've worked with this charity on other projects, Sam, so I thought you'd really enjoy this," said Ms Tibbott.

Sam got the impression that Ms Tibbott regarded her as an activist-in-training. If ever there was a rally to attend locally or a protest with regards to climate change or civil rights, Ms Tibbott would just happen to pass a flyer Sam's way.

"Thanks, miss," said Sam. Sam had volunteered at the charity over the last two summers; she wanted to be a human rights lawyer and had originally volunteered because it would look good on her personal statement for uni applications, but she'd loved it so much she'd kept going back to help out.

Of the three of them, Sam was the most driven. Robert thought this was because she was an only child and got one hundred per cent of the parental encouragement available. And while Sam accepted this was probably partially true, she knew that it was mostly the fire of ambition in her stomach that spurred her on. Miss Tibbott was right; she wanted the world to change for the better and she wanted to be one of the ones to do it.

Milly

Ms Tibbott handed Milly her envelope. "I thought this would help with your writing," she said. "It'll give you a real insight into circumstances that we don't often get to see!"

Ms Tibbott was very supportive of Milly's ambitions as a writer and championed her work whenever she could. It was Ms Tibbott who had encouraged her to start her blog: @off-centre-oddity. It wasn't attached to any social media platforms where people from school might find it; she wasn't a sadist. But the follows didn't matter; she liked that her words were floating about in the ether for people to find, or not. In her real life, Milly felt like she had no voice at all, but through @off-centre-oddity her voice was loud and clear.

Milly opened the envelope and her stomach dropped. *Oh no!* she thought. Suddenly it seemed as though the whole classroom was watching for her reaction. She felt her chest tighten.

"What's up with you?" asked Sam.

"Nothing," said Milly too quickly.

Robert peered over her shoulder at the letter. "Oh, mate," he said.

Milly raised her eyebrows and sighed.

It was Sam's turn to look. She pursed her lips. "We could ask to swap if you like?" she offered.

"It's no biggie," Milly lied. It was a biggie. It was the biggest biggie. Milly had been placed at the food bank on Millers Hill; the place her family had been relying on for their food this past two months. She kept telling herself she wasn't embarrassed about it, but she definitely didn't want the whole class to know.

"Look who you're partnered with!" Robert hissed, pointing to the name at the bottom of the page.

"Oh crap!" she breathed.

"I'll let that one pass because this is an extreme case, but in future consider saying 'oh cringle' instead," said Robert.

Sam poked him with her pen.

"Ouch!" he said. "Grinch-bag!"

Milly looked over to the window where Laurence Bashir – hottest boy in sixth form and possibly the world – was sat, and found him staring back at her. She flushed instantly. Laurence picked up his sheet of paper and waved it at her to signify he knew they were partnered, then dropped it back on to the table as Cassia parked her Kardashian backside down on his desk and began to talk animatedly at him.

Milly buried her head in her arms on the desktop. "Wake me up in January," she mumbled.

"Look on the bright side," said Sam.

"There is no bright side," came Milly's muffled voice. "There is only darkness. This is shaping up to be the Worst Christmas Ever!"

"You're always moaning that Laurence doesn't know you're alive," Sam said. "And, well, now that you're partnered with him, he's going to realize that you are *actually alive*!"

Laurence Bashir and Cassia had an on-off thing going on that lately had seemed much more off than on. He was popular and so naturally he hung out with the coolest people, of which Milly was definitely not one. But unlike many of his counterparts, Laurence was not unkind to those in the lower echelons of school society. He didn't seem overly interested in matters of social politics, although Milly reasoned that your social standing was likely to play on your mind a lot less if you were the one at the top of the ladder.

Robert

"So," Robert began, in an attempt to draw Milly out of her panic-brood. "It's late-night shopping this Saturday, who's up for it? I hear there's going to be a snow machine and the word on the Christmas street is that the reindeer corner will be making a comeback."

"Me," said Sam. "I'm up for it! I want to pet a reindeer; they're so cute!"

Milly grunted from beneath her hair, her head still clamped to the desk.

"I'm sorry, what does that mean?" Robert asked. "Grunt once for 'yes' and twice for 'no'."

Milly stuck two fingers up at Robert but grunted once to indicate that she was up for it. "I'm working at the Windmill," she mumbled into the desk. "I'll meet you after."

"There's only one teensy problem," said Robert. "Nadia is working in reindeer corner - she's my woman on the inside."

Robert saw Sam's mouth draw into what he had come to know as "the pout of doom" and he gulped. Sam and Nadia had been together for a few months and it hadn't ended well. Robert and Milly both knew that Sam was secretly still hung up on Nadia, but Sam would never admit it. It didn't help that they had to see each other each morning in tutor group. Sam had made ignoring Nadia an art form. When they'd split up, Robert had been deep into his whole unrequited love thing, and having Sam lean on him for heartbreak support had not helped to cure him.

Sam jutted out her chin in defiance. "It's fine," she said curtly. "It'll be the perfect opportunity for me to give her her Christmas present."

Milly raised her head off the table and peeled her hair away from her face. "You're getting Nadia a Christmas present?" she asked.

"I'm almost afraid to ask, but what kind of present were you thinking of getting?" asked Robert.

"A dog poo in a box," said Sam.

"A what in a what?" asked Robert.

"A dog poo in a box. Maybe with a black ribbon wrapped around it to match her black soul."

"I forbid you from giving Nadia a dog poo in a box," said Robert. "Wrapped in ribbon or otherwise."

"Cat poo then," said Sam.

Robert shook his head.

"Rabbit poo?"

"Sam!" said Milly.

"Oh, for Frosty's sake! Where's your inner Grinch?"

Ms Tibbott was back at the front of the class trilling enthusiastically about how these placements were chances to form great new friendships.

"You really have to admire her enthusiasm," said Sam.

"Somehow I can't see me, Trinity and Miranda forming a great friendship," said Robert.

"I should hope not," said Sam. "You're *our* geek and we're very territorial."

Across the room, Tom grabbed the paper out of Laurence's hand and read it, exclaiming loudly: "So, you and Milly Parker feeding the poor together! Sounds sexy!"

Cassia barked out a laugh. "As if!"

Milly looked as though she was actually trying to burrow into her desk while Laurence snatched the paper back, saying: "Dude, don't be such a loser!"

Robert suspected that Tom, like Laurence, had probably never worn a hand-me-down in his life. Most of Robert's clothes trickled down to him from his older brother. When he was younger his mum had even tried to palm him off with his brother's old boxer shorts, but Robert had drawn the line at wearing second-hand pants. It was an important victory in the Barlow household, as his mother never again tried to make her children share undergarments; Robert felt proud to be flying the flag for underpant autonomy. He had considered putting this achievement on his personal statement for his university application, but Sam had forbidden it.

The class quietened down and the rest of PSHE was taken up with Ms Tibbott giving an overview of each placement's function and the roles they played within society. Milly, Sam and Robert sat, each lost in their own thoughts as they contemplated the weeks ahead.

Chapter 3

Sam

Ten to five and it was already fully dark. The street where Sam and her mum lived was twinkling with fairy lights strung around shrubs and ornamental trees in front gardens. The glistening triangle outlines of Christmas trees glowing behind lacy net curtains was a vision of warmth on a cold evening.

Sam clicked the front gate open and bumped into her mum's boyfriend, Bill.

"Hello, Sam love," said Bill.

"Hi, Bill. You not staying for dinner?"

Bill looked back towards the house as if the answer might be strung up in the windows. "Not tonight, love."

"Are you all right?"

"Course I am, sweetheart," said Bill, forcing a smile.

"Right then, I'll be off." He looked back at the house again and Sam was sure she saw his shoulders slump. "I'll see you then." He gave Sam his signature wink, which Sam had grown to recognize as an endearment. Sam liked Bill. She often thought that if she could choose a dad, it would be him; she wouldn't know her own dad if he was stood in front of her.

Sam closed the door behind her. The air smelled of orange and cinnamon candles and Michael Bublé was crooning "It's Beginning to Look a Lot Like Christmas" out of the stereo; no Christmas in their household was complete without Mickey Boob. The black Christmas tree in the corner of the lounge – which Milly referred to as *a sexy tree* – was dripping with silver lights, electric-blue tinsel and cerise-pink glittery baubles; it was the Ru Paul of Christmas trees.

"I'm in the kitchen, babes!"

Sam found her mum, wearing her "Too Hot to Handle" apron and standing on tiptoe in her pink fluffy mules and leaning over a large, steaming saucepan of curry.

"Hi, Mum. Mmmm, that smells good."

"Nani Amaira's chicken dopiaza," she said.

"I just saw Bill."

"Did you?" said her mum with forced nonchalance.

"It's not like him to turn down one of your curries."

Her mum turned round, wooden spoon in hand. "He's got other plans tonight." She smiled too brightly.

"Have you two had a row?"

"No, no. Not exactly."

"What then?"

Her mum shook her head as though in despair. "He wants us to move in together."

This was the news Sam had been hoping to hear for the last two years. "That's great!" she said.

"Is it?"

"Isn't it?"

"I don't know if I'm cut out for playing happy families," said her mum. "And besides, it's you and me, babes, the Terrific Two for ever!"

"But it won't be for ever, Mum, I'll be going to uni next year."

"Well, if you go to Canterbury, you can still live at home."

"But what if I go to London or Nottingham?"

"You'll need a home to come back to in the holidays."

"Yeah, but the rest of the time you'll be by yourself. And I'm sure Bill won't ban me from the house in the holidays. I thought you liked Bill?"

"I do! I really like him. It's just. Oh, I dunno. We've never needed anyone but us. I don't want to give up my independence."

34

"He's here all the time anyway, so it makes sense for you to move in together. Bill knows you're a *very independent woman - you've* told him enough times!"

Her mum laughed. "True enough, babes, true enough."

"So what did you say to him, when he asked?"

"I told him it'd be a shame to spoil a good thing, but I promised to think about it."

They had always been the Terrific Two. Before Bill, there'd never been anyone else. Sam's dad hadn't been on the scene since she was a baby; she didn't even remember him. He and her mum had been high school sweethearts, but things went sour pretty fast when her mum found out she was pregnant. They'd given it a go but, in the end, Sam's dad just couldn't hack being a teenage parent. Sam could kind of understand it; she wouldn't want to be a parent yet. Her dad left, not just them but the whole area, started again somewhere new, where - Sam guessed - he could pretend he'd never had a kid. Her mum didn't talk much about it, but to say her dad hadn't been a nice person to live with was probably an understatement. Chats about her dad always ended with her mum saying that some things were for the best, and that it was better not to have a dad at all than to have one who didn't want to be there.

Her mum was fierce - in every way, especially when

it came to hers and Sam's relationship ... and shoes. But sometimes Sam felt that her mum had poured so much of her energy into the Terrific Two that she hadn't left any for herself. And ever since Sam had begun applying to universities, the weight of that responsibility had hung heavier on her mind. If her mum's fear of commitment drove Bill away, would Sam be able to leave her too?

Milly

"Did you tell your mum about your placement?" asked Sam.

Everyone else in the house was asleep and Milly was video calling Sam from beneath her duvet. Sam had her hair in a topknot and was wearing fleecy Disney pyjamas; she looked like she belonged in an Ariana Grande video.

"Yeah," said Milly. "I think she was kind of pleased about it, like me helping out at the food bank somehow makes up for us having to use it?"

"What about your dad?"

"God, no! He'd just use it as another stick to beat himself with. I'll let Mum tell him."

"Are you serious about not going to the ball?"

"I guess. There're too many obstacles in the way – it would be easier just to blow it off. It's not that much of a big deal really when you think about it."

"Come on, Mills, this is me you're talking to. Don't pretend like you haven't watched *The Prom* on Netflix like a hundred times, and let's not forget your guilty obsession with *High School Musical 3*! The Christmas ball is like all your prom dreams come true."

"Do you have to remind me how much of a dork I am?"

"I'm your best friend, that's my job. I am here to cut through any reindeer poop you might be trying to spin."

"I think my mum really wants me to go. She's worried I'll regret it if I don't, and I don't want to give her anything else to worry about."

"As always your mum is correct. And if neither of us finds dates we can go together."

"Maybe you could ask Nadia?" Milly suggested.

"Why would I ask Nadia?"

"Because you two still fancy each other."

"Puufrrruuh! I don't think so!"

"*I do* think so, and Robert agrees."

"Yeah, well, once bitten twice shy."

"It was *only* a kiss."

"Only nothing."

"Have you dropped any more mega hints to your mum about going to Nottingham uni?"

"My mum does not pick up on subtlety. Maybe I'll just pretend to go to Kent University but really I'll go to Nottingham; pop back every other weekend with a postcard or a fridge magnet of Canterbury Cathedral to cover my tracks..."

"Cos leading a double life is sooo much easier than just telling your mum you want to move away."

"Exactly."

"Chicken!"

"Mama Chowdhury is a complex woman. She wants me to be independent and dependent all at the same time."

Milly's computer screen began to bleep, and Robert joined the conversation.

"All right, biatches!" he grinned. "Just got back from band practice. What did I miss?"

"Bertram, we've discussed this. This is not *Mean Girls*, and we are not your biatches," said Sam.

"If anything, you're ours," said Milly.

"Don't encourage him," Sam chastized.

"Miranda sent me a message saying she was looking forward to working with me. What do you think that means?" Robert asked.

"That she's looking forward to working with you?" offered Milly.

"There must be more to it than that," Robert mused.

"She's probably just being friendly," said Milly.

"Or is it a trap?" asked Robert. "You know, lure me in with friendliness and then use it against me somehow with Cassia, to make me look an idiot."

"You don't need Cassia for that," said Sam dryly. "Robert, as always, you are thinking too deeply about this!"

Milly heard her dad's tread on the stairs and the door to her parents' bedroom open. She listened. The knot of sickness that had taken up residence in her stomach squeezed. *Maybe it'll be all right tonight?* she thought. But within moments, the familiar sound of hushed, muffled arguing began to seep through the wall.

"Are you listening?" Sam broke Milly's reverie.

"What? Sorry? No, I got distracted. What did you say?"

"I said, are you going to ask Laurence for a lift to the food bank?"

"No! Why would I do that?"

"Cos he's got a car and the food bank is across town?" said Robert.

"Can you even imagine what an uncomfortable journey that would be? What would we even talk about? No way, I'll get the bus."

Robert picked up his phone and his eyes widened. "Now Miranda's asked if I want to meet her outside the community centre. What do you think *that* means?"

This was greeted with groans and laughter from Milly and Sam. Sam threw a sock at the screen. The call ended and Milly pulled the duvet up around her chin. It was cold in the house. They were on heating rations; a quick blast in the mornings *to take the chill off* and then a couple of hours early in the evening. By nine o'clock it was properly chilly again, and by ten, everyone took to their beds to escape the cold. Milly uploaded her latest blog, pulled her dressing gown up around her ears and closed her eyes, imagining her words bursting out into the universe, waiting to be found like a message in a bottle.

@off-centre-oddity

To an outsider my family would look so normal – boring even – that no one would ever give us a second glance. Middle-of-the-road types, with a nice house and a garden big enough for a trampoline. Not at all the type of people anyone would expect to be relying on the kindness of strangers in order to eat.

But what is a type? Why are we so keen to slap labels on people?

I had never thought very deeply about food banks. I felt sorry for the people who couldn't afford to eat and had to use them. My mum would always pop a few extra bits in the trolley to leave in the food box outside the supermarket. I didn't have to think about food banks any more than that because I wasn't one of those families. Until I was.

Most people don't grow up thinking one day I'll need to use a food bank. That isn't how it happens. It isn't inevitable and it isn't anyone's fault. Life happens and sometimes that's where you end up. We are all only ever a step away from falling down. No one is immune; we are all the type.

Food banks should not be regarded as belonging to someone else's life. Food banks are a part of my normal, boring-looking family's life. I am so grateful to all the people who don't believe that food banks are somebody else's problem; from now on I'll be their type.

Sam

Sam brushed her teeth in the tiny bathroom filled with expensive beauty products. As she checked her face in the mirror, she noticed a spot the size of the North Pole growing on her chin. She opened the cabinet to get two cotton buds and the tea tree oil with her mum's wise spot advice ringing in her ears – "Never squeeze a spot with your nails, babes, it's a sure recipe for a breakout" – and stopped short; on the shelf next to the tea tree oil was a small bottle of pills with her mum's name on it. Sam picked them up. She couldn't remember the last time she'd looked on this shelf, but she definitely hadn't noticed any pills there before. Why hadn't her mum mentioned anything? The name was long and nonsensical, so she googled it. Beta blockers, apparently. She googled beta blockers – *To aid in the control of heart rhythm, high blood pressure and angina.*

Sam could feel her own heart start to race, and with trembling fingers, she replaced the bottle where she had found it. A hundred jumbled thoughts raced through her mind: Did her mum have heart problems? Did Bill know? Is that why Bill had asked her to move in with him? Was her mum going to have a heart attack? Was her mum going to die? And at the tail end of these thoughts came another, more selfish thought which darkened Sam's cheeks with shame even for thinking it; how can you go away to uni if your mum is sick? Sam's heart was secretly set on going to Nottingham Uni. She'd been trying to get around to discussing it with her mum, but the time was never right. She was starting to think the universe was on a mission to keep her tied to her mum's sexy-slogan apron strings.

As she climbed into bed – spot unpopped and pulsating – Sam wondered why her mum wouldn't confide in her about something as important as a heart condition. They were the Terrific Two, for baubles' sake! They didn't keep secrets. Although, apparently, they did. She could only think of one reason why her mum would keep something like this from her: because it was too serious for her to want to burden Sam with.

Sam fell into a fitful sleep and dreamed about being at the Magical Snow Ball with only her pants on and a paper plate to cover her boobs, while Nadia snogged a faceless boy in the corner by a Santa's grotto and Bill whirled her mum – who was lying in a hospital bed – around the dance floor by the bed rail, the *beep beep beep* of the heart monitors adding percussion to the Indigo Tigers set, while Milly swung on a trapeze above their heads.

Chapter 4

Wednesday 2nd December

Robert

Robert liked and commented on @secretgeek's latest Instagram post while he waited for the rest of the band to set up. He'd tuned his electric guitar and was plugged into the amp ready to rock; in this case, ready to Christmas rock. The Indigo Tigers were more used to covering Queens of the Stone Age than Slade, but a gig was a gig. He took a shot of the band setting up on the stage in the sixth form hall and uploaded it. Almost immediately he received a like from @secretgeek, followed by likes from Sam and Milly. Getting a like from @secretgeek could make his day; it was like biting into a KitKat and finding solid chocolate. Was it weird that he had a crush on someone whose only personal photograph was her with a green face and whiskers?

"Hi!"

Robert looked around and saw Miranda standing in the wings, stage right.

"All right?" said Robert.

"Are you excited about the placement?"

"I guess." Miranda was still looking at him, so he asked: "Are you?"

"I guess. I'm kinda nervous."

Miranda's Canadian accent was strong, and Robert liked the way it sounded. It seemed other-worldly compared to the variations of British accents all around them: almost musical.

"You'll be fine," he said brightly. He was finding it hard not to be distracted by her sweet half-smile. He wished the other guys would hurry up with their soundchecks. This conversation was Awkward As.

"So, you follow @secretgeek?"

Robert frowned. What, was she stalking him? Great, he was going to be stuck at placement with bunny-boiler-minion. "I do, yeah, do you too?"

"MIRANDA!" Cassia's voice cracked the air like a whip. Miranda jumped and scurried off into the darkness offstage.

The Indigo Tigers had permission to practise in the

sixth form hall after school. Cassia was busily snapping shots of herself in events-planner mode. Robert's news feed was filled with @cassiakeepsitreal; #somethingoutofnothing #someonesgottadoit #makingthemagichappen. She was prolific in creating social media content. Robert thought it ironic that the most fake person he knew had an account with "keeps it real" in her handle. Miranda caught up with Cassia, who began to bark out orders at her.

"BARLOW!" It was clearly Robert's turn to be yelled at. He made his way to the front of the stage and Cassia climbed the steps to meet him.

"I need a set list from you, stat!"

"OK." Robert nodded. "We haven't quite ironed out all the covers yet, but I can get a list of the definites to you tomorrow."

"Fine," said Cassia. "I don't want anything too tacky, OK? This is a big deal. Don't ruin it."

"Cassia, you know I can play."

"It's not you I'm worried about."

"They're a good band, I promise."

"They better be," she snapped and turned back down the steps. "I need that list by tomorrow," she called behind her.

They'd actually been friends in primary school – and even for a time after they'd started secondary school. But while

Cassia's social stock went up, Robert's remained static, and soon it was as though they'd never been friends at all.

Robert watched as Miranda scuttled along behind Cassia, feverishly drawing and making notes in her sketchbook. The rest of the mean-minions were tasked with hauling around large whitewashed boards and backdrops for Cassia to decide where best to place each one. Robert watched Miranda work, her hand flying across the paper as she translated Cassia's inspiration on to the page. From his position up on the stage, her sketches looked pretty good. She bit her lip as she drew and wrinkled her nose as she squinted towards where Cassia pointed.

He'd never really paid much attention to Miranda; she was just one of several mean-minions who tittered and pouted and nodded like pigeons when Cassia held court. He remembered being curious about her when she'd arrived at the start of sixth form, her accent setting her apart instantly from the regular newbies coming in from other schools, but within a week she'd been assimilated into Cassia's group and there wasn't much opportunity to get to know her after that. Plus, if Cassia was Miranda's idea of an ideal friend, then she probably wasn't his.

But then, when the band struck up, Miranda looked up at him and smiled, and it was so unexpectedly lovely that

Robert almost fluffed a chord. He shook himself mentally. *She must be buttering me up so I'll be her mate at the community centre,* he thought.

Practice went well. The lead singer struggled a bit with the highest notes on the chorus of "Don't Let the Bells End" by the Darkness, and Paul McCartney's "Wonderful Christmastime" needed a bit more work, but otherwise Robert felt they were in pretty good shape. Cassia and co had left after their first couple of numbers and Robert could feel his fellow band members relax at their exit.

Sam was waiting for him after practice. "You sounded pretty good," she said as they pushed through the double doors and into the cold evening. "I could hear your racket from the library."

"Thanks," said Robert. "How come you're here so late?"

"I had an essay to finish."

"Swot," said Robert.

"You won't be saying that when I'm a high court judge."

"I guarantee you, I will. No Milly?"

"She had to get back to sit with Tara."

"Where's her dad?"

Sam shrugged.

"In the house – but not present, according to Mills."

"Do you think she's really going to skip the ball?" asked

Robert. "You know she's been secretly dreaming about being Cinderella Barbie since she was five, right?"

"Yeah, I know. She's worried about the cost of getting a dress. I think she's trying to convince herself that she doesn't care."

"I'm not sure it's working. But you'll be there, won't you?"

"Are you nervous about the gig?" asked Sam incredulously.

"A bit, maybe. It's one thing playing at parties and village fetes, but being here... I don't know, I guess I just feel a bit exposed playing in front of our entire peer group. Does that make sense?"

"Perfect sense. Of course I'll be there. But I'll be dateless, so you'll have to dance with me when you've finished being a rock star."

There was a time when the very idea of slow dancing with Sam would have caused Robert to break out in hives. Now, though his heart still beat a little faster, it was a relief to finally be on the other side of his unrequited love obsession for her.

"No worries," he said casually.

"Unless you've got a hot date lined up?"

"I mean, I don't like to brag but I've had a lot of offers," said Robert. "In fact, I've been having to beat them back with a large candy cane. But I'll ignore the sounds of their breaking hearts because you need my dancing skills." He busted out an awkward moonwalk as he said this.

"You're a true friend, Bertram."

"I know."

"Come on then, you can walk me home."

"Gee, thanks."

"Mum made you a doggy bag of pakoras last night. I forgot to bring them to school, but you can pick them up now instead."

"What are we waiting for?" said Robert, picking up the pace. Ms Chowdhury's pakoras were legendary. Luckily for him, she thrived on feeding people, and Robert was only too happy to be fed. He was already planning on eating most of the pakoras on his way home and hiding the rest in the bottom of his wardrobe; the Barlow siblings were like a cross between bloodhounds and gannets where food was concerned.

Milly

There were multiple strings of angst tugging at Milly's brain at the moment and all of them seemed to be yanking in different directions. She hardly knew which worry to obsess over first. Her usual list of worries: too tall, too thin, no boobs, invisible to boys, Cassia being a cow, exams, university, future career, global warming and zombie apocalypse had been added to lately by more pressing concerns: the K.O.C. going AWOL, Mum going into some sort of happy-happy tailspin, no dress for the Christmas ball, no date for the Christmas ball, one black hair discovered by left nipple. And now this: working twice a week at the food bank with Laurence Bashir. LAURENCE BASHIR! And all the unthinkable possibilities for further social mortification this presented. What if the people at the food bank recognized her? What if they said: "Oh, Milly Parker! How did you enjoy your last food box? Were those economy beans OK?" She could just imagine Laurence laughing about it with Cassia afterwards.

Milly had helped her mum to prepare the spaghetti bolognese, and they all sat round the table to eat. Mum was too bright, as if her forced enthusiasm could mask Dad's gloom.

Jasper answered questions about his day in a series of monosyllabic grunts. Milly wondered when he'd gone from being her dopey younger brother to a sullen, greasy-haired grump. Only Tara seemed oblivious to the uneasy atmosphere, as she chatted about spelling tests and unicorn glitter.

"I've been looking online for dresses, Milly," said Mum. "You know, you can pick up a decent second-hand one really

51

cheaply. And if it needs a bit of adjusting, I'm sure it won't be anything Nan can't handle."

"Thanks, Mum. But I'm still not sure I want to go."

"Really? I would have killed for them to have a ball at my school!"

"It's just so much hassle, and it's not like I have anyone to go with anyway."

Her brother snorted his derision.

"Go with Robert," said Mum.

"Poor Robert," Jasper mumbled. Milly kicked him under the table. "Ouch!" he grumbled. "Cow-bag."

"Enough," said Dad quietly.

"Mum, I don't think Robert wants to be the consolation prize."

Milly knew that Robert would go with her if she asked, but that wasn't the point. Besides, she clung to the hope that someone would spot how awesome her best mate was and fall for him so he had a proper date.

"But you've got to!" said Mum. "You'll regret it if you don't. And anyway, you need to go so that you can look back at the photos when you're old like me and wonder where it all went wrong!" She laughed, but it was cut short as Dad let his cutlery clank on to the plate and left the table.

"Noel!" she called after him. "I didn't mean ... I wasn't

saying. . ." But Dad had disappeared into the study and closed the door. The study was where her dad spent most of his time these days; hiding away from his family – or so it felt to Milly – only venturing out when nobody was around, like a ghost. His low mutterings as he spoke into his mobile phone on the other side of the study door were often the only indicators that he was home at all.

And so ended another uncomfortable dinner in the Parker household.

Sam

Robert left with a small tub of pakoras, but not before Sam's mum had made him sample a bowl of warm saag aloo.

"To keep you warm on the walk home," she'd said. "But don't spoil your dinner – I don't want your mum calling me up to complain that you're too full to eat your tea."

They'd all laughed at that, even Bill; it was common knowledge that Robert's stomach was a bottomless pit. He was like one of those cats that goes from house to house, scrounging treats, even though he is perfectly well fed at home.

Robert was tall – though not as tall as Milly – with a mop

of curly brown hair that was forever dropping over his eyes. He was good-looking, but he didn't seem to know it, and he goofed about so much that most other people didn't notice either.

Where Sam and Milly had had an unconventional beginning to their friendship – they had bonded after an excruciating cross-country mishap in year eight, which saw Sam headbutted by an angry cow and Milly, in her haste to avoid the same fate, fall backwards over a small hillock into an enormous pile of cow poo – Robert had won Sam over with his easy-going manner, his complete disregard for fads and his fearlessness in the face of peer pressure.

Sam had been relieved when she'd come home to find Bill helping her mum in the kitchen.

"Your mum tells me you're going to be volunteering for the refugee Christmas charity," said Bill, laying out black sequinned placemats on the table.

"Yep," said Sam. "I start on Friday."

"I'll have a chat with the guys at work, see if I can get some donations."

"That would be great, thanks."

When they were settled at the table and Mum had brought over the leftovers, ready for seconds, Bill said: "I've been meaning to have a chat with you both."

Oh, baubles! thought Sam. She saw her mum tense and fiddle with the strap on her diamante bracelet.

"We've spent the last two Christmases here, and they've been great. So, this year, I thought I'd like to share the love and have you both over to mine instead."

Sam eyed her mum. They'd never had a Christmas anywhere else. The silence was growing uncomfortable. Sam looked at her mum imploringly. *Say something! Don't just leave him hanging!*

After another minute of listening to the clock ticking and the dull mumblings of next door's TV, Mum finally spoke. "Well, Bill, you've taken me by surprise there! It's an interesting offer..."

"I'm asking you to spend Christmas Day with me, not laying down a business proposal," laughed Bill.

"We can spend Christmas Day together here," said Mum brightly. "You don't need to put yourself out."

"I'm not putting myself out, Nish," he said. "I'd like you and Sam to spend a couple of days at my place over Christmas."

"A couple days now, is it?" said Mum, arching a sculpted eyebrow.

"Well, I thought you could come over on Christmas Eve and maybe stay till Boxing Day, or whenever you like. I'd love you to stay longer but I don't want to push my luck."

"I think it sounds really nice, Mum," said Sam.

Mum shot her a look as though she'd just thrown her dinner out of the window.

"It'll be fun!" Sam went on.

Bill smiled. "Sam's on board," he said. "What do you say, Nish? Let me treat you for a change. I've never had a proper family Christmas in my house, so you'll be doing me a favour, making some memories at my place that aren't just of me!"

Wow, he's really trying to sell it, thought Sam. *Come on, Mum, give the guy a break!*

"Well," said Mum. "It's ... I will certainly think about it. I just have to check a few things ... but I'll say a tentative yes. Thank you."

"I'll take a tentative yes over a flat-out no, any day," said Bill giving Sam a conspiratorial wink.

He really was a keeper, Sam thought. If only her mum could see it!

Milly

Milly sighed and turned over in bed. The moon shone through the curtains, full and perfectly round. *What am I going to talk about with Laurence at the food bank?* she wondered. They would have to say something to each other if they were going to be working together. Milly's total panic of saying something stupid in front of someone popular generally made her say something stupid. Her usual strategy was to let Sam and Robert – who had more than enough to say – deal with the vocals while she did her absolute best to stay invisible.

But Sam and Robert wouldn't be at the food bank with her. And it wasn't only Laurence's coolness that was freaking her out. Laurence was the guy of her dreams. Laurence was, she suspected, the guy of many girls' dreams. He was taller than Milly, which was a huge plus, and he had these big, sparkling brown eyes and ... oh, that smile! It was the friendliest, warmest, most Hollywood smile she had ever seen. His Middle-Eastern heritage – on his dad's side, which she knew from parents' evenings – had blessed him with olive skin and dark, shiny hair, which fell over one eye when he looked down. She conjured his image in her mind and let out a wistful sigh. *Stop it!* she berated herself. *He is out of your league, Milly. The best you can hope for is that you don't get the horror-hiccups or vomit on his designer shirt if he speaks to you!*

Laurence

Laurence's double bed faced the large picture window. In the winter, he didn't bother closing the curtains at night, so he could lie in bed and look out at the stars. Tonight, the moon was bright against the coal-black sky. He wondered if his brother had any kind of view from his window. He couldn't think about it, it made him too sad. The lump in his throat felt like he'd swallowed a golf ball, and trying to not cry made his head pound. He thought about something else.

He was a bit nervous about volunteering at the food bank. He didn't know what to expect. Laurence had never had to think about where his next meal was coming from, and in some ways that made him feel a bit guilty. Of course, it wasn't his fault that his family had money, but sometimes it made him feel removed from his friends; he couldn't relate to their lives and it made him feel like he had to apologize for his own. His dad had wanted him and his brother to go to a fancy private school somewhere near Hastings, but his mum had put her foot down; she wanted her children to go to state school and experience *real life*.

Laurence thought about Milly Parker, the girl he'd be working with. Funny how he'd known her since year seven and yet they'd never really talked; he guessed they'd have to start now.

Though it pained him to admit it, he'd never given Milly, or anyone not directly in his circle, much thought until recently. School had pretty much been one long party for him; he was one of the most popular guys at Millers Field High and he knew it – everyone either loved him or wanted to be him. People looked up to him, and when they saw him and Cassia together, he knew they saw them as *life goals*. It had felt good for a long time; so good he could easily drown out the nagging voice of his conscience. But since the trouble with his brother, all that popularity, all those admiring glances, felt kind of hollow. What was it all for? And all the jokes he'd let slide at other people's expense, all the snide remarks that came out of Cassia's mouth which he'd laughed along with, telling himself they didn't do any harm – they were *just bants* – suddenly felt heavy on his chest. His smug contentedness had worn thin and left him hungry for something more fulfilling. Perhaps working at the food bank with shy Milly Parker was the change of perspective he'd been searching for. Maybe it would sweeten the bitter sadness that had become his constant companion these last few months.

Chapter 5

Milly

On Thursday, the posters for the Christmas ball went up and the atmosphere in the sixth form common room kicked up a notch. Suddenly all the talk was whether a bias cut or a body-con gave better shape, and if hair up or down was hot this season.

The flirting went next level too, as everyone who didn't already have one in the bag hunted out potential dates. Even the super-scholars – serious girls who looked down their noses at literature written after 1901 and knew what the Higgs boson particle was – seemed to have decided that the Christmas ball was their time to shine. There was, Milly noted, a sense of this being a chance to throw off the shackles of your assigned pigeonhole and show the other groups what they'd been missing. It was a tempting thought. Milly had always loved those transformative moments in movies where the plain girl walks down the stairs in a killer dress and mouths fall open with audible gasps, like Hermione at the Yule Ball in *The Goblet of Fire*, or when the invisible girl is suddenly seen, like Lara Jean in *To All the Boys I've Loved Before* – though with Milly's luck she'd end up covered in pig's blood like Carrie in, well, *Carrie*.

It felt like Cassia had commandeered all forms of social media and saturated them; TikTok, Instagram, YouTube and Snapchat were awash with pictures and stories relating to every aspect of the ball, as well as her sudden ascent to being lead singer of the Glee Club, which until Tuesday she would have avoided like supermarket own-brand coffee. She had taken to finishing every post with #entrepreneur #influencerswanted #eventplanner #nextbigthing #teeninfluencer.

The common rooms, a series of converted attic rooms, which ran the length of the sixth form building, were a hub of activity; anyone with the smallest amount of crafting talent was put to work. No one could deny that with Cassia in charge, corralling people into service, the job was going to get done and get done well. The smell of paint pervaded as large wooden screens were decorated with scenes of frozen landscapes, and a fabric backdrop the full width of the hall was being painted in sections to show a snowy castle in the mountains.

Milly and Sam were on paper-chain duty. Sam flopped back on to the threadbare sofa, a python-like coil of looped paper covering her feet and one side of the chair.

"I can't do any more," she said. "I ran out of spit half an hour ago. I think my tongue is swelling up."

"Don't expect sympathy from me," said Milly. "My blood levels are ninety per cent paper glue." She threw herself back next to Sam.

Laurence walked past laughing with Tom and Ethan. Milly tried to melt into the sofa cushions. She'd thought she was safely hidden until Laurence looked back and said: "See you tomorrow at the food bank."

Milly tried to sit up but the springless sofa had half swallowed her and she ended up waving her arms and legs like a daddy-long-legs, and what came out of her mouth was a strangulated, "Ooop, yep, cool beans!" which she finished with a snorty squeal that sounded like a pig having its tail pulled. Tom and Ethan exploded into laughter. Laurence looked at her quizzically and gave a half wave.

"Er, yeah, right," he said and walked through to the next common room.

Milly heard Ethan, still laughing, shout, "Man, what a loser!"

"Oh god!" moaned Milly, pulling the paper chains over herself so that she was completely covered.

"As your best friend, who adores you unconditionally, I have to say, you did yourself no favours there, Mills," said Sam.

"I panicked! That's what panic does to me."

"But cool beans? Is this like one of those Christmas change-up movies? Have you switched places with a thirty-nine-year-old dentist who never left home?"

"I don't know where it came from," said Milly from behind her hands. "I go full dork under pressure."

Robert came up to the common room after his French lesson and dutifully picked up the paper chains and began to lick and stick.

"When do Flory and Nemo get home?" asked Sam.

Everyone in Robert's family had a nickname; it was a thing his parents did. Each child got named at birth for the official records but then soon after were given nicknames, and their real names were only ever used when they were in really big trouble. Robert's nickname was Bertram.

"Nemo's back from uni on Thursday but Flory doesn't fly in until the nineteenth," said Robert. Flory was one of

Robert's many sisters. She was in the army, currently working in Estonia.

"Have you had to give up your room?" asked Milly.

"Yeah. I'll be sharing with Dot and Curly. It could be worse: Toast sings in her sleep and Spider sleepwalks. She woke up in Nan's bed the other morning."

"How is your nan?" asked Sam.

Robert shrugged. "She has good days and bad days. She likes having all the kids around. She doesn't know who half of them are, but she likes them anyway."

"I don't know who half of them are and I've known you all my life," said Milly.

"Why did your parents bother with actual names if they only call you by your nicknames anyway?" asked Sam.

"Would you want the name Widget or Toast on your passport?" Robert replied.

"Fair point," Sam conceded.

Miranda and Trinity walked through the common room arm in arm.

"Does Cassia know they're out by themselves?" Sam whispered.

"Hi, Robert," said Miranda, coming forward to perch on the edge of an armchair. Trinity pursed her lips and remained at a safe distance in case uncool was catching.

"All right?" said Robert.

"First day of placement tomorrow. Are you ready for it?"

"Um, I suppose so, yeah."

"So, can I meet you outside, before we go in? I'd feel better not going in by myself."

"What about Trinity?"

At hearing her name, Trinity rolled her eyes disdainfully.

"Oh, well, Cassia wanted us all to be with her in the choir, so Trinity asked Ms Tibbott if she could change."

"But you didn't?"

"No." Miranda gave a swift, nervous look in Trinity's direction. "I wanted to help at the community centre." She bit her lip and looked hopefully at Robert.

"Oh. Right. Sure then, no worries," said Robert. "I'll meet you outside the centre at one o'clock?"

Miranda's face broke into a broad smile. "Great!" she said, jumping up from the chair. "Thanks. Things are always so much better with a friendly face beside you."

Robert watched them leave. "Have you ever noticed how nice Miranda's smile is?" he asked.

Sam

Sam flopped back on to her teddy fleece pillows. Robert and Milly's faces looked out with concern from her laptop. Her mum was downstairs watching *First Dates*. Bill hadn't been over, and from her mum's evasive manner, Sam guessed they'd had another *discussion* about moving in together.

"How long have they been seeing each other now?" asked Milly.

"Two-and-a-half years."

"Do you think not moving in with Bill would be a deal-breaker for him?" asked Robert.

"I don't know. I hope not. I like having him around. It feels kind of like I imagined it would be to have a dad, ya know? Although obvs I'd never tell Mum that."

"Obvs," agreed Robert.

"Even stupid stuff, like us all sitting on the sofa eating popcorn on a Saturday night watching *Strictly*, it feels nice. And he makes Mum laugh."

"Does he want you guys to move in with him or would he move in with you?" asked Milly.

"I don't know. Mum wouldn't really talk about it. I don't think we'd move in with him, though. She'd either make him move in here or they'd pool their resources and get a place together with prenups drawn up in case it all went tinsel-up."

"His place probably wouldn't be big enough to house your mum's shoe collection anyway," said Robert.

"She will NOT compromise on wardrobe space," Sam agreed.

"Have you had a chance to talk about uni yet?"

"Nah, the Bill stuff has sort of got in the way."

"Or are you avoiding it?" asked Robert.

"I guess a lot depends on if Bill splits up with her over this moving-in stuff. I can't very well say, 'Hey, Mum, I know you just got dumped but I'm also planning to leave you. See ya!'"

"You can't not go to Nottingham just because you're worried about your mum. It's not fair on you," said Milly.

"Yeah, but we're the Terrific Two! I can't just leave the band and let her be the Woeful One."

"Do you think that your mum thinks that *you're* the one who will be upset if *she* is the one to break up the Terrific Two by moving in with Bill? While all the time *you* think that *she'll* be upset if *you* break up the Terrific Two by going away to uni? So then *neither* of you is doing what each of you would like to do for fear of upsetting the other?" asked Robert.

"Huh?" said Milly.

"Bertram, I don't know what you just said, but if you put

it in writing for me, I'll decipher it and get back to you on it tomorrow. Ooh, speaking of tomorrow, Mills, how are you feeling about food-banking with Laurence?"

Milly gulped audibly, a proper cartoon gulp. "You know how I get when I'm nervous."

"Fear-farts?" asked Sam.

"Yup."

"Terror-tinkles?" asked Robert.

"Every time I think about it," agreed Milly.

The term "terror-tinkles" was coined by Milly's mum many years ago to explain Milly's excessive use of the toilet when she was nervous. The fear-farts were self-explanatory. She also suffered from the horror-hiccups, which were guaranteed to arise at the most inopportune moments.

"Thank god you didn't take up his offer of a lift!" said Sam.

"You'd have had to drive with the windows down," added Robert.

"It's not funny," Milly groaned. "Why is my body always trying to sabotage me?"

"I sneeze when I drink anything fizzy," Sam offered helpfully.

"My feet smell like cheesy popcorn in smart shoes," said Robert.

"That's a cute thing," argued Milly. "The sneezing, not your popcorn feet, Bertram, that's just gross!"

There was a knock at Sam's bedroom door and her mum came in with a mug of hot chocolate topped by a small mountain of pink and white marshmallows. She saw Robert and Milly on the screen and bent down. "Hello, my darlings, how are you?"

"Fine thanks, Ms Chowdhury," Robert and Milly chimed in unison.

"Oh, you two, when are you going to start calling me Nish? I think I've known you long enough now to drop the formalities. And what are you three Macbeth witches cackling about this evening?"

"Milly's fear-farts," said Robert, without missing a beat.

Milly flushed. Sam snorted into her hot chocolate.

"Oh, babes," Sam's mum sympathized. "You still struggling with them? I know what it's like to be a slave to your lower intestines. Have you tried peppermint tea? It works absolute wonders for my IBS..."

"Eweeee, TMI, Mum!" Sam yelped.

"Bodily functions are nothing to be ashamed of," said her mum.

"Yep, thanks for the hot chocolate, Mum, love you!"

"Oh, all right, I can take a hint. Goodbye, my darlings!"

she trilled and wiggled out of the room, her pink fluffy mules flapping as she went.

"Close your mouth, Bertram," said Sam.

"Your mum is hot, though," he replied.

"Bertram, stop it!" squealed Sam. "And anyway, your fantasy is a girl dressed as Mrs Grinch; you are not exactly a good judge of what is hot."

"No, I think Robert's right, your mum is probably the hottest mum we know," admitted Milly.

"What a claim to fame," Sam groaned.

There was a ferocious banging on the door to Robert's bedroom.

"What the fir trees?" said Sam.

"Is there an earthquake?" asked Milly.

Robert came close up to his laptop, so that mostly just his mouth and nostrils filled the screen. "Worse!" he whispered.

Sam and Milly leaned closer to their screens as Robert's bedroom door slammed open and several holdalls flew through the air, one of them knocking Robert sideways off the bed.

"BERTRAM!" yelled a deep voice, before a bear of a man in sweatpants and hoodie jumped on Robert and began feverishly applying a noogie to the top of his head. "I've missed you, loser!" he yelled, planting a big lip-smacky kiss on Robert's forehead. Then, seeing the laptop on the chest of drawers, and Sam and Milly looking out of it at him, he leaned over and grinned at them. "Sam, Mills, how *you* doing?"

"Hi, Nemo," said Milly. "How's uni life?"

"Ah, you know, parties and chicks, chicks and parties!" He winked.

"You are so gross," said Sam. "Do girls actually fall for your macho BS?"

Nemo laughed and threw an arm round Robert, pulling him close into his side. Robert looked small in comparison to his brother, his dark hair still standing on end from its recent noogieing but he didn't seem unhappy to be being squeezed by Nemo. In fact, Sam thought he looked goofily happy to have his big brother home and she felt a pang of longing.

"More than you might imagine," Nemo grinned. "And now, if you don't mind, ladies, I've got to evict my little brother from his bedroom. Say bye, Bertram!"

"Bye, Bertram!" Robert beamed into the camera and the screen went black.

"I envy him sometimes," said Sam. "Having all those siblings for company."

"I guess the grass is always greener."

"Guess so."

***

Sam lay in bed flicking through the Nottingham University prospectus she kept hidden under the mattress. What was she going to do? Should she give up on this dream? Her mum had given up plenty for her, so wasn't it only fair that she should be prepared to give up something in return, especially with this heart thing going on? Sam had been dropping massive hints to her mum that she knew about it and left gaping gaps in the conversation for her mum to fill in the truth, but her mum would not be drawn. Maybe she should talk it over with Milly and Robert. But would that be disrespectful to her mum? She sighed. She'd still go to uni, she'd just go to the closest one. She could still have a university experience, and there was a lot to be said for staying at home; think of all the money she'd save. But no matter how much she tried to reconcile it, deep down she felt like she was settling. When she laid it out in its simplest terms her choices were clear: break her mum's heart (possibly literally) or break her own.

Chapter 6

Friday 4th December

Laurence

Laurence came down the final flight of the sweeping staircase at 7.30 a.m. to find his mum on the half landing, wrapping the bannisters with fresh ivy from the garden.

"Good morning, darling!" she trilled.

"You're starting early," observed Laurence. The thick carpet was soft and bouncy beneath his bare feet, but the draught from the huge stained-glass window, which ran the depth of the hallway, blew cold around his ankles. That was the problem with big, old houses: draughts.

"Your dad's got a Christmas mixer tonight, lots of important people coming, so everything has to be just right."

"Can't let the side down," said Laurence. "Wouldn't want anyone thinking we weren't perfect."

Laurence's dad was a barrister, quite an important one by all accounts, and that meant putting on a show at Christmas – it would be cocktails, canapés and butt-kissing the "right people" through till the twenty-fourth. Laurence hated it. He hated that his home wasn't his own at a time when everyone else seemed to be hunkering down with their family and enjoying the festive season.

He hated that he was on show, like some sort of prize racehorse. And he hated the snobbery that simmered beneath all his father's intimate gatherings. Laurence had always disliked his father's *mixers*, but at least he'd had company with his misery; this year he would be suffering them alone.

As he passed his mum, she let go of the greenery she was holding and took him by the shoulders, kissing his forehead and smiling at him. "Have you contacted your brother?" she asked quietly.

"I messaged him last night."

"Good," she said, and Laurence could see that beneath the bright exterior she was on the edge of tears. "He needs to know that he's still a part of this family, even though he can't be here in person."

"Has Dad spoken to him?"

His mum let go of her hold on his arms and went back to her ivy. "Not yet," she said. "He just needs a little time."

"It's not really about what *he* needs at the moment, is it?" said Laurence.

"Don't be too hard on him. Let's not forget your brother's part in all this."

"As if any of us would ever be able to."

Laurence reached the bottom of the stairs, crossed the parquet floor of the entrance hall and carried on down a hallway that led to the kitchen. He glanced in at the dining room as he passed by. His father was sat at the table, the *Financial Times* obscuring most of his face, the toast in the rack beside him untouched. Laurence made to move quietly on his way, but the large paper lowered, and his father's steely gaze landed on him.

"Ah, Lou, there you are. I've got a mixer tonight, and I'll need you to show your face, so make sure you're in and for god's sake make sure your shirt is ironed."

"Good morning to you too, Dad," said Laurence.

"Don't start, Laurence, I've got a hell of a day today. Now listen, we're holding a formal Christmas party week after

75

next, black tie. You're welcome to bring a guest – someone suitable."

"Someone suitable?" Laurence asked.

His father stared at him. "You know what I mean. Don't make me out to be some sort of snob."

"Aren't you?"

"I don't want to fight with you, Laurence. There are going to be some important people coming and I'd very much like for you to join us. I know that these things make you uncomfortable, which is why I am happy for you to bring a guest. All I ask is that she doesn't have multiple tattoos and piercings."

"I don't understand why that would make them *unsuitable* company," said Laurence. He didn't want to start the day on a fight with his dad, but his dad consistently said impossibly ignorant things that made him angry "So I can bring a racist bigot but as long as she's dressed *suitably,* that's fine? It's so superficial, Dad, can't you see that?"

"Why not bring Cassia? I've invited her uncle; he's a local counsellor. It could help to grease the wheels for a new building project I'm trying to push through with some colleagues if you invite his niece."

"I'm not with Cassia any more, Dad, and I don't want to be any part of your *greasing the wheels.* It's not exactly ethical, is it?"

"Your idealism is admirable, Lou, but you will learn that it doesn't always translate so easily into the real world." His dad shook the paper and addressed him from over the top of his glasses, which rested halfway down his nose, in a manner which Laurence suspected he used to address defendants in the courtroom. "And if you want *superficial* you need look no further than the designer labels strewn across your bedroom floor that cost more than most people's weekly food shop. When you stop being driven by appearances, then you can lecture me on superficiality; until then, you need to own the distasteful knowledge that you are more like me than you care to believe."

He raised the newspaper, ending the conversation. Laurence left the room but not before a stab of sadness caught in his throat as he noticed that this year there were only three stockings hung above the fireplace instead of four.

Robert

There was no such thing as a gentle easing into the day in the Barlow household. The noise began at 5.30 a.m. when Widget sounded the alarm by screeching "MA MA MA MA MA!" and bashed her toys against the bars of her cot until someone came to get her. This was closely followed by Dot and Toast competing from their separate bedrooms to see who could sing nursery rhymes the loudest – among the favourites were "Barf Barf Back Seep", "Hairy Mary Quite Confairy" and "Wind The Boffin Uff" – unfortunately they rarely sang the same rhyme and never in the same key.

At half-past seven Robert's two eldest sisters dropped his nieces and nephews off before heading off to their places of work. Breakfast time in the Barlow family kitchen made the cream pie fight at the end of *Bugsy Malone* look like afternoon tea at the Ritz.

Robert dutifully helped his parents dish out toast and cereal to the unruly mob and left them to it, preferring to spend a few quiet moments with his nan before the feeding frenzy was over and his siblings began rampaging through the house again.

"Morning, Nan," said Robert, handing her a cup of tea and a plate of peanut butter on toast.

"Morning, Bertram dear," said Nan. "What have you got to show me today?"

Robert got out his phone and his nan swapped her glasses for her reading specs. Robert pulled up a video of a skateboarding competition in America, where the ramps were as high as buildings, and held it for his nan to watch.

She loved this stuff: videos of people on roller coasters, free runners jumping over rooftops, BMX racing – if it was fast and scary, Nan loved it. Nan made little chirrups of delight as she watched another video, this time of a bungee jumper with a GoPro camera on his helmet.

"Woo! Lordy!" she said, leaning back to take a sip of tea. "Now let's look at Paint Girl?"

This was Nan's name for @secretgeek. Robert had once shown her a drawing she'd done of Rosa Parks as a winged goddess, and his nan had been so captivated, she'd wanted to see more; she scrolled through @secretgeek's Instagram page so often that Robert could probably write an essay on her painting techniques. But he liked that his nan remembered Paint Girl when she forgot so much else. As long as she remembered this little morning ritual of theirs, Robert knew he still had a piece of his nan. Quite often by teatime she would be muddled again; she would call him Peter – her brother's name – and ask him questions that he couldn't answer, though he would try his best to give her a response that she'd be satisfied with. It was unsettling to see someone you love look at you like a stranger. But something about mornings seemed to reset her memory button, and so long as that was the case, Robert determined to keep showing her videos of adrenalin junkies and @secretgeek's superheroes.

As a way to help with Nan's memory, the family had set up a file called Nan's Book on the iPad. This file contained old and new downloaded photographs, as well as pictures of family holidays, articles on gardening, recipes, knitting patterns: all the kinds of things that Nan liked in one place, so that she could scroll through them whenever she liked. Robert had added a Paint Girl section to Nan's Book, where he added screenshots of @secretgeek's artwork, so that Nan could look at the pictures when he wasn't around.

The sound like wild buffalo stampeding along the hallway signified that it was time to leave for school. Robert retrieved his phone from Nan, swapping it for the iPad, and took a quick photo of Nan looking at Paint Girl. He uploaded it to @oneinten on Insta and tagged @secretgeek with the heading "No age limit on art lovers!" After topping up Nan's tea and putting on the TV – his nan regularly threatened to give Philip Schofield a smacked bottom, but she adored Holly Willoughby – he left to meet Sam and Milly.

Chapter 7

Sam

Sam left school before lunch, having given Milly one final pep talk about working with Laurence.

The Christmas Box charity had its headquarters in a section of an old aircraft hangar on a disused airfield, just outside of town, so Sam took the bus. Since being decommissioned, the airfield had become a kind of mini business park, with a farm shop and café, a fireplace specialist, a hot tub showroom and a garden centre.

The bus pulled into a layby next to a set of large metal gates, hung with signs for the businesses within. Sam called her thanks to the driver and walked through the gates. Both the garden centre and the farm shop were strung with fairy lights and had fresh Christmas trees for sale outside. Sam's mum wouldn't have a fresh tree; she didn't like the needles dropping on the carpet. Sam bought a sausage roll and a hot chocolate from the café before entering the hangar.

To the right of the space stood three large shipping containers, labelled "Girl", "Boy" and "Unisex". To the left was a long metal table and chairs, and boxes of Christmas wrapping paper rolls dotted the floor. An open door in the steel wall seemed to lead to an office/kitchen area and it was from here that a stream of Christmas pop music emanated. Across the back wall there were two sheds that looked like they had been teleported in from someone's garden.

"Hello!" Sam called. Her voice echoed around the cavernous space.

"Be there in jiffy!" came a voice from behind the wall.

Sam took a bite out of her sausage roll and heard a cooing from above. She looked up to see three pigeons perched on the beams, their beady eyes intent on her lunch. She grinned at them and took another bite. "You'll get nothing from me," she called up to them. "I don't share my food with no one."

"Laying down the ground rules?" said a voice with a familiar East London accent.

"Tula! I didn't know you'd be here."

"Ah, but I knew you were coming." She grinned. "The school called the office. I'm helping down here with the Christmas boxes once a week."

"Are you still working with the council?"

"Yep, still fighting the good fight."

Sam had met Tula in the summer when she was volunteering with the refugee charity. Tula worked with local councils, helping refugee families with the copious and often confusing form filling required for things like housing and schools.

"Let me grab my tea and I'll give you the grand tour," said Tula, disappearing into the office and returning with a steaming mug which had the words *I may look like I'm interested in what you're saying, but I'm actually thinking about Christmas* written on it. "It's pretty self-explanatory," she said, pointing to the containers. "We have to keep everything covered because of the pigeons. Expect to get pooped on at least twice a day." She pointed to the brightly coloured scarf covering her afro. "The containers are for the boxes that come in ready made up. We sent lists out to shops and community centres in November with gift ideas and the types of things that would be appreciated. Some of the donations come in singly," Tula pointed to the sheds

83

at the back, "and they go in there and we put the boxes together ourselves."

"Have you had much in yet?" Sam asked.

"We've had a few bits, but it's always quiet the first week of December. Once the schools start collecting, it'll get really busy."

"So are we putting boxes together?"

"You got it, sugar. Kitchenette, toilet and office are through there." Tula pointed to the door she had come out from. "And that's it. Oh, and wear layers. It is brass monkeys in here!"

Sam and Tula settled down to covering shoeboxes in Christmas paper.

"What unis did you apply for in the end?" asked Tula, dumping a pile of toys from the shed on the table.

"Kent, London, Nottingham, Warwick and Aberystwyth."

"Good choices. Any you're leaning towards?"

Sam gave an involuntary sigh. "That's where things get tricky."

"How so?"

"My mum."

"You don't want to leave her?"

"It's not that. I mean, I'll miss her and stuff. She's kind of tricky. I don't know if I should go away."

84

Tula pulled a face. "It's just you and your mum, right?"

Sam nodded.

"Always been that way?"

Sam nodded again.

"And you're telling me a woman who brought up a kid single-handed can't look after herself?"

"My mum is," Sam made quote marks in the air, "*a very independent woman!*"

Tula laughed.

"But it's like... Oh, it's so hard to explain!" Sam threw her arms into the air and two pigeons took fright, firing poops simultaneously, which landed just centimetres away from where she was sitting.

"Lucky miss!" said Tula. "Carry on."

"I feel like she's invested so much of her life in me that the least I should do is stick around."

"Listen to me," said Tula. "I'm not saying your mum won't have that whole empty nest thing going on when you leave. I know I did when my kids first left home. But we know it's coming; that's what we're aiming towards. We don't bring you up to be home-grown bezzie mates for ever. Us mamas and papas grow you strong so you can go out there and live!"

"She has this habit of pushing people away, so if she hasn't got me..."

"If you want my advice, talk to your mum about your worries. She might surprise you."

Sam smiled but remained unconvinced.

Milly

Milly had considered arriving at the food bank early to ask the volunteers, if they *did* recognize her, not to mention to Laurence that her family used the food bank. But then she decided that this was offensive to them, as it suggested she thought they were indiscreet, and also it made it look as though she was ungrateful for their help. OMG! Why did everything have to be so complicated? She wished she could just have one emotion per quandary, instead of seventeen conflicting emotions for every element of her life.

She'd been on edge all morning and could barely concentrate during lessons due to her mind playing out the many excruciating ways she could embarrass herself that afternoon. After stopping to use two public toilets on the way, she had arrived at the food bank to find Laurence already waiting on a mustard-coloured easy chair. God, why did he have to be so gorgeous? This was going to be awkward enough without having palpitations because he was giving off hotness pheromones all over the place.

The food bank was in an old church hall, and despite having been refurbed and painted, the smell of musty curtains and cold damp floorboards still hung in the air. Milly had been here several times with her mum when her dad wasn't feeling up to going.

In front of the counter, round tables and school-assembly-style chairs dotted the grey carpet. The food bank doubled as a drop-in centre for people who needed help with their benefit forms or their food vouchers. Three tables were currently occupied, the low hum of voices just audible over the Christmas music playing through speakers set high in the corners of the room. Two small children delved delightedly into a large wooden toy chest by the tea station. The long counter had tinsel pinned to its front, and behind it, shelves up to the ceiling were filled with bags of shopping.

"Hi," said Laurence, standing to greet her. "I got here early. I was worried about where to park. I'm glad you're here, this kind of thing always makes me a bit nervous." He smiled at her and Milly was taken aback to think that someone like Laurence would feel nervous about anything. He was wearing a black hoodie and jeans, and it didn't go unnoticed by Milly that the hoodie was plain, with not so much as a designer tag in sight. She wondered if this had been a conscious thing.

Milly smiled and hiccupped. She clapped her hands to her mouth. *Really??? Now??? Give me a break!*

"Hic! Sorry. Hic! Nervous. Hic! Reaction," she managed to mumble behind her hands.

Laurence laughed. "You too? My brother gets those. I've never met anyone else who gets anxiety hiccups. I've never been here before, have you?" He looked at Milly and then added, "Nod once for 'yes' and twice for 'no'."

Milly – her mouth clamped shut to try and inhibit the hiccups – was struck by a sudden crisis of conscience. But she smiled through a hiccup and nodded twice for "no". *You've done it now, Mills*, she thought to herself. *You are officially a liar!*

"Hi, guys," said a breezy woman with a strong Yorkshire accent, wearing a bright yellow sweatshirt. "I'm Sarah, one of the supervisors." Her eyes lit briefly in recognition upon seeing Milly, and Milly tensed, waiting to be outed. But Sarah looked away and said: "You must be Milly and Laurence, from Millers Field."

Milly realized she had entered into a pact of silence with Sarah, and she relaxed a little, although she felt a bud of unease unfurl in her stomach at the notion that she had begun her placement with Laurence on a lie.

"It's great to have you here," said Sarah. "We need all the help we can get. It's always extra busy around this time of year. Let me show you around and then I'll leave you with Magda to get started."

Milly and Laurence followed Sarah behind the counter and through a door which led to a large storeroom, with aisle upon aisle of floor-to-ceiling shelves full of tinned and dried goods. Laminated signs marked where one foodstuff ended, and another began. Milly had never seen so many bags of fusilli pasta in one place. It was easier to make surprised and interested noises here, since Milly genuinely hadn't been into the storeroom before; the storeroom was a guilt-free zone. She was surprised at how heavily her one tiny mistruth was playing on her mind.

Sarah opened her arms wide. "This is the kindness of strangers, right here," she said. "Ordinary people popping one or two extras in their trolley each week at the supermarket, to help a complete stranger who's struggling. It can be a hard place to work," she said. "You'll hear a lot of sad stories and you wonder how life can be so unfair. But then you come in here and you see the goodness of people's hearts stacked from floor to ceiling, and you know you're part of something special."

After a brief tour, Sarah handed them over to Magda, a

friendly looking woman with glasses thick as bottle tops and an Eastern European accent. Magda showed them how to put together the bags of food to make sure that every person had enough for a few meals and a couple of treats, like biscuits or crisps.

"Will you be here for the party on the eighteenth?" Magda asked.

"Party?" asked Laurence.

"Yes," said Magda. "We do it every year near Christmas. Christmas isn't a good time for everyone, so we try and combine handing out the Christmas food bags with a bit of a do. That way, if someone maybe won't be seeing people over the festive period, they've at least seen a few friendly faces in a bit of a party atmosphere."

"That's so thoughtful," said Milly.

"Well, thoughtful tends to go hand in hand with this place," said Magda, playing it down. "You'd be welcome to join us. It's all hands on deck up to Christmas and it really is a case of the more the merrier."

"It sounds great," said Laurence. "But we've got our sixth form Christmas ball on the eighteenth."

"Oh my," said Magda. "Well, you can't go missing that! A Christmas ball, how wonderful! We didn't have anything like that when I was at school," she said wistfully. "It was all snogging behind the bike sheds and bad home perms; and that was just the boys!"

Magda went off to make tea, leaving Laurence and Milly to make up the bags.

"Who's your date for the ball?" Laurence asked.

"No one. I mean I haven't got a date, but it doesn't really matter because I haven't decided if I'll go yet."

Laurence frowned. "I thought everyone was going. It's all Cassia and Trinity have talked about for months!"

"It may have escaped your notice but I'm not like Cassia or Trinity." She smiled.

"Are you unsure about going because you don't have a date or because you just don't want to?"

"I'd go without a date," Milly said as nonchalantly as she could. "I just don't know if I'm a Magical Snow Ball kind of person." As lies went, this one was the size of the community Christmas tree on the high street.

"Surely *everyone* is a Magical Snow Ball kind of person!" Laurence said, smiling. "I think you should have a rethink; we should all be there."

Milly wondered what it must be like for people like Laurence, for whom the idea of *not* attending the Magical Snow Ball would never enter their heads. Those people who have the supreme confidence that they will, without a shadow of a doubt, have a date for the ball, and not the slightest worry that they won't be able to afford clothes for the night. What would it be like to live in their world?

Robert

The community centre was essentially a prefab which had been thrown up after the war and added to over the years, so that it resembled a hodgepodge of different-shaped buildings stuck together like a bad Minecraft experiment – it was unlikely to ever be featured on *Grand Designs*.

Miranda had been waiting outside for Robert. The smile that broke out over her face upon seeing him had stopped him in his tracks, as though he'd walked into an invisible electric fence. *Holy nutcrackers, she's lovely!* he thought.

Of course, he had seen Miranda pretty much every day for the last two years, but this was different; he'd never been the actual focus of her attention before. She had always been two steps behind Cassia, looking pointedly away from him, as though to distance herself from whatever diatribe Cassia was spouting that day. But now under the full force of her attention, Robert felt like he needed sunglasses.

"Do you think they'll like us?" Miranda asked

breathlessly, as they headed down a brown-carpeted corridor towards the sounds of screeching children.

"I expect they'll be glad of the help."

"Not the play leaders," said Miranda. "The children!"

"You're worried about the children?"

"What if they don't like me?"

"Why wouldn't they like you?"

"They might think my accent's funny."

"Have you heard how kids talk?" Robert laughed.

They pushed open a set of double doors and the noise of twenty screeching pre-schoolers crashed over them like a wave. Chaos was Robert's natural habitat, but Miranda looked like she might bolt. He smiled reassuringly at her.

"Come on," he said. "You'll be fine. Just lean in and accept the mayhem."

Miranda smiled hesitantly and followed him into the room. Pam, the senior play leader handed them a printout each detailing the afternoon structure. This was "free play" which explained the speeding tricycles, sand flinging, kids dressed as wizards and dogs, and general running about with arms flailing, screeching at the tops of their lungs like the early-bird shoppers on Black Friday. Ten more minutes of this would be followed by storytime, painting and sticking inspired by the story, then a kind of toddlers' jazzercize class, and finally the afternoon would end with one last storytime.

"Have you always wanted to be a teacher?" Miranda asked as they tried and failed to separate the play dough back into its original colour pots once the children had all left.

"Pretty much," said Robert. "I know it sounds corny, but I like the idea of helping to get kids interested in reading and learning, so they see education as fun. I blame reading *Matilda* too many times as a kid."

"You see yourself as Miss Honey?"

"She was an inspirational teacher!"

"That's so cute," said Miranda.

Robert felt himself blush. *Heavenly silver bells!* Cute? Cute was a Shih Tzu in a handbag; he didn't want to be *cute*, he wanted to be heroic, like Captain America in primary school teacher form. "How about you?" he asked.

"I want to teach art to children, maybe become an art therapist? It's such a good way to help children express themselves. I guess I kinda think that if I can help them express themselves as children, maybe they'll be less repressed as adults?"

"Good luck with that," laughed Robert. "I don't think I've ever met a non-repressed adult."

"Which is exactly what I want to change," said Miranda.

Jumping juniper berries! She's a revolutionary! That is geekily hot! He realized he was staring. *Say something!*

"So you like art?" he said. *Doh! Obviously, she likes art, she wants to be an art therapist!*

"Sure," said Miranda.

"I didn't know that," said Robert.

"Oh yeah, well, I kinda keep it on the down-low."

"Why?" asked Robert.

Miranda sighed as they laid out the plastic sheets on the table for tomorrow morning's painting session. "I don't want people to judge my work based on who I am. I like to be anonymous; you know?"

Miranda's phone pinged with an Insta update from @cassiakeepsitreal. Miranda held her phone so that Robert could see the story; Cassia was stood in front of a semicircle of elderly people, singing a "Silent Night" solo while the choir and Glee Club stood behind her humming. She had, to use a cliché, the voice of an angel; too bad she didn't have the personality to match.

"For someone who sulked when she was given her placement, she's certainly changed her tune ... no pun intended," said Robert.

"That's what she's good at – she can turn any situation to her advantage."

At that moment hashtags began to swim along the screen: #givingback #christmasjoy #discoverinfluencer #influencercommunity #lifestyleinfluencer #starinthemaking #astarisborn.

"Hashtag *giving back*?" Robert pulled a face. "That's so fake."

Miranda stifled a laugh.

"She's always had a great singing voice, though," said Robert. "I'll give her that. As kids, we planned to start a band together when we grew up."

"You and Cassia?"

"Hard to believe, right. Yeah, we used to be mates. Went to the same music teacher, did recitals together and stuff."

"I am shocked by this revelation."

"That was before she crossed over to the dark side," said Robert. "You're not like Cassia at all, though. How can you stand her?"

"Things are never that simple," was all Miranda replied.

Chapter 8

Milly

Milly and Laurence had found their rhythm and there were now two rows of pre-prepared food bags lined up on the floor behind them. The steady routine had calmed Milly's horror-hiccups and she found Laurence surprisingly easy to talk to – so long as she didn't remind herself that he was cool and gorgeous. She didn't know what she'd expected from Laurence really, maybe a bit of mild showing off about the exotic holidays he'd been on, or some humble bragging about his success on the sports field. But neither of those things had occurred.

"I've never really thought about food banks before," said Laurence. "Not properly. It makes you think, doesn't it?"

"Yeah," said Milly, trying to ignore the sudden coil of unease in her stomach. How was she going to get out of this one?

"I feel kind of bad."

"In what way?" Milly asked.

"Well, I mean, we never have to consider how lucky we are, do we? Imagine having to rely on somewhere like this just to be able to eat. It's not until you see it for yourself..."

"It's a good job it's here," said Milly non-committally.

A burly man in a hi-vis jacket came in through the back door carrying a stack of Quality Street tins. He lowered them down on the table.

"Some of the local stores are donating Christmas goodies," he said. "Everyone deserves a few treats at Christmas," and he headed back out the way he'd come.

"I love the big tins of chocolates at Christmas," said Milly. "We all fight over the orange creams. And whoever loses at Monopoly or Cluedo has to eat the coconut ones as a forfeit; it's kind of a Christmas tradition, although I think my mum probably started it because she can't stand having the dregs left in the tin after Christmas."

Laurence smiled. "I think your mum and my mum would get on well," he said.

"How about you?" Milly asked. "Any Christmas traditions in your family?"

Laurence ran his hand through his hair and Milly noticed a faraway look in his eyes. "We used to," he said after a moment. "But I'm not sure they'll still apply." Milly was about to ask why when Sarah blustered back in.

"OK," she said. "Now people will come in and show you a voucher, which entitles them to collect some food. The most important thing is that you greet everyone with a smile and a cheery hello! The last thing anyone needs is to be met with a face like a slapped backside. Some people want to talk, some don't. Let them lead the conversation. A lot of folks are embarrassed by having to come here, people are proud by nature. Our job is to make sure nobody feels like a charity case."

"But they are a charity case," said Laurence.

"If you had a massive boil on your forehead, would you want people to keep coming up and telling you about it?"

"No," said Laurence.

"Well then. Our customers know they're down on their luck right now – they don't need soppy sympathy faces making them feel worse. We are here to empower people, not dehumanize them. Right!" Sarah raised her voice to the team. "Doors are about to open, so let's bring some joy!"

Milly was no stranger to the way this side of the food bank worked but she could see that for Laurence it was a real eye-opener. She tried to imbue her expression with a kind of casual fascination that would look to Laurence like this was her first time too, but after three separate people asked her if she was feeling OK, she decided to stop overthinking it and get on with the job in hand.

Sam

Tula pulled the iron door of the hangar shut and locked it. "Get in," she said motioning to her car.

"Are you sure?" asked Sam. "I live in the opposite direction from where you need to go."

"I don't care where you live, it's dark and I'm not having you waiting around for a bus."

Sam was about to pull open the car door when a figure loomed out of the darkness.

"Hello!" said Robert brightly.

"Jeez! You scared the tinsel out of me," yelped Sam. "What are you doing here?"

"It's dark, I've come to escort you home, my lady." Robert grinned, bowing low.

"You came all the way over here just to see me home?"

"Of course."

"You still want that lift?" asked Tula.

"No thanks," said Sam. "Apparently my knight in shining armour is here."

"Lucky you," laughed Tula. "Well, I'll be seeing you!" and with a quick wave she had pulled out along the gravel drive.

"I didn't know you'd be offered a lift," said Robert sheepishly. "Now you've got to wait in the cold for a bus with me."

"I appreciate the thought," said Sam, smiling. "Thank you, you're very sweet. Weird, but sweet."

Robert let out a gasp of exasperation. "That's the second time today someone has applied a word to me that can also be used to describe a hamster or a pigmy marmoset."

"Huh?"

"Miranda called me cute earlier."

"Did she?" Sam was grinning and nodding knowingly. "Well, I guess you are cute in a gawky kind of way."

"It isn't good!" said Robert. "Cute and sweet are words to describe lambs and ducklings, not guys."

"There is nothing wrong with being a nice guy, Bertram. Trust me, being mean to keep girls keen is so last century. Girls like guys who listen, and who tramp halfway across town to make sure their mate doesn't have to stand in the ice rain alone in the dark."

"Snain," said Robert.

"What now?"

"That's what this weather is, half snow, half rain: snain."

"Isn't that sleet?"

"Snain is better."

Sam rolled her eyes. "Anyways, what do you care whether Miranda thinks you're *cute* rather than buff like Thor?"

Robert shrugged. "I don't! It would just be nice, once in a while, to be seen as more than a friend."

The bus pulled up and they climbed on, leaving the dark industrial estate and the snain behind them.

Milly

At five-thirty, Sarah said they could go, while she and the other volunteers got ready for the next lot of customers due in at seven o'clock.

"I'll give you a lift home," said Laurence.

"Oh, no, you don't have to, it's all right."

"I know I don't have to, I want to!" He smiled at her and Milly's legs turned to marshmallow.

"Come on," he said. "Surely getting a lift must be better than walking home in ice drizzle? Or am I really that bad?"

Milly snorted, tripped over her own foot and face planted on to his chest.

"I'll take that as a yes to a lift?" he said, laughing as he helped her back upright.

Laurence's car was old enough to still have a choke function and ashtrays inserted in every door, but he seemed very proud of his vintage vehicle. The engine roared and shuddered when he turned the key in the ignition before settling into a loud purr. At some point someone had installed a CD player into the dash and the passenger footwell was littered with CD cases.

Once in the car, Milly desperately tried to think of something to say. Laurence was concentrating on the road; the least she could do was pick up the conversation slack.

"Mind if we put the radio on?" she asked. She was stalling for time and hoping radio noise would fill the empty silence while she thought of something to say.

"Sure, go ahead."

Milly reached over and pressed the button for the radio. The DJ's voice filled the car, overly bright and excitable: *And now, since the most wonderful time of the year is almost upon us once more, here's a little something to get those festive bells a-jingling!* Wham's "Last Christmas" filled the car.

"I love this one!" she said. "Have you seen the video? Super retro hairdos."

Laurence shifted in the driver's seat and rubbed roughly at his eye. "Actually," he said, "do you mind if we turn it off? I'm not massively into Christmas songs."

"Oh, sure, yeah, no problem. Sorry." Milly switched off the radio – mentally kicking herself for exposing her festive geekdom – and the car was plunged back into silence. Now she felt so super awkward that her brain had completely deserted her, leaving only a black hole of panic and a jumble of words and half-formed sentences, which couldn't possibly be made into a coherent line of conversation. She clasped her hands in her lap and noticed her palms were clammy with anxiety.

"It's not that I hate Christmas or anything," Laurence's voice punctured the quiet. "It's just there's stuff going on ... at home ... I don't feel so much like celebrating this year."

You've got stuff going on? Milly scoffed inwardly. *What could possibly be going on in his perfect world?* she wondered – maybe Santa wasn't going to bring him the jet ski he'd asked for. Then she gave herself a talking to; money wasn't everything, and even fabulously good-looking rich people weren't immune to problems.

"Sorry you've got stuff going on," Milly said, feeling like his statement needed an answer but not knowing how to give one without sounding like she was prying. "I'm finding it hard to get into the Christmas spirit myself this year."

"What killed Christmas for you?" Laurence asked.

"Oh, it's not dead, it's just ... different."

"OK, what's made Christmas different for you?"

Now was her chance to tell him about the food bank, and her families money worries and the potential for there to be no Christmas at all at this rate. But could she trust him? What if he told everyone at school? What if everyone found out and began to treat her like a pariah ... more of a pariah than she already was for just being herself? Milly was aware that he was waiting for an answer, so she said: "Consumerism."

She saw Laurence raise his eyebrows.

"How about you?" she asked.

"Capitalism," he replied, and after a moment they both laughed. Milly had the feeling she wasn't the only one holding something back.

"But you, Robert and Sam love Christmas, don't you?" said Laurence. "I noticed Robert has already started with the cheesy jumpers. I have to admit I'm a bit envious of your commitment to Christmas each year. You always seem to be having a better time than the rest of us."

Wait. What? Laurence Bashir is envious of us? And more to the point, Laurence Bashir notices us? Milly's world was turning on its head. Was it possible that while she watched the *beautiful people* like some live-action reality show, they were watching her right back?

"Oh, yeah, well, I guess we do have a nice time. It's kind of silly, I suppose, but..."

"I think it's great!" said Laurence. "You don't care what anyone thinks of you."

At this, a laugh of shock escaped her. "Pah! Are you kidding? I worry about what everybody thinks – in fact, I worry about *everything*! But whether we go nuts about Christmas or not, we're still the invisible dweebs, so it makes no difference, we might as well be having a good time." Milly was shocked by her own candour.

"I don't think you're invisible," said Laurence, a little defensively Milly thought. "*Or* dweebs."

"Oh, come on," said Milly. "If you weren't stuck with me at a placement, would we be hanging out? Would you even talk to me? How many times have you come and sat with us and just hung out?"

Laurence spluttered. "Well ... I mean ... you don't talk to me either! And you could come and sit with us anytime you like, but you don't."

Milly laughed incredulously. "No, we couldn't! Can you imagine if we came and plonked ourselves down next to you, with Tom and Ethan, and Cassia's crew? There'd be an uproar. Trust me, I'm an overthinker, and I've given this a lot of thought; the cool kids can *deign* to spend time with the uncools but it doesn't work the other way around. It's the unwritten class system of high school."

Laurence was quiet for a moment. "I've never thought of it like that," he said at last.

"You've never had to; you're *cool*."

"Is that how high school feels to you?"

Now it was Milly's turn to be quiet while she contemplated Laurence's question. "It's not so much how it feels, as how it is," she replied carefully.

Neither of them said anything for a while, but strangely the silence didn't feel awkward any more.

"I'm sorry if I've ever made you feel … like an outsider," said Laurence. By now they had pulled up at the end of Milly's cul-de-sac.

"It's OK," Milly replied. "It's not really any one person's fault. I guess we all participate in our own way by not trying harder to change things." *Great, Milly, way to go mega deep! What a dork. No wonder I'm not cool.* "Anyway, thanks for the lift," she said as brightly as she could to try and breeze away her previous emo-statement.

"Yeah," said Laurence absently. "Sure. No worries. You're welcome."

Milly: How were your placements?

Sam: Pretty good actually, apart from constantly dodging the pigeon poop! 💩

Milly: 😳

Robert: The community centre was good. I got to lead the final storytime. I read *The Gruffalo* and did all the voices; the kids were well impressed!

Sam: 😄 I'll bet. Mills, did you tell Laurence about your family using the food bank?

Milly: It didn't come up.

Sam: What do you mean it didn't come up? You were IN the food bank!

Milly: I'll tell him in my own time, it's no big deal.

Robert: If it's no big deal, why didn't you tell him?

Milly: Any thoughts on who you might ask to the Christmas ball?

Robert: 🧑

Sam: 🙀 How about you?

Milly: If I do go, I'll probably go solo.

Robert: How did it go with Laurence anyway? No unfortunate bodily incidents?

Milly: Fortunately not! He's surprisingly not a jerk.

Robert: I didn't think he would be.

Sam: You didn't?

Robert: Nah, I get a good vibe off him. I think he's trapped by his reputation.

Sam: Deep.

Milly: How about you and Miranda?

Robert: Also, surprisingly not a jerk.

Sam: Bertram's got a crush! 🤍🤍🤍🤍

Robert: I do not have a crush on Miranda.

Milly: Sweeeeeeeeeet!

Robert: Will everyone stop saying I'm sweet!

Sam: Sweeeeeeeeeeeeeeeeeeeeet!

Robert: Oh, kiss my glittery baubles!

Milly: 😂😂😂😂

Sam: Don't forget, it's late-night shopping in the high street tomorrow night. We can come meet you after work, Mills?

Milly: It's a date!

Laurence

Laurence and his mum ate their dinner on a tray in front of the TV in the snug, avoiding the large table in the dining room and the old pine table in the kitchen. This was a new arrangement, unspoken but understood by both of them; the empty chairs at the tables were like spotlights illuminating the people who were missing. It was hard to enjoy a meal with a void glaring at you.

When they'd finished, Laurence picked up their trays and his mum opened the window and lit her after-dinner cigarette – she'd given up smoking ten years ago and taken it back up again in the spring.

As he made his way down to the kitchen, the front door opened and the familiar sound of a heavy briefcase being placed on the parquet flooring, and the shuffle as his dad shrugged out of his coat, met his ears. He knew he should turn and greet his father, but somehow he couldn't bring himself to do it, just like his father couldn't bring himself to get home on time for dinner.

"Good evening, Lou."

Laurence heard the clack of expensive shoes following him down the hall. "All right?" he replied.

"How was your placement at the food bank?"

Laurence turned, two dinner trays still in his hands. "How did you know I had a placement?"

"Your mother told me. Contrary to popular belief, Laurence, I do like to know what's going on in your life."

You could have fooled me, Laurence thought, but he kept it to himself. "It was good, thanks."

"I'm glad. It's good to give something back. I think sometimes we forget how lucky we are."

"I doubt James is feeling very lucky." It was a low blow and Laurence knew it, but honestly, what was it with his dad – being all community-spirited but not giving enough of a crap to call his own son. His dad winced; blink and you'd miss it, but Laurence saw his words wound his dad before his courtroom mask slipped back into place.

"James will be getting three square meals a day," said his dad, his voice so cold it seemed to suck all the warmth out of the hallway. "That's more than can be said for a lot of the people who are driven by circumstance to visit the food bank."

Laurence knew he was right, but he wasn't going to tell him that. "Maybe you should ask around the law courts, see if any of your old Cambridge chums can spare some pennies for the poor."

"I really don't know when you started hating your privilege," said his dad wearily. "Or me for that matter."

112

"Your dinner's in the oven," said Laurence. "It's probably still hot. You could eat it with us in the snug; we were going to watch a movie..." He left the offer hanging there, a rope thrown across the gap. But his dad shook his head.

"I've got work to do; I'll eat in the study."

The rope fell.

Laurence lay in bed that night thinking about his brother as usual, but also about Milly. Her words had been like a door into another world, a completely different perspective to the school experience he'd had. There was more to Milly Parker than the shy girl hiding behind her hair. He guessed he'd always known that on some level, but he'd never bothered to pursue it further. He was curious about her, and he wanted to hear more of what she had to say. He recalled the way she had looked at him in the car, like she was trying to see past what his mouth was saying to the truth behind it. Milly's face was the last thing his mind conjured before his eyes closed and sleep took him.

Chapter 9

Saturday 5th December

Milly

The Old Windmill Café was packed with late-night shoppers when Milly called her goodbyes at the end of her shift. The winter evening blew its icy breath in her face as she clung on to three cups of hot chocolate and scanned the crowd for Robert and Sam. She spotted them by Robert's knitted Christmas bobble hat poking out above the crowd, and she was glad she'd forced herself to make the effort to wear her Rudolf scarf.

They were watching a dance troupe perform to a live band playing 50s rock 'n' roll. Robert looked back and saw

Milly. He tugged Sam's arm and they pulled away from the audience and gratefully took their drinks.

"Thanks, Mills," said Robert. "I've been freezing my baubles off out here!"

"There's a Christmas gig at the Windmill on the fifteenth," said Milly. "My boss just put a poster up. Fancy it? It's ticket only, but I reckon I could swing us a discount."

"Count me in," said Robert. "I've got a holly and berries print shirt that's been waiting for the right occasion."

Sam rolled her eyes. "I'm up for it," she said, sucking chocolatey froth through the hole in the lid. "We just saw your mum a minute ago."

"Yeah, she dropped in earlier for some cake. I think she's meeting your mum." Milly nodded at Robert.

"Your dad didn't fancy it then?" Sam asked.

"He's got a headache. He's about as cheery as my brother at the moment."

"Cracking Christmas crackers!" exclaimed Robert. "That's like a minus ten on the cheery scale."

"Tell me about it! Of course, there's every chance my brother will grow out of his misery when he stops fighting puberty. But I'm a bit worried my dad's Grinchiness might be permanent. He wouldn't even help put up the Christmas decorations."

"And the outside of the house?" asked Robert.

"Nothing," said Milly. "Ours is the only house in the cul-de-sac not decorated; you know how the neighbours are always trying to outdo Dad."

"And failing," added Sam.

"Exactly!" Milly agreed. "This year they've brought their best game, and my dad? Nada. The K.O.C. is officially MIA."

The road was closed to traffic for the evening. They walked slowly down the high street – slowly being the only option with so many people herding along – through the snow-machine blizzard and alongside the queue for Santa's grotto, being housed as usual in the shop that sold tea towels, flannelette nighties and massive, tummy-hugger pants, owned by two very jolly old ladies who smelled of lavender.

Several of Robert's siblings and nieces and nephews were waiting noisily for their turn to see Father Christmas. Milly's sister Tara was holding hands with Toast, while their mums chatted beside them. Sam, Milly and Robert waved and moved on.

"Maybe I should join them," said Milly. "Ask Santa to help my dad find his King of Christmas spirit."

"I'll come too," said Sam. "See if he can grant my wish to make my mum less pig-headed."

Robert caught sight of Laurence and Tom through the

crowds up ahead, walking down the hill in their direction. "There's your new mate," he said, nudging Milly.

"Heavens to holly berries!" Milly exclaimed.

"Nice," said Robert, approving of her festive swearing attempt.

"What's the prob?" asked Sam.

"I don't know what the rules are?"

"Huh?"

"I mean are we just food bank friends, or are we like actual people friends? Because if we hadn't been at the food bank together then we would still be on the same terms we were for the last seven years, and we would possibly smile at one another as we passed, at the most we might half-heartedly wave, but now I don't know what the rules are."

"As usual, Milly, you are overthinking this," said Sam.

"I second that," said Robert. "Just be yourself."

"What?" Milly almost shrieked.

"Well, no, all right, maybe not the *yourself* you are around other people, that's just weirdly mute and starey. Be the *yourself* you are around us," said Robert.

"Bertram's right. You got on well with him at the food bank, so there is no reason why you can't say hello and expect a hello back. Only a dirtbag would talk to you in one place and blank you in another."

Laurence

Laurence had just eaten his own weight in shiitake mushroom ramen in the Sushi Shack and was feeling pleasantly full as he tramped down the hill towards the centre of the high street, where the main late-night shopping festivities were taking place.

"There's your placement pal," said Tom, picking a bean shoot out of his front tooth.

Laurence looked down into the crowd. Milly was wearing her hair in two long plaits, with a striped bobble hat fastened to her head. He wondered how he hadn't spotted her earlier; she seemed to stand out from the crowd as though she had a silvery haze surrounding her. At least that's what it looked like to him. Or maybe she'd just walked under a street lamp. Either way, now he'd spotted her, he couldn't seem to turn his eyes away. He steered their course so that they would casually bump into Milly and her friends.

"What are you doing?" said Tom.

"Nothing," said Laurence. "I just thought it would be nice to say hello. You know, after we spent the whole afternoon together yesterday, it would be kind of rude to blank her."

"You don't need to blank her, mate, but you don't need to be her best mate either. Unless..." Tom nudged Laurence with his elbow. "Have you got the hots for Milly Parker?"

"What? No! I just thought I'd say hello."

Tom narrowed his eyes at Laurence. "I know that soppy look," he said grinning smugly.

"Naff off!" said Laurence laughing. "Anyway, what if I do like her? It's up to me, isn't it?"

"You'll get no argument from me, mate. But Queen Cassia might have something to say about it."

Laurence was about to protest that Cassia had no bearing on who he liked, when the queen herself emerged from the tanning salon and made a beeline for him.

Oh, nuts! thought Laurence.

"Hi, Lou!" Cassia trilled. Laurence's heart sank.

"All right, Cass," he said, trying to be as unfriendly as possible without actually being unfriendly. After all, it wasn't Cassia's fault that she was the last person he wanted to see right now.

"We're heading down to Starbucks for gingerbread lattes," said Cassia. "Want to join?"

"Ah, no thanks, Cass. I'm full of ramen – can't face a big drink right now."

"So don't drink," she simpered. "Just join."

It was too late to change course; in a few short steps Milly would be in front of him. If he stopped to speak to her now, Cassia would no doubt be her mean self and say something hideous that would make Milly shrink away, like one of those ferns that curl in on themselves when touched, just as she did in class. He would have to settle for a wave and a smile and hope that she didn't think he was snubbing her.

Milly

Milly had been pulling all her bravery around her, bolstered by her friends' positivity lectures, and was determined to smile and call a friendly yet effortlessly casual "Hi!" when they reached Laurence. And if his response to that was positive, she might even attempt some really awkward small talk about the weather and the excellent late-night shopping turnout. And then she saw Cassia and her bravery dissolved faster than a sherbet fountain.

The distance between them grew smaller and smaller until it was impossible that either party wouldn't have seen the other. Cassia was laughing about something, waving her arms about, the mean-minions completely in her thrall.

"Hi, Miranda!" called Robert, ever the optimist. "Busy tonight, huh! How tired were you yesterday after all those kids?" He laughed and rolled his eyes.

Miranda gave a half-smile and looked away. Milly saw

Robert's face fall and her heart squeezed for him. It was only for a second and then Robert plastered on his signature carefree smile, but Milly and Sam knew the encounter had knocked him.

Sam grabbed his arm. "Don't you just hate rude people?" she said loudly, looking squarely at Miranda who was looking squarely at the floor.

Milly couldn't speak, paralysed by the fear that always came over her when faced with confrontation. She watched as Cassia's mouth curled into a cruel smile.

Laurence

Laurence watched the scene play out before him. He needed to get Cassia away before she had a chance to attack. Milly looked like a fawn dazzled in the headlights. If he tried to make conversation with her now, it would only make Cassia's attack more potent. Was he a coward? Or was he just trying to handle the situation the best way he could to minimize casualties? The latter he hoped.

He had to distract Cassia. He looped his arm through hers. "Come on," he said in as breezy a tone as he could muster. "Let's go to Starbucks, hang out for a bit." It was enough to throw Cassia off her stride. She looked down at his arm linked with hers and smiled up at him.

"You got it, babe," she cooed. "It reeks of loser up here anyway."

As Laurence passed by, he tried to catch Milly's eye. He wanted to smile at her, to tell her with his eyes that he was only doing this to rescue her from the sting of Cassia's tongue, but Milly didn't look at him. She had turned to look back towards the Old Windmill at the top of the hill with its sails white against the dark sky, like he wasn't even there. His ramen noodles felt like snakes writhing in his stomach.

Milly

Milly couldn't quite believe what had just happened. She tried not to show the crushing disappointment she felt at Laurence's blatant rebuff.

"Well," she said, trying to make her voice sound light. "I guess we know what the rules are now."

"I guess so," agreed Robert.

The evening somehow felt a bit tarnished after their meeting with Laurence and Miranda; it was a given that Cassia would behave like a complete Krampus but the other two had taken them by surprise. They still had a good time, but the encounter had left a sour aftertaste, which no amount of chocolate pretzels could eradicate.

Robert

Milly and Sam had been picked up by Sam's mum. Robert was helping his parents herd the family away from the high street and towards home; no mean feat with several overtired clan members who were overwrought by their first glimpse at Father Christmas this season and crashing hard after too much chocolate. Toast had her arms wrapped around Robert's neck and was bawling, "I don't want to leave Santa!" loudly into his ear. They were just about to turn down Ford Road when Robert heard his name being called over the sounds of the snivelling child in his arms.

Robert turned to find Miranda running down the road towards him. His older sister, Beany, looked round too.

"I'll take this one, shall I?" she said, detaching Toast from him. "Catch us up, yeah?"

"Yup," said Robert. "Won't be a minute."

Beany followed after the rest of the family and the road was suddenly quiet.

"Robert!" gasped Miranda, bending down and clutching her knees as she caught her breath. "Been ... looking ... for ... you ... needed ... to ... say ... sorry!"

Robert didn't say anything but waited until she had caught her breath. After a moment, Miranda stood up straight.

"I've been looking for you," she said.

"You kind of left me hanging earlier with everyone," said Robert. "I mean, I'm used to being the butt of the joke but usually I'm the one making it."

"I know, I'm sorry. I just... It's complicated with Cassia, you know? I'm always one step away from being kicked out of the group. I have to be really careful."

"I only said hello!"

"I know."

"So, what, you can't say hello to someone without Cassia's prior approval?"

"I don't know. It's complicated."

"You've said that already."

"I had a really nice time with you yesterday."

"Me too," said Robert. "That's why it felt like such a kick in the jingle bells!"

"In the jingle bells?"

"We have a festive swearing policy, it's a thing."

"Right."

In spite of himself, Robert had to give Miranda credit for accepting this without explanation.

"I'm sorry I ignored you," said Miranda. "I panicked. Can we start again?"

"Will Cassia let you?"

Miranda looked at the floor. Robert sighed. Why was he giving her a hard time? He liked her, didn't he? And she had just run like a woman being chased by a polar bear to find him. So why was he being a jerk about it? "Sure," he said. "We can start again."

"Thank you!" She smiled, and Robert felt his heart skip a beat.

"But you might want to think about whether you want to be friends with someone who makes you too scared to say hello to people."

Miranda nodded and looked away. "My dad's waiting for me," she said. "I'll see you Monday?"

"See you Monday," said Robert.

And with that, Miranda began pelting back the way she had come, leaving Robert to ponder whether he felt pleased that Miranda had cared enough to find him, or nervous that he might just be swapping one unattainable crush for another.

Milly

Oh to be Cool!

I have often wondered who decides what Cool is? Is there a secret governing body? Are we assigned our status at birth? Or is there a hidden section in the eleven-plus which you either pass or fail? For many of us, our fates are decided on the first day of secondary school and our labels follow us around the corridors for the next seven years.

What is Cool?

Cool is an enigma, hard to pin down, elusive. It would appear to be classless. Intelligence isn't a factor; A* and E-minus students are equally welcome. It doesn't appear to be openly racist, sexist or homophobic. And yet, Cool is discriminatory and elitist. Only the select few may enter the dizzy heights of Cool, but since nobody actually knows what the entry requirements are, it's almost impossible for anyone not already Cool to become a member.

Outside of school, Cool is subjective. For example,

I think Historian Dr Suzannah Lipscomb is Cool, but my friend would argue that no one is as Cool as Rylan. And that's OK, because in the real world everyone is welcome in the Cool gang. But not so in school. In school we are stereotyped: geek, nerd, dork, emo, brainiac . . . you get the picture. And everyone knows stereotypes are a trap that is almost impossible to climb out of.

What would it be like to be in their shoes? Life certainly seems easier for those guys. Maybe it's a confidence thing? Or some intangible aura or vibe that only the blessed few have been gifted. I'd sure like to know what it is I am lacking.

Who knows, maybe on the outside things will be different. Maybe my Cool lies just over the school walls. I'll keep you posted.

Chapter 10

Sunday 6th December

Sam

Sam finished reading Milly's latest blog and left a comment. She and Robert didn't share @off-centre-oddity blogs on their social media because Milly was too worried that people at school might guess it was her. But Sam's mum always shared them on her social media accounts, and that in itself was enough to get Milly's words out there.

Sam was lying on her bed in her PJs. Bill had stayed last night, and they had all breakfasted together. He'd left just before eleven a.m. and later she and her mum would go to her grandparents' house for dinner ... *feast* would be a more appropriate word; all the aunts would be in the kitchen with her nani, and dish after fragrant dish would be brought out to the table to be devoured by noisy relatives. Sam's hair was always deeply infused with the scent of toasted cumin seeds and the floral smell of her nani's rose candle by the time they left.

She cropped a selfie of her, Robert and Milly standing in the blizzard caused by last night's snow machine and posted it to Instagram. Within seconds it was liked by Nadia, followed by a comment: @nadiamoonchild Fab pic. Dreaming of a white Christmas? 🌨️🎄

Sam looked at the comment. It was almost begging for a response. She imagined Nadia sitting in her bedroom holding her phone, staring at the screen, hoping for a comment.

It annoyed Sam how much she loved and loathed getting responses from Nadia on her posts. Even a like made her heart beat faster. It was infuriating! Nadia had betrayed her in the worst way possible. What did she think was going to happen by her constant liking of Sam's posts? Did she think Sam would suddenly forgive her? But then behind it, another thought crept in, almost a whisper; how would she feel if Nadia gave up liking her posts? Would that be worse than the likes? Sam begrudgingly had to admit that it would.

Nadia had cheated; Sam had seen it with her own eyes, out of her bedroom window! Of all the places Nadia could have gone to cheat on Sam, she chose the park across the road from Sam's house. Anyone would think she'd wanted to get caught. The cheating wasn't even the worst of it; Nadia had been snogging a guy! He was Nadia's ex-boyfriend, Jake. What a punch in the tinsel. Somehow that made the betrayal even worse.

Sam couldn't seem to get over the break-up. No matter how mean she was to Nadia, no matter much she ignored her in tutor group, it didn't seem to hurt any less. The simple fact was that Sam had really liked Nadia. It wasn't like they had broken up because Sam had got bored or changed her mind; she was really into Nadia, and Nadia had broken her heart.

Usually, Sam would ignore Nadia's comments on her posts, but this time – she was calling it being caught up in the season of goodwill – her finger hovered over the heart-shaped like button, and before she could change her mind, she clicked on it. The response from her friends was instantaneous.

Robert: Did your finger slip? You know you just liked a Nadia comment, right?

Sam: It's Christmas, I thought I'd show her who was the better person.

Robert: How gracious of you 🫤

Milly: She's persevered long enough, she deserves a like.

Sam: Whose side are you on?

Milly: Yours, always. But deep down in your cold, cold heart you still like Nadia and she obviously likes you too.

Sam was desperately trying to come back with a feasible sounding denial.

Sam is typing...

Sam is typing...

Sam is typing...

Milly: Don't bother trying to deny it.

Robert: We know your truth, girlfriend!

Sam: Eat tinsel, bauble brain.

Robert: Nice festive swearing! I'm so pleased you're both embracing the jolly season even though you're feeling Grinchy. Miranda apologized for ignoring me, by the way.

Milly: And did you forgive her?

Robert: Of course I did, I'm not Sam!

Sam: Gee, thanks.

Milly: I guess Miranda's got bigger baubles than Laurence!

Sam: Did you actually expect an apology from him?

Milly: I guess not.

Robert: This surprises me. I expected better of Laurence. I've always thought he was an OK guy.

Sam: That's because you are delightful, and you judge everyone by your own standards.

Robert: Delightful??? That's worse than sweet and cute!! What am I, a cartoon rabbit?

Milly: Squirrel.

Sam: Fawn.

Robert: Great, so I'm Bambi. No wonder I haven't got a girlfriend!

Milly

Milly had her hair tied up in a messy topknot and her baggiest old clothes on as she tidied her bedroom. She didn't often tidy her bedroom, and usually only under duress, but today she was feeling all kinds of het up, and tidying seemed to be the only thing to take her mind off it. She didn't know why last night was bothering her so much. She'd gone through her entire high school life without caring if the likes of Laurence Bashir acknowledged her or not. OK, that was a lie, she did care, but she had learned not to let it bother her; she let their obliviousness bounce off her like hail on an umbrella. So they'd spent an afternoon together, big deal! She was sure Laurence wasn't moping about his mansion thinking about her!

When the doorbell rang, she ignored it, until Tara came into her room, swinging a Barbie by the hair. "There's a boy on the doorstep."

"A boy?" asked Milly. "Is it Robert?"

"Nope. Not Robert. It's a different boy."

Milly froze. "For me?"

"Yep."

Milly ran down the stairs, slowing at the last few so as to appear nonchalant when she reached the door. It wasn't until she saw Laurence standing before her in perfect brilliance that she remembered she had wild hair and shapeless – possibly food-stained – clothes on. Her hand fluttered up to her topknot, but there was nothing to be done about it. If she pulled it out now her hair would look full Bellatrix Lestrange.

"Um, hi," said Laurence. His tone was quizzical as though he was surprised to find her here.

"You know where I live," said Milly. *Oh, sugar plums! Way to state the obvious, Milly! Tell him your name next, why don't you!*

134

"I asked Miranda and she asked Robert for your address. I dropped you off up the road on Friday, so I had a fair idea, but I didn't want to go knocking on every door in the cul- de-sac to find you!" He grinned but it looked fragile.

"Right." Milly didn't know what to say. She was still stinging from last night's rebuff. What was his problem? Did he have multiple personalities or something?

"I wanted to apologize for last night," he said.

Milly almost jumped backwards. Was he reading her mind? "Right," she said. *Stop saying right! Say something else, you sound like an automaton!* "OK." She mentally slapped her forehead.

Laurence was swinging his arms. He looked cold. Should she invite him in? Would that be weird? "It was damage limitation," he said, as if this was supposed to explain everything. Milly cocked her head to one side, her topknot listed over with it.

"I knew Cassia was about to go off; I recognize the signs. I just wanted to get her away from you guys as quickly as possible before she made a scene. I wanted to talk to you, but it would have made things worse, fired Cass up even more. I don't think she even realizes what she's like half the time."

"Are you defending Cassia or apologizing?" Milly asked hesitantly.

"I'm apologizing," he said, smiling.

"So, are you and Cassia together?" *Whaaaaaatttttt! What did you just ask? Why would you ask that?*

"No!" He almost snapped the word out in his hurry to answer. "We're friends, kind of, not really, but we've known each other a long time. I'm rambling. I'll stop."

Milly was going all kinds of melty on the doorstep watching the most confident guy in the school fumble over his words.

Laurence drew in a deep breath. "The thing is, I like you and I'm sorry that I didn't talk to you last night. The problem was with me, not you. I will try to do better."

He smiled and Milly held on to the door frame to stop herself from falling down in a Victorian swoon. *He likes me he likes me he likes me...*

"Apology accepted," she said as casually as she could. If her smile got any wider it was in danger of swallowing her ears. She wished she wasn't dressed like a badly packed Santa sack.

"Cool," said Laurence. He flashed Milly another smile and her knees dissolved. "So, are we cool then?"

"We are cool," said Milly. "Although, I should warn you that no one in the history of ever has described me as being cool."

Laurence laughed. "I think you're pretty cool," he said.

Milly squeaked involuntarily, it was high-pitched and loud, as though she had a guinea pig living in her throat. Laurence looked at her quizzically.

"Sorry about that," Milly guffawed. "I squeak when I'm happy, I guess?"

Laurence laughed again. "I'll keep that in mind," he said. "I'll file it along with the horror-hiccups," and he gave her a smile that was so cheeky that her throat guinea pig almost broke out into opera. "Well, that was it," he said, shrugging. "I just wanted to explain myself."

"Did you want a cup of tea?" Milly asked. *A cup of tea? Yeah, you're real cool, Milly!*

"I would actually love one," he said, "but I've got to go somewhere with my mum. Thanks anyway." There was that smile again. *Keep it together, Milly!*

"I'll see you at school tomorrow," he called as he walked away, pulling his jacket up around his ears against the cold.

Milly floated up the stairs and through the rest of Sunday, even her dad's absence during the family movie afternoon – *The Muppet's Christmas Carol* – couldn't crack her snow-globe mood.

Chapter 11

Monday 7th December

Laurence

Cassia had just sat back down having given the Magical Snow Ball update to the tutor group. It was only 8.40 a.m. and already Laurence had managed to argue with his dad – which in turn had upset his mum – and prang his car on one of the metal barriers in the sixth form car park. It was his own fault; he'd been distracted by the sight of Milly Parker hurrying along the path, the breeze teasing at her hair, long loose curls lifting about her face as though defying gravity. Jeez, what was happening to him? Was he thinking in poetic prose now? No wonder he'd clipped the barriers.

Ever since Milly had told him on Friday that she

didn't have a date for the ball, Laurence had found himself increasingly drawn to the idea of asking her to go with him. The thought had begun simply as a logical solution to their common problem; after all, he didn't have a date either, so they may as well go together. Not like a pity date, more like a charitable gesture. But the more he'd thought about it, the more he began to realize there was nothing charitable about it; he liked her, he *really* liked her. This had taken him by surprise. Milly was not, after all, his usual type and yet he was drawn to her, there was no other way to put it. And it wasn't only because she was pretty, though she was exceptionally pretty – now he had actually taken the time to give her more than a cursory glance, he had realized this – it was that he found himself wanting to hear more of what she had to say, and he wanted her validation on the things that he said. This was new; he'd never been too concerned about other people's opinions. He hadn't needed to be; people tended to agree with him. Of course, there was the minor matter of her thinking she might not want to go to the ball, but Laurence couldn't shake the idea of Milly in a ball gown, his arms around her, slow dancing... *Get a grip!*

Cassia kept pouting in his direction and taking every opportunity to walk past him and touch his arm or hand. As she'd sashayed past *again* a moment ago, she had reached out and brushed her hand along his jawline. Laurence was bemused. They'd broken up ages ago and he'd given no indication that he wanted to get back together again. And yet she seemed to keep draping herself over him like a highly perfumed dustsheet.

He looked over at Milly, sat as usual with Sam and Robert. Her hair was the most amazing colour, like ripe apricots. He wondered how he'd not noticed it before. He was pleased he'd mustered the courage to go and see her yesterday. He'd hated the way things had been left on Saturday night; there were enough misunderstandings in his life. When she'd held his gaze with those pale grey eyes, he'd found himself uncharacteristically lost for words.

"So, Lou," said Cassia, loud enough for everyone to hear. Laurence hated her using his nickname; it implied an intimacy he didn't feel. "How did you get on with Milky on Friday? Fun, was it?"

Laurence glanced at Milly and saw her cheeks flush pink as she looked down at her desk and tried to pretend she hadn't heard. He didn't like it. He'd never been keen on Cassia's random attacks, but this felt different. Something bloomed warm in his chest: protectiveness? "It was good, thanks, Cass. It's an interesting place. Thought-provoking," he replied coldly, in the hopes she would lay off.

"Thought-provoking?" Cassia laughed too loudly. "And what about Milky? Was she thought-provoking and interesting?" She was smiling archly, as though she expected him to be in on the joke with her.

Laurence opened his mouth to defend Milly, but Sam beat him to it. "More interesting than you'll ever be," she snapped from across the room.

Dammit! He'd missed his chance. Now it looked like he didn't care.

Cassia shot Sam a look. Laurence wanted to implore Sam not to get into a war of words with Cassia. He'd found it appealing once, thought she was sassy, but he'd come to realize that what Cassia spouted was meanness, not sass.

"Leave it out, Cass," said Laurence, cutting across her before she could spit a retort.

"Oh my god!" Cassia looked at him mock affronted. "One afternoon with Milly Parker and you've been infected with dweeb!"

Cassia's entourage tittered; though not Miranda, he noted.

"There's just no need for it, Cass," he replied calmly. "And in answer to your question; yes, *Milly* is interesting and thought-provoking."

A little gasp ran around the class. This was as good as

a public proclamation of defiance. Cassia's face puckered in annoyance, while across the room, the teeniest beginnings of a smile played at the corners of Milly's mouth.

Not for the first time in recent weeks, Laurence felt sure there was more to life than being the most popular guy in the school, no matter what Cassia would have him believe.

Milly

Laurence caught up with Milly as she was walking to her next class. "Hey," he said, walking up beside her.

Milly jumped into the air like she'd been electrocuted and dropped the pile of books she'd been carrying. Loose papers covered with her scrawled notes shot out across the busy corridor and were trampled underfoot by stampeding students. Just once she'd like to not be a klutz.

Laurence set about gathering the papers. "Sorry," he said. "I didn't mean to make you jump."

"Don't worry about it," Milly said, picking up her books. "It happens all the time. I get caught up in my own thoughts and forget there are other humans in the vicinity."

"I guess that's why you get good grades."

Milly looked at him quizzically.

"You know," he said. "You can concentrate while all hell's breaking loose around you. I get distracted too easily."

"Oh," said Milly, wishing she could think of something witty to say. "Being boring has its perks, I suppose."

"I don't think you're boring," said Laurence, straightening the collected papers and handing them back to her. *Ask her to the ball, ask her to the ball*, his brain kept egging him on, but he felt weirdly nervous; he'd never asked someone out without being absolutely sure that they'd say yes – and with Milly he had no idea which way it would go. He wasn't sure his ego could handle a rebuff.

Meanwhile...

All coherent words had left Milly's brain and she stood gawping at him like a demented reindeer. *He doesn't think I'm boring! That might just have been the nicest thing any boy has ever said to me. Jumping jingle bells, how sad is that?*

Laurence raised his eyebrows as though waiting for her to say something. Milly realized this was how conversations usually went; one person speaks and the other responds.

"Thanks," she said.

Laurence smiled.

Phew! Good response, she thought.

"I wanted to apologize for Cassia," said Laurence.

Now it was the turn of Milly's eyebrows to raise. "Why are you apologizing for Cassia?"

"Because sometimes when she talks, she gives the impression that she's speaking for all of us. But she's not and I just want you to know that we don't all think the way she does. It's like guilt by association."

He ran his hand through his perfect hair and looked into the middle distance. He looked utterly gorgeous. Milly had never seen anyone make thinking look this hot. Laurence seemed to find his words and Milly tried to regather her wits.

"What I'm trying to say is, please don't judge me by the things that come out of Cassia's mouth."

"OK," she said, smiling and hoping this was the right response.

Laurence smiled too and seemed to relax, as though he'd been building himself up for this conversation. In his head he was scrambling for ways to bring things around to the ball without making it look like a conscious effort. "So, are you still anti Christmas ball?" he asked. *Not bad. Keep it casual, test the water.*

"I wouldn't say I was *anti* exactly," Milly replied. *Try, dying to go but desperately wanting to convince myself otherwise.*

"Maybe you'd feel more enthusiastic if someone asked you to be their date?"

Milly laughed. Was he mocking her? "Maybe, but I won't hold my breath waiting for *that* to happen!"

"Why not? You must have thought about someone you'd like to go with?"

Milly looked up into his dark brown eyes and almost dropped her books again. She suppressed a hiccup. *You you you! I want to go to the ball with you!* her brain screamed but she said: "Sure," in her squeaky-throat guinea-pig voice, while trying to hold her breath.

"You're trying not to hiccup, aren't you?" Laurence smiled.

"*Hiccup!* Busted. *Hiccup!*" Milly managed, one hand clamped over her mouth.

Laurence laughed. "Because I was just thinking that if there is someone you'd like to go to the ball with, he might want to go with you too," he said, willing her with the power of his mind to understand what he was getting at.

"Right," she said through her hand. *What is he going on about?* "Wait..." A horrifying thought popped into her head. "You're not trying to set me up with someone are you? Because I. That's. Really not. Like, no way, noooooooo way!" The hiccups ramped up a notch.

"No, relax, it was nothing like that. I just thought, if you liked..."

"Actually, no, there's nobody," she said far too quickly. She needed to squash any ideas he had about matchmaking.

·"Oh, but you just said there was someone."

"Yeah, I got confused, thought you were talking about something else. I do that," She raised her eyebrows and crossed her eyes in a *hey I'm so goofy* way.

Laurence felt deflated. "OK then," he said. "Cool, glad we got that straight. So, do you want a lift to the food bank tomorrow?"

"*Hiccup!* Yes. *Hiccup!* Please. *Hiccup!*"

"Great! I'll catch you later," said Laurence and strode off down the corridor, leaving Milly and her hiccups to mull over what had just happened.

Robert

When Robert went to his locker to grab his biology books, he found a note wedged in the door.

Meet me after school by the wooden bridge.
I've got a great idea for storytime tomorrow
afternoon.
Miranda xx

Robert was intrigued. Obviously, she could have asked him this morning at registration, or even during their English class, but then he supposed Cassia would have been present. Really, could Cassia actually stop Miranda from talking to him? Sure, she was a mean girl, but come on! She wasn't actually the queen!

At ten to four, Robert found Miranda waiting for him on the bridge. The stream was iced over at its edges, and the splashes from the fast-running water in the middle had formed long, skinny icicles which drooped from the grasses and reeds clinging to the bank like a frozen waterfall.

"Hi!" Miranda said chirpily, her breath white in the cold. "I think it's going to snow."

Robert looked up at the sky; it certainly looked laden with something.

"I doubt it's snow," he said. "Probably more snain."

"Huh?"

"Never mind."

"In Canada it *knows* how to snow. I miss the snow. I think the Canadian weather could teach the British weather a few things."

"Except how to rain," said Robert and Miranda laughed.

"No, you Brits have got the rain down for sure!"

"Do you miss Canada?"

"Sometimes." She looked straight into Robert's eyes and he felt his heart skip. "And sometimes not so much."

Robert grinned. *Stop grinning like an idiot! Say something!* "So, storytime," he said.

"Yes! I've got an idea. Have you heard of *We're Going On a Bear Hunt*?"

Robert laughed. "Are you kidding me? With all my siblings? I know it off by heart!"

"Great!" Miranda smiled. She had a sequinned tea-cosy hat pulled down low over her ears; she looked VERY cute. "So, I was thinking we could read it together, only while we're reading it, we get the kids to do it with us and we do the actions, you know, like..." Here she began to take giant, balletic steps as she recited, "We have to go OVER it!"

"Are you making me do some sort of interpretive dance thing? I've gotta say, this looks a lot like interpretive dance."

She laughed at him. "No! We'll just be doing the actions of the story: over it, under it, through it ... all of that stuff. The kids will love it."

"They probably will," said Robert. "But we're not recording it. If I find a video of myself doing interpretive dance on TikTok there'll be trouble."

Miranda grabbed Robert's arm and began to pull him along. Robert let himself be pulled. *This is flirting! She is definitely flirting with me. A mean-minion is touching my anorak! This is not a drill, I repeat, this is not a drill!*

"I promise, no secret filming," Miranda giggled, leading him off the bridge and up the muddy riverbank path, which ran parallel with the high street.

"Where are we going?" Robert asked.

"I thought you could walk me home."

"OK. Where do you live?"

Their feet were squelching and slipping in the mud that was too wet to freeze.

"On the new estate past the Old Windmill."

"Ooh, posh," said Robert.

"Not really," Miranda laughed.

"Wouldn't it be better to walk up the high street? It's almost dark, one of us is likely to end up in the stream."

"This way's quieter," said Miranda.

"That's because all the sane people are walking up the nice, concrete pavement."

"I think Cassia said she was getting coffee after school in the high street..."

"So?"

"I just don't want to bump into her right now, that's all."

Robert laughed. "Why? Are you ashamed to be seen with me?"

But Miranda just giggled and hugged his arm tighter, and Robert decided that only an idiot would pass up the opportunity to risk a broken ankle with the hottest of the mean-minions.

Sam

Sam and her mum were catching up on *Made in Chelsea* with a bowl of sweet and salty popcorn nestled between them. Bill was supposed to have come over for dinner but *apparently* he had to work late.

"Have you thought any more about Bill's moving-in suggestion?" Sam asked.

"Yes."

"And?"

"I'm still thinking about it."

"Aren't you worried that if you keep him hanging on too long, he'll give up?"

"No, babes, I'm not. If he's serious, he'll wait."

"But don't you think you might be hurting his feelings? It might come across like you don't care that much."

Mum paused *MIC* and turned to face her. "Is that what I've taught you?" she asked. "To give in to people just so that you don't hurt their feelings?"

"No, but … Bill isn't people."

"And what about my feelings? Don't they count?"

Sam could see her mum turning the tables on her. Her avoidance of things she didn't want to discuss was legendary. No wonder she hadn't told Sam about her heart condition.

"Why are you so closed off about this?" Sam asked.

"Do you really need to ask that?"

"Yes, I do! Everyone always tells me, don't ask about your dad, don't press too hard. And I know that it was really bad, but he's been gone for years!"

Her mum sat up straight and pulled her shoulders back. This was peak Mum, pulling up the drawbridge and cutting off the conversation.

"Do I get all up in your grill about your love life?" Mum asked.

"I don't have a love life," said Sam.

"You might have if you stopped being so pig-headed."

Sam bristled. "And where do I get that from?"

Her mum smiled archly. "Touché!"

"Can I be honest with you, without you getting cross?" Sam asked.

Her mum's lips thinned into a line, but she nodded.

"I worry that you'll regret it if you push Bill away."

"If I do, they'll be my regrets, not yours," said her mum. "I appreciate that you like Bill, but this is my business."

"Is there ... is there something you're not telling me?"

"Like what? I haven't got another fella on the go, if that's what you're implying. Just because I'm not jumping to move in with Bill, doesn't mean I've got someone else on the go."

"Oh no, Mum, I wasn't thinking that at all."

"Well, what then, babes? What is it you think I'm hiding?"

How was she going to do this? Her mum was either getting the wrong end of the stick on purpose, or Sam hadn't made her question clear enough.

"I found something," Sam began, slowly, testing the water. "In the bathroom."

Her mum looked blank for a moment and then she laughed.

"Oh, that!" she chuckled. "I thought I'd hidden that in the bin. It was a false alarm, babes, nothing to worry about. I won't be springing any brothers or sisters on you!"

"Wait. What? You thought you might be pregnant?" Woah! She hadn't seen that coming. How many secrets was her mum keeping?

"I was worried for a moment there, but it's OK. Don't you worry," said her mum, grabbing Sam's face and laying kisses all over it. "You're my only baby!"

***

Later, when she was alone in her room, and had calmed down from the shock of finding out her mum had taken a pregnancy test, she realized she was still no closer to getting her to fess up about her heart condition. Maybe it was time to bring Robert and Milly in on this; they'd tell her what to do. Or they'd tell her she was being nuts. Perhaps she was. Was she putting obstacles in her *own* way? Sam sighed and took another online virtual tour around Nottingham University. Was she pushing her mum towards moving in with Bill, so that she could go off to uni guilt-free? She ran a self-diagnostic, weighing up her thoughts and feelings, and decided that no; her motives were pure. But it didn't change the fact that if her mum was sick, she would feel a lot less guilty about leaving if Bill was around.

Robert

Robert was in a quandary. He was lying on a mattress on the floor in Dot and Curly's room, since being evicted by his elder brother returning home from uni. Curly had given him his Peppa Pig to help him sleep, but Peppa was being no help whatsoever; never trust a pig in a dress to solve your problems for you.

As he lay beneath a Paw Patrol duvet cover, he was relieved that his desperate feelings for Sam had finally settled back into the friend zone where they belonged. This was a good thing. Not so good, was his latest unfeasible crush. Miranda. Miranda the mean-minion. This would never do. Having unrequited love for a lesbian was one thing, but fancying a mean-minion, that was practically a criminal offence.

There was only one thing for it. He burrowed under the duvet and video called Milly. "Are you asleep?" he whispered.

"Does it look like I'm asleep?"

"Your eyes are puffy."

"Well, I was asleep and then a moron video called me, so now I'm awake."

"I saw you chatting with Laurence earlier."

"He was offering to give me a lift to the food bank tomorrow. And he was apologizing for Cassia this morning, which was a bit weird. I mean, Cassia is responsible for her own actions, don't you think?"

"Maybe he feels tarnished by association?" Robert suggested.

"Maybe. He's a nice guy underneath all that handsome."

"I told you he'd be cool about you using the food bank. If you can look past the Armani labels, he's all right."

"I still haven't told him about the food bank thing."

"Oh, that's a bit weird, isn't it?"

"I just haven't found the right moment yet."

"Didn't it come up at all in your conversation about the *food bank?*"

"Why did you call me?"

"Yeah, right, sorry. I think I like Miranda."

Milly sucked in a breath and let out a small squeal. "At last!" she whispered. "You fancy someone who isn't your gay best friend ... or Mrs Grinch! This is awesome!"

"She's a mean-minion, though."

"Nobody's perfect."

"So, what do you think? Would someone like Miranda go for someone like me?"

"Why not? You're not bad-looking ... from a distance."

"Gee, thanks."

"I'm kidding! If you like her, go for it. She'd be lucky to have you."

"Thanks, Mills. I'm not great at this stuff."

"Nor me."

"I mean, how can you even tell if someone likes you?"

"Do you make her laugh?"

"Yes. But that doesn't count. I make you and Sam laugh all the time, it doesn't mean you fancy me."

"We're laughing *at* you, Bertram. That's different."

"Cheers."

"Look, I think you just go with the flow and see where it leads you."

"Ha! Says the person least likely to go with the flow ever!"

"Do as I say, not as I do."

"Yes, Mum."

"Is that Peppa Pig in your bed?"

"It's not mine."

"Does that make it OK?"

"Soooo judgey!"

"I'm going to sleep now, again."

"Night, Mills."

"Night, Robert, night, Peppa."

Chapter 12

Tuesday 8th December

Sam

Despite the electric blow heaters, the old aircraft hangar was so vast that it was still only barely warmer inside than outside. The pigeons sitting on the beams above, with their heads tucked under their wings, seemed to agree.

Donations were beginning to pick up, even since Sam's last visit on Friday. The space was starting to look like a minimalist Santa's grotto, as boxes covered in bright, shiny Christmas paper invaded the bland space with pops of joyful colour. As well as the present boxes, the charity received winter coats, shoes and blankets, to be dished out at the same time as the gifts.

Sam was working with Libby, a seasoned aid worker with a first-hand perspective on the kinds of perils refugees faced. She had only been back in Britain since November.

"My poor old mum was starting to make noises about how I'm never home for Christmas," said Libby. "So I thought I'd give her this one."

"I bet she was pleased," said Sam.

"You have no idea!" Libby laughed. "You'd think the queen was coming to stay!"

Sam felt a niggle of guilt as she imagined her own mum sitting at home alone, nights on end, if she went away to uni. If she didn't speak to her mum soon about the prospect of her leaving home, she would end up living with her mum for ever. An image of the two of them quietly knitting together on the sofa filled her mind, Sam with her grey hair pulled back into a neat bun, one of their twenty cats sitting on her lap and getting fur on her pleated tweed skirt, *The Antiques Roadshow* on the telly. She shook herself and shuddered.

"It's freezing in here, isn't it?" said Libby in agreement with Sam's silent shiver.

"Yeah," Sam agreed.

"Ms Tibbott tells me you want to study Human Rights Law," said Libby.

"Does she?"

Libby laughed. "Ms Tibbott and I go back a long way. Rainy old Kent isn't the only place she's been a teacher, you know."

"Really?"

"Uh-huh. She's seen her fair share of the world. She also said you worked for this charity in the summer?"

"Yeah, we arranged park days and picnics, you know, to try and help people make new friends. I didn't do much really, just made sandwiches and set up games for the kids."

"Don't listen to her!" said a voice that sent a thrill through Sam's stomach. "She's too modest; she worked really hard all summer."

Sam turned to see Nadia standing in the doorway, her arms filled with brightly papered boxes.

"Oh, hey, let me help you with those," said Libby, rushing over to relieve Nadia of her load.

"There's more in the car," said Nadia.

"Great! I'll get you to write down where these are donated from for our records, if you don't mind," said Libby.

"Sure, yeah. It's my dad's shop. Croft Stores. He puts up posters in the shop every year. His customers are really generous."

"Lucky us," said Libby. "Sam, can you help this..."

"Nadia," said Sam.

"You two know each other, great!" said Libby. "Could you help Nadia bring in the rest of the boxes, please, and I'll go grab the paperwork."

Sam wanted to be hardened to Nadia's charms, but it wasn't easy. She had practised being aloof for so long that she could pull off a pretty convincing cold stare by now, but making her heart as hard as her outer shell wasn't as easy. She was annoyed that it skipped a beat when she heard Nadia's voice and skipped another when she caught sight of her. She was still angry, but it was hard to keep the fires of hate stoked when Nadia was standing there looking so nervous.

Sam swallowed her feelings down hard and brushed past her. "You coming?" she called back.

Nadia followed Sam out and opened the boot of her dad's car to reveal more boxes. "My dad was going to bring them, but I was talking to Robert..."

"Robert?"

"Yeah, they had band practice in our garage." Nadia's elder brother was the drummer for the Indigo Tigers. "Well, anyway, he told me you had your placement here, so..."

Sam made a mental note to lick the samosas her mum was making for Robert before she handed them over tomorrow. "So here you are," she said, gathering an armful of boxes.

"I'm sorry," blurted Nadia. "I don't know how many times I can say it. You never let me explain."

"You didn't need to explain," said Sam with what she hoped was a cool nonchalance. "I saw it with my own eyes; I didn't need you to draw me a picture as well."

Nadia had tried many times to state her case, but Sam wasn't interested. Once a cheat, always a cheat. It had been hard to begin with to ignore Nadia during tutor time and PSHE lessons, but practice makes perfect, and now she had spent so long denying Nadia's very presence that she barely even noticed her; or so she told herself.

"Shouldn't you be at a placement?" Sam asked.

"I'll go in a minute." Nadia smiled as they headed unsteadily, beneath the weight of several heavy boxes, back into the hangar.

Sam wanted to ask where her placement was, but her pride was too thick in her throat to form the words.

As if reading Sam's mind Nadia said: "I'm working at the soup kitchen. Last week I was on spud-peeling duty. This week they're going to let me loose on actual cooking!" She shrugged and gave a nervous little half-laugh, and Sam had to fight really hard not to join her. "You know how I like to experiment with new flavours!" she said, looking at Sam like a puppy hoping for a treat.

This time a laugh escaped Sam before she had time to check it. She certainly did know all about Nadia's love of experimental cookery; the taste of her Brussels sprout and clementine tofu surprise had lingered long after they'd abandoned it to the bin.

"Lucky them," said Sam as they schlepped another load of boxes. "And rather them than me!"

"They weren't all bad," said Nadia, craning her neck above the load and raising her eyebrows. "My octuple chocolate cookies were a triumph." She smiled at Sam and it was like the sun had broken through the pewter clouds. Sam's breath caught in her throat.

"Yeah," she said briskly to hide her feelings. "They were good. They were basically just pools of chocolate, though."

"What's better than that?" asked Nadia. She signed the paperwork and began to walk backwards towards the door. "It was nice talking with you," she said. "I'll probably have more boxes to bring next week, so I might see you then. I mean, I'll see you at school ... but you know ... I miss you. Anyway, Byeeee!" Nadia gave the goofiest children's TV presenter wave that Sam had ever seen.

"See ya," Sam called, causing Nadia to break into such a joyful smile that for the second time in as many minutes Sam's breath was whipped clean away.

"Friend of yours?" asked Libby as the door to the hangar closed.

"Used to be."

"Looks like she'd like to be friends again if you ask me."

Sam wanted to say, "Yeah, well I didn't ask you!" but what she actually said was, "It's complicated."

"It's a simple as you want to make it," said Libby, pulling out a fresh roll of holly berry wrapping paper. "The families we work with, some of them haven't seen their loved ones for months, years even. They've got thousands of miles and oceans of politics and bureaucracy between them; *that's* complicated."

Sam didn't answer and Libby didn't say any more on the subject. They chatted about Christmas plans and family while they worked. Later, when Libby went into the kitchenette, Sam pondered her encounter with Nadia. Was she really still angry with Nadia? Or had she been so long in a cycle of dislike that it had become a kind of habit? Maybe she only thought she hated Nadia because she still liked her so much. Hate was an easier emotion to channel than dealing with the hurt of liking someone who broke your heart.

Milly

Milly climbed into Laurence's car after the food bank with considerably less trepidation than when she accepted his offer of a lift before their shift.

She had mercifully dialled her nerves down to intermediate fear by lunchtime, and even the horror-hiccups had slowed once they were on the road. It had been a busy afternoon and not just for her internal organs. More and more people were visiting the food bank for the first time, and Milly's heart went out to them as they awkwardly navigated this new reality they found themselves in. It was getting close to Christmas and the financial stress of the holidays was visible on lots of faces.

Milly had been surprised by Laurence's compassion. Laurence, it seemed, was full of surprises.

"Do you want to pick some music?" Laurence asked as he pulled out on to the road. He had offered to give her a lift home, and since it had just begun to snow Milly was happy to accept. He drove carefully, as the fat flakes fell.

"Sure." Milly bent down and began to pull the mess of CD cases at her feet into a pile. "I can't believe it's snowing! It looks nice against all the Christmas lights in the streets. Pity it never settles."

"Yeah, I don't remember ever having a white Christmas." He wondered if it was snowing where his brother was. And would he be able to see it?

"Not outside movies," Milly agreed. She pulled a pile of CDs on to her lap and began to sift through them. "But I live in hope!"

There was the mix of indie, grunge and rock music that she had expected, but then something else caught her eye. "What is this?" she asked, holding up three Christmas compilation CDs. "I thought Christmas was dead to you."

"Oh, that, yeah." Laurence half-smiled. "I seem to be stuck somewhere between wanting to forget all about it because of the memories and wanting to cling to it because of the memories. I know. I'm a massive contradiction."

"So the memories are painful?" Milly asked tentatively. "You don't have to talk about it if you don't want to."

"Actually, it's the opposite. The memories are great. That's why I didn't want to listen the other day, especially to that song. It reminds me of how Christmas used to be and then I think about how it'll be this year and ... it hurts that it won't be the same."

"I'm sorry," said Milly. "I didn't mean to pry."

"No, I'm glad you asked. I want to talk about it; I just haven't had anyone to talk about it with. Until now."

Milly thought she might faint. Was Laurence going to confide something to her that he hadn't been able to speak about with any of his friends? He had pulled the car over to the side of the road and parked.

Laurence bit his lip and wondered if this was the right thing to do; if he was somehow betraying his family by divulging their dirty secret. But there was something about Milly that made him feel he could trust her. And if he didn't talk about his feelings soon he was going to implode. He would just have to take the chance.

"If I tell you something," he began, "can we keep it just between us?"

"Of course," said Milly.

"My brother, Jamie. He's in prison for embezzlement."

Milly was shocked. She'd never known anyone that had gone to prison. All she knew about prison was from watching *Orange Is the New Black*. She had not seen the conversation taking this turn and she didn't know what she was supposed to say.

"Oh, I'm sorry. Are you close?" Not that it made much difference, she supposed. She was sure she would miss her brother if we went to prison, even though he was the biggest bah humbug in the south-east.

"Really close. He's my best mate. Obviously, I don't condone what he did, but I miss him so much."

166

"Of course you do! He's your brother. My brother is a right pain in the bum, but I'd still miss him if wasn't around."

"We had this thing we'd do at Christmas..." Was he really going to tell Milly this? "You'll think it's stupid."

"Why don't you let me decide? It can't be any worse than my mum making us all listen while she reads us *The Night Before Christmas* every Christmas Eve." *Did I actually just tell him that?*

"That's kind of cute," said Laurence. He was warming more and more to Milly. "OK. I can't believe I'm actually fessing up to this. Literally nobody else knows about this."

"Well, now I'm really intrigued."

"So, every year, we'd learn all the words to a cheesy Christmas hit and then perform it to our parents, with actions and everything, like a musical on Christmas Day. It's just one of those silly traditions, you know?"

"It doesn't sound stupid," said Milly. "I mean, it sounds hilarious! But that's what makes Christmas special, I guess: all the silly family traditions."

Laurence felt pleased and relieved. He was right to trust Milly. "Last year we did Wham. We bought mullet wigs and everything."

"So that's why you didn't want to listen to it when it came on the radio," said Milly.

"It took me by surprise. I didn't know what to do. I've been avoiding listening to it, and then suddenly it was coming out of the speaker."

"When did it happen?" Milly asked. "When did your brother go to prison?"

"June. It was a big scandal. The company Jamie worked for is pretty big and, what with my dad being a barrister, it was *shamed barrister's son* and all that." He laughed mirthlessly.

"I don't remember hearing anything about it." Milly was sure something like that would have been in the local news. If it had got out, it would have spread through the common rooms like wildfire.

"It was all hushed up, at least as far as the media was concerned," said Laurence. "My dad has connections." He said this as a means of explanation.

Milly wondered what it would be like to live in a world where your family had *media connections*.

"But within the industry and my dad's line of work, it was pretty big news," Laurence continued. "Mud sticks, you know. My dad's lost clients."

At least he's still got a job, Milly thought and then chided herself. Money wasn't everything, she knew, but it sure helped.

"How did your folks take it? I guess they're missing your brother too."

"My dad won't talk about him. Jamie's name has become a dirty word in our house. It feels like he's trying to erase him from our lives, like a stain to be scrubbed out."

"That's hard to deal with," said Milly. "How is your mum coping?" She thought of her own mum: holder-together of all things in a crisis.

"She cries a lot. It's almost like she's afraid to talk about him in case she upsets my dad. But why are we all so worried about upsetting him? He acts like he doesn't even care! I'm sorry, I didn't mean to dump all this on you, it's just that I feel like I can talk to you."

"It's OK," said Milly. "I'm happy to listen. Well, not *happy* obviously. I mean, I'm happy that you feel you can trust me."

"I do," said Laurence. "I haven't told anyone at school about this stuff. Not even Tom."

"It's a lot to keep bottled up."

Laurence nodded. Milly couldn't imagine how she would have coped these last few months without Robert and Sam to talk to.

"It feels like my family has divided into camps," Laurence went on. "You know what I mean?"

Milly knew exactly what he meant. But she didn't want to eclipse his pain by telling him about her family woes. Or maybe this was the time? Now might be the perfect moment to tell him about the food bank and clear the fuggy cloud of omission that was hanging above her head.

"I completely understand," said Milly.

"I knew you would," Laurence said, smiling shyly at her.

Do it now, tell him now! Tell him! Milly shouted to herself.

Ask her to the ball, ask her now, do it, do it! Laurence steeled himself for the big question.

"My family have been..."

"So, I was wondering..."

They both said at the same time.

"Sorry," said Laurence, "you go first."

"No, it's fine, what were you going to say?"

"I was just going to ask..."

Thwack! A snowball hit the windscreen, making them both jump. A group of year nines ran off down the road laughing.

"Holy nutcrackers! That scared the tinsel out of me." Milly was clutching her chest.

"Holy nutcrackers?"

"Festive swearing. It's another tradition: only Christmas-related swearing throughout the whole of the jolly season. Robert is very committed to the cause, and I don't like to let him down."

"That sounds like a tradition I can get on board with,"

Laurence laughed. Milly liked making him laugh.

They were quiet for a moment.

"So, you started saying something before the car came under snowball fire?" Milly said.

"Yeah, um, I..." Laurence's bravery had left him. "I have completely forgotten what it was!" He slapped his head in mock frustration. "How about you? You mentioned something about your family?"

Suddenly it didn't feel like the right time any more to blurt out her family's business. The moment for sharing had faded like the snowball melting slowly down the windscreen in the warmth of the heaters.

"Do you know what, I can't remember either! I guess it can't have been that important."

Laurence started the engine again and drove Milly home. The snow was falling thick enough now to warrant the windscreen wipers being on, and though it didn't seem to be sticking to the ground, garden walls and post boxes began to look like they'd been thickly iced in a layer of white fondant.

As she watched his car turn out of her cul-de-sac, Milly couldn't help feeling pleased that, for all his popularity, it was her he'd chosen to confide in.

Sam

Bill had come over for dinner, but Sam could sense that things weren't as they should be. It was friendly enough, but the unspoken words were hanging in the air, screaming silently, like wraiths trapped between worlds. She knew her mum was wild about Bill and Bill was potty about her mum, so why was her mum being so stubborn?

She left the "grown-ups" watching *Love Actually* after pudding and messaged the group.

> **Sam:** Super weird atmos downstairs. Why are adults so crap at being adults? 😕

> **Milly:** Should we hold an intervention? 😗 We could do my parents at the same time.

> **Sam:** Any movement on the K.O.C. front?

> **Milly:** The K.O.C. is still AWOL ☹

> **Robert:** Toast and Dot have decorated my bed...

He sent a picture of his mattress covered in tinsel, baubles and various Christmas-themed soft toys, including a giant Rudolf.

Robert: Apparently, I have to sleep under it to give me Christmas dreams. If the K.O.C. doesn't make an appearance, you're welcome to borrow my siblings ... you can have them on permanent loan.

Milly: Adorable!

Milly is typing...

Milly: OMG!!!

Milly is typing...

Sam: ??

Milly: Laurence just PMed me on Insta.

Robert: Holy Santa hats!

Milly: He said he really enjoyed spending time with me this afternoon!

Sam: 🎉

Robert: It's a Christmas miracle!

Sam: It's a Miracle on Food Bank Street!

Milly: He's probably just being friendly. We had kind of a deep discussion earlier.

Sam: Friendly schmendly

Robert: Not too friendly I hope 😜

Sam: So you've told him about the food bank then? That's great! And he was cool about it?

Milly: 😶 Um. No. I didn't tell him about the food bank.

Robert: MILLS!!!!!

Sam:

Milly: I know, I know. I'll tell him.

Sam: Do it quick. The longer you leave it. . .

Milly: Oh god, terror-tinkles! BRB

Sam: While we're alone, is there anything you want to fess up to, Bertram?

Robert: Huh?

Sam: Nadia turned up at the hangar today, you told her where I was.

Robert: Oh yeah. Soz about that. She kinda put me on the spot, and you know I'm a rubbish liar.

Milly: I'm back! Ooh, you spoke to Nadia, what happened?

Sam: I didn't try to kill her.

Milly: Progress.

Sam: She keeps wanting to *talk*!

Robert: Maybe you should listen.

Sam: Maybe you should kiss my North Pole!

Robert: Ooh brutal! That is my new favourite festive swear.

There was a knock at the door.

"Yes?" called Sam.

"It's only me, Sam love," said Bill. "I'm gonna push off now, just wanted to say goodbye."

Sam pulled the door open without thinking. She wanted to say something, but she wasn't sure what. Bill was at the top of the stairs. He stopped when he saw her, and Sam didn't know how to proceed. She and Bill talked a lot but not about real stuff. They liked to gang up on her mum and take the mickey, and they got into big discussions about politics and *Love Island*, but they didn't do feelings or anything like that. Bill was looking at her. He smiled, and Sam found her voice. "Have you and Mum had a fight?"

Bill looked like he wanted to say something, but he didn't. "No, love, nothing like that. I've got an early start, that's all."

"Oh, OK. I'll see you tomorrow?"

Bill rubbed the back of his neck and looked at the carpet. "Um, not sure. Maybe. I'll see how late this job keeps me." Bill was a Section Engineer in construction. "I just wanted you to know," he began, looking deeply uncomfortable. "That whatever happens with me and your mum, I think of you as a daughter. And, what I'm trying to say is ... I'll always be around for you, if you need me." He sniffed and cleared his throat. "Anyway," he said with gruff joviality. "I'm off. See you later, love."

"See you later," said Sam. It was all she could muster; she was in danger of crying. She watched him walk down the narrow hallway, and as he reached the top stair, she realized she couldn't leave it like that. She called out: "Bill!"

Bill turned back to look at her.

"Thanks," she said. "That means a lot. And ... if I'd ever had a dad, I'd have wanted him to be like you."

Bill smiled at her and gave her his signature wink and carried on down the stairs. Sam closed her bedroom door and threw herself down on the bed. Was that a goodbye-goodbye?

It certainly felt like it. She buried her head in her pillow and let out a frustrated scream. Her mum was blowing it, and Sam didn't know how to stop it.

Chapter 13

Wednesday 9th December

Sam

"Listen up, people!" Cassia commanded from the front of the class. Thirty sets of lips zipped themselves shut and all eyes turned obediently to the front of the class.

"Thank you," said Cassia sweetly. "There's a lot still to be done. Some of the other forms are building a papier mâché mountain range and the icicle chandeliers are beginning to take shape, but there's a shedload still to do. So I've written up a rota to make sure everyone pulls their fair share of the weight."

Cassia clicked her fingers and the mean-minions jumped up and began handing out sheets of paper with lunchtime ballroom duties.

Sam looked down at the paper and saw her name with Nadia's printed in for this lunchtime. Sam glanced over at Nadia, and Nadia smiled tentatively. Sam nodded back. From the corner of her eye, she saw Cassia clock the exchange.

"I took the liberty of putting you two together." Cassia's voice was syrup. "I know you had a lovers' tiff a while back but I'm sure you can be civil for the greater good."

Sam knew full well that Cassia hadn't put her with Nadia for any kind of good, great or otherwise. Everyone knew that Sam and Nadia's split had been acrimonious, and Cassia would have delighted in putting them together and then settling back to watch the fireworks. Sam often wondered what had happened in Cassia's life to make her such a prize pain in the candy canes. Robert had once told her that Cassia was supposed to have gone to some private boarding school when they left primary, only she'd failed the entry test and landed here instead – lucky them.

"It's like the Christmas gods are conspiring to get you and Nadia back together," said Robert.

"Don't let Cassia hear you referring to her as a god," said Sam. "Her ego is big enough. And anyway, we're not getting back together. She's still a cheating liar."

Robert shrugged, making it clear that he didn't believe

her. Sam wished she could siphon off just a little of his candour. People thought she was tough, but inside she was a mass of feelings she didn't know what to do with.

Milly

Milly had just shovelled in a mouthful of smoky bacon crisps when Laurence plonked himself down on the sofa beside her. "So, I've been thinking," he said, unaware that his sudden appearance had induced a major crisp crisis.

Should she chew quickly and get them swallowed and out of the way? But this would mean Laurence would hear her crunching. She was pretty sure loud fast crisp crunching was not sexy. Should she suck the crisps then? Until they were soggy enough to mash down and swallow? *Stop overthinking!* she yelled at herself as she semi-covered her mouth and chewed while smiling at him and looking engaged, hoping she didn't too much resemble a cow chomping grass.

"I want to do something to help at the food bank," Laurence continued, completely oblivious of the crisp crisis.

Milly swallowed and thanked the universe that she hadn't choked and spat wet crisps over Laurence-hottest-hot-of-hotness.

"Like what?" she asked. The winter sun spilled through the common-room window, making Laurence's black hair shine like a raven's wing. Milly had an overwhelming urge to lean over and give him a sniff. She bet he would smell delightful... *Focus, Milly!*

"What if we ask everyone in sixth form to donate at least one Christmassy food item? Imagine how much stuff we'd have!"

Milly was impressed. It was a good, thoughtful idea. She almost felt bad promoting it since her family would probably benefit from some of the goodies. "That's a brilliant idea," she said. *Tell him you use the food bank! Tell him, tell him!*

"I'm glad you like it. It feels like we should actively be helping, you know? By the law of averages, there's probably some kids *in this school* whose family have to use the food bank. I think it's important that we show we care. There's a stigma around food banks that shouldn't be there."

Milly nodded emphatically and Laurence smiled. "We can float the idea tomorrow at registration," he said.

If only he knew! Milly thought. *Do it now, now is the perfect moment.*

"If your family had to use a food bank," she began tentatively, "would you keep it a secret?"

"I don't know," Laurence said. "I guess it's nobody's

business really."

Milly took a deep breath and opened her mouth to speak but Laurence got there first.

"Listen, um, about yesterday when I told you about Jamie. I just wanted to say thanks."

She'd missed another chance. *How long before it was too late to tell him without looking like a total liar?* she wondered.

"For what?" she asked.

"For listening." Laurence was looking at his hands. "And you know, for being so understanding," he went on.

"That's what friends are for," Milly said.

Laurence smiled up at her from beneath long black lashes. *Heavenly choirs of angels!* "You're a really kind person, Milly," he said.

Milly blushed ferociously.

"I don't really have anyone I can talk to about this stuff," he went on.

"What about Cassia?"

"Cassia?" Laurence almost spluttered. "You don't share your deepest and darkest with Cassia, trust me."

Milly could believe it.

"Tom's a good guy and we have a laugh, but that's it, you know? We have banter, but we don't have conversations. I guess you have actual conversations with Sam and Robert."

"I suppose we do. I mean, it's not all deep, existential stuff, but I've never come across a problem I couldn't tell them about."

"You're lucky," said Laurence, and Milly could see that he meant it. "Jamie was my go-to person for all that stuff and we both know where he is right now."

Milly nodded. She wanted to put her hand on his, but she settled for a friendly arm rub. Laurence shook himself as though melancholy could be shaken off like water from a dog's coat.

"Anyway, I just wanted to say thanks and," he looked shy again, "I'm really pleased we got placed together at the food bank."

"Me too," said Milly, hoping he couldn't smell her smoky-bacon breath.

Laurence left the common room and Milly wondered how she'd just let another perfectly good opportunity to tell him about the food bank slip past.

Sam

Sam had expected to mind more about being paired with Nadia at lunchtime, but although her habitual reflex was to fume and think evil thoughts about her ex-girlfriend, she was surprised to find she didn't mind so very much. She'd tried to brood about it through French, but her heart wasn't in it. Was she softening towards Nadia? Was all Robert's talk about the Christmas spirit tamping down her rancour?

They were put to work on painting the life-sized magical snow carriage white, ready for it to be adorned with silver stars.

"How did Cassia even get hold of a *magical snow carriage*?" Nadia asked.

Sam could hear the nervousness in her voice and felt a little guilty. "There's a magical snow carriage store in town," she said and was gratified to hear Nadia laugh. "But actually, I heard her mum knows someone in the theatre who offered to loan it out for the ball."

"That was lucky."

"I think Cassia is one of life's lucky people," said Sam. "Nothing ever seems to go wrong for her."

"That we see," said Nadia. "What's projected out to the world doesn't always tally with what's going on on the inside."

"I guess not," said Sam.

"Are you going? To the ball I mean."

"Yeah, I think so. Milly's hung up about not having a

date, but I don't mind going on my own, to be honest."

"Well, you Chowdhurys are *very independent women!*" said Nadia with a smirk.

Sam couldn't help but smile at having her mum's favourite saying repeated back to her. She didn't know if it delighted or annoyed her that Nadia had known her so well.

"We are that if nothing else," Sam agreed. "How about you? Are you going?"

"I think so."

Sam was burning to know if Nadia had a date, but she didn't want to seem too interested. After all, what did she care?

"Have you got a dress sorted?" she asked instead.

"Yes. My mum made us all go to London for a *prom day out!*" Nadia grimaced.

"Nice."

"I'm the baby of the family, aren't I? My sisters are so much older than me that it's like having four mums sometimes."

"I have enough trouble handling one!"

Nadia laughed. "It was like 'Say Yes To the Dress': they made me come out and twirl in every gown and then critiqued it, loudly!"

"That sounds like a nightmare."

"It wasn't so bad. Noisy, but not so bad. I'll miss them when I go to uni."

Sam remembered when they were looking at unis together in Nadia's lounge earlier in the year. It was a whole family affair, not just Nadia's parents but her sisters, aunties, uncles and everyone had an opinion – even on Sam's choices – and they'd given them at the tops of their voices. Sam envied Nadia for being able to choose a university hundreds of miles away, with her parents' full blessing.

"They still ask about you," said Nadia, as though reading Sam's thoughts. "My parents. They're always interested in how you're getting on."

Nadia hadn't come out to her parents, so they had always just assumed that she and Nadia were best friends, which she supposed they kind of had been, for a while anyway. They must wonder why she stopped coming round. Maybe they assumed they'd fallen out ... maybe over a boy ... which was exactly what had happened.

"How about you?" Nadia asked, calling her back from memory lane.

"How about me what?"

"Have you got your dress?"

"Yeah, you know my mum and dress shopping."

"How sparkly did she want you to go?"

"Left to her, I would have been wearing a full-sequinned crinoline gown with matching shoes and a parasol."

Nadia laughed and nearly dropped her paintbrush.

"Please, please go with the parasol!"

"Only if you get one to match!"

Sam marvelled at how easy it was to fall back into conversation with Nadia, even after all this time.

"Did you go for a maroon dress?" asked Nadia.

"How did you know? Are you stalking me?"

"No! I just remember that's your favourite colour."

"Oh." Sam felt strangely exposed by this reminder of their shared intimacy. "You remember that, huh?"

"It's no big deal," Nadia said quickly and busied herself painting.

Sam felt something shift inside her, like a thaw after the long winter months.

Robert

"But the glitter has got to be biodegradable," said Miranda. "That is like my one stipulation and I will not be moved on it."

Holy holly berries! Was there nothing wrong with this girl? Apart from the obvious mean-minion thing. But still, Angel Gabriel! And she was an eco-warrior!

Robert wondered if he looked as starstruck as he felt.

"Absolutely," he agreed casually. "Biodegradable all the way."

They were sitting in the Old Windmill Café after school, working on their lesson plan for Friday. They had decided to make toilet-roll Father Christmases with the children and teach them about reusing and recycling at the same time.

Miranda's phone blipped. Miranda's phone blipped a lot.

"Cassia again?" Robert asked.

"Uh-huh," Miranda responded while writing at an almost superhuman speed.

"She keeps you on a pretty short leash."

Miranda looked up at him, her eyebrow raised. "Is that how you see me? A dog on a leash?"

Robert put his hands up. "Sorry, that was really inappropriate. No, absolutely not. No dogs involved. I've never. I mean, don't think you're... Can we just forget I said anything about a leash?" Robert could feel his shame muscles flexing and he was fighting hard not to crawl under the table and go foetal.

Miranda looked at him, straight on, and he could see her deciding whether to let him off the hook. His expression must have been all kinds of contrite because a few seconds later she smiled and said: "Sure. Cassia's messaging me because I'm missing Glee Club practice – she's making sure I know where to meet her later."

"I didn't know you were in Glee Club."

"I wasn't, but then Cassia got roped into doing this singing thing for her placement and so she wanted us all to join in with extra-curricular stuff."

"Why?"

Miranda's expression became thoughtful for a moment. "It's kinda like she decides what's cool and what's not. And I guess she thought Glee Club wasn't cool, but she has to do it, so if we all do it too, then it becomes a thing, like a choice, and then it becomes cool. Does that make sense?"

"So if Cassia chooses to do something it becomes cool?"

"Yeah, kinda. She has that power, you know? There are people who predict what the next zeitgeist will be and then there are the Cassias of the world, who by their sheer force of will, *determine* what the next zeitgeist will be."

"That's deep. I didn't know Cassia was so deep."

"Oh, she doesn't know she's doing it. In her mind, she just wants to boss high school, and this is how she does it."

"And what did she say about you missing Glee Club to do lesson planning?"

Miranda looked sheepish. "I told her I had the dentist."

Robert raised his eyebrows.

"She can be kind of mean," Miranda said in explanation. "Sometimes I just don't want to have to deal with her drama. It's like she has opinions on EVERYTHING and if you do something that she doesn't like, you'd better be ready to state your case."

"Can I just ask: why are you friends with her?"

Miranda laughed. "She's not all bad. There's another side to her that people don't see. And besides, she's been good to me. I owe her."

"This might not be my place to say, but I'm not sure you're doing the whole friendship thing right. Surely you shouldn't feel you *owe* someone for their friendship?"

"Maybe *owe* isn't the right word. It's more about loyalty. You can understand that, surely? You're loyal to Sam and Milly, right?"

"Well, yeah," Robert conceded. "But our friendship is give and take. From what I can see, you're doing all the giving and Cassia is on the take."

"Then maybe *you* need to look closer. Cassia made me part of a group. Being taken in like that means a lot when you arrive at a new school and you look and sound different to almost everyone. I felt protected in Cassia's gang, and if that meant I had to put up with a little social regulating, then so be it."

Robert felt a twinge of guilt. "I'm sorry if we didn't make you feel welcome when you arrived. I never really thought how hard it must have been for you; you seemed to slip so easily into school."

"If I made it look easy, then I'm one hell of an actor!" She laughed. "I guess I've had a lot of practice. We moved about a lot with my parents' jobs."

"And how about now? Are you still OK being socially regulated?"

"It's a small price to pay for fitting in."

"Is fitting in really that important?"

"I know you think I'm shallow," said Miranda.

"I didn't say that."

"Do you know how many schools I've been to?"

Robert shook his head.

"I've been to nine different schools since I was seven years old," said Miranda, her voice defensive. "Do you know what it's like to always be the new kid? I've been bullied, beaten-on, ostracized; I've spent the equivalent of years being some mean girl's emotional punchbag. I've had the wrong eye shape, accent, hair, clothes – you name it, I've been on the wrong side of it. So don't tell me that *fitting in* isn't that important. You look at me and think I'm selling my soul but it's not like that: it's self-preservation."

Robert was momentarily stunned into an uncharacteristic silence. "I had no idea," he said quietly.

"Why would you? You never asked. You looked at me and made a judgment and drew out my whole personality by what you thought you saw."

Robert's insides were squirming. He prided himself on being the nice guy, the one everyone liked. He knew he'd got off lightly with the popular gangs and the bullies down the years because he made people laugh, he was harmless, he was – and this was a painful one to admit – ineffectual. And the worst of it was, he played up to that character because it made his life easier. He had an easier time of it than Sam and Milly for sure.

"I think I get you," said Robert. "I mean I'm white, so I can't even imagine, but the self-preservation part, I get. It's easier to be popular."

"I don't want you to get the wrong idea about me. I'm not using Cassia to make myself popular. Do I like being popular? Hell yeah! I'd take it over being terrorized any day of the week. I've done my time being too afraid to look up from the floor. But believe it or not, there are actually a lot of things to like about Cassia. She's a big character, and there's a lot of

193

safety in hiding behind it. Equally, she could make my life really difficult if she wanted to, so I need to toe the line. Do you understand what I'm saying?"

Robert nodded. He was starstruck by Miranda. He wanted to talk with her until they'd used all the words in the world and then he wanted to talk some more. "I do," he said, hoping that she could see how much he meant it. "I really do. I admire your honesty. And I want to be honest too. I did judge you. I did think you were shallow and an airhead. I always imagined you in a kind of carefree Barbie-bubble. And I'm sorry. If it's any consolation, I feel like a giant anus right now."

Miranda smiled. "An anus? Really?"

"A giant anus. Huge!"

Miranda laughed. "Don't beat yourself up," she said, reaching her hand out to touch his. "I didn't mean to make you feel bad, I just needed you to understand why maybe I make allowances for Cassia that you wouldn't."

"I do," said Robert and he meant it.

Chapter 14

Thursday 10th December

Laurence

Ms Tibbott hadn't arrived yet but most of the class were already in the registration room. It was 8.20 a.m. This was the morning that Milly and Laurence were going to ask the class to bring in food donations for the food bank. Milly looked as though she'd just seen the ghost of Christmas past; her eyes were wide in what Laurence had come to know as her *nervous as hell* look.

"Hey." Laurence pulled a chair round to sit by Milly. "Are you freaking out?"

"Does it show?"

"A bit," he said, playing down that she looked about ready

to lock herself in the stationery cupboard. "Would you like me to do the talking for both of us?"

He watched Milly's shoulders loosen their grip on her ears.

"Really?" she asked hopefully.

"Sure. It doesn't bother me."

Milly collapsed her head on to her arms dramatically, her long hair splaying out across the table. "I'm such a loser!" she groaned. "I was worrying about it all night."

Laurence laughed. She was so cute, he wanted to reach out and brush her hair off her face, but obviously that would be creepy and weird. "You're not a loser," he said.

Milly turned her head and looked up at him through a veil of strawberry-blonde waves. Laurence felt his chest constrict. He'd like to ask her to be his date for the ball, but he could see this wasn't the time, so instead he asked: "Were you really worrying all night?"

Milly nodded. "I'm not good at public speaking," she admitted. "Or even five minutes of front-of-the-class speaking."

As if to press the point, her face turned a pale green. *Woah, she really means it!*

"Look," Laurence said, gathering his thoughts, "I don't mind talking in front of people and you do, so it makes perfect sense for me to do the talking. It's no biggie, honestly."

"Thank you," Milly said, sitting up. She gave him a look like he'd just rescued a drowning lamb.

Ms Tibbott breezed into the class.

"I need the loo!" Milly said, jumping up and dashing out of the classroom.

"She gets very nervous," Robert whispered across to him.

"I'm already familiar with the horror-hiccups," said Laurence.

Robert nodded sagely.

"Laurence, come away from loser corner, I need to pick your brains about something," came Cassia's penetrating voice.

"Sorry, mate," Laurence said, getting up. "It's easier not to argue."

Robert gave Laurence an understanding nod.

Laurence knew that Cassia's sass was her armour. When her parents divorced it was MESSY. She and Laurence had been together while it was happening, and Laurence remembered being stunned at the time at how two supposedly intelligent adults could be so blinded by hate for each other that they used their own kids as weapons. Cassia and her brothers had been pulled from pillar to post, used as pawns in their parents' private war.

Cassia had always been popular and maybe even a little mean, but the divorce changed her, and eventually even Laurence couldn't reach her. He guessed that school was the only thing in her life that she felt she had any control over; it didn't excuse her behaviour, but it did go some way to explaining it. There were times, plenty of times actually, when Laurence wanted to tell Cassia to just go to hell. But how could he?

Still, he thought, as she talked at him about the schedule of events for the Magical Snow Ball, there was only so long you could keep acting up because life had dealt you a bum deal. He hoped the Cassia he remembered would find her way back to the surface one day.

Milly got back into the classroom just before her name was called for the register. When Ms Tibbott closed the book, Laurence stood up and walked to the front of the class.

"Hey, everyone, Milly and I have had a thought we wanted to run by you." He chanced a glance at Milly, whose cheeks had flushed to a deep rose. She smiled at him and for a moment he almost forgot what he was saying.

"Um, so, yeah, we've been doing our placement at the food bank and we thought, maybe we could ask everyone to bring in one or two Christmassy food items as a donation? I've got a list from the food bank of things they especially need, which I'll stick on the noticeboard in the common room, but anything you can afford would be great: a box of sweets or biscuits, that kind of thing. A lot of people need help, so this would be a Christmas gift for someone who really needs it."

Milly was squirming with unease. Firstly, she couldn't afford to contribute to her own idea, and secondly, there was a chance that her family would end up with some of the things donated. Her family really did need all the help they could get, but still, it felt all kinds of wrong asking her classmates to donate. The glances in her direction as Laurence spoke felt accusatory, even though the rational side of her brain told her they couldn't possibly be.

Laurence finished speaking. The response was unanimously positive; even Cassia seemed to like the idea. Ms Tibbott was beaming. "This is a wonderful idea, you two!" she gushed. "And if you want to get your families involved too, the more the merrier. You can bring your gifts in on Tuesday or Friday mornings and Milly and Laurence can deliver them when they go to the food bank. Bravo, you two!"

Milly was smiling at him really hard. "Good work!" she whispered as he walked back past her to his seat.

"Cheers," he said.

Laurence left for first period on a high. He hadn't expected helping other people to make him feel so good inside. For the first time in quite a while, he didn't feel aimless.

Milly

Things were starting to get weird at school. The dynamic was changing and not everyone was happy about it. Cassia's usual sour expression had upgraded from lemon to lime.

Since the start of the community placements last week, the clear delineation between groups was beginning to blur as people who would never have previously mixed were breaking ranks and swimming into uncharted territory. The common rooms were basically a free-for-all, with absolutely nobody adhering to the unwritten guidelines of social rank.

The sky outside was gunmetal grey and hail and sleet pelted down by turns. Milly was writing out an essay plan on the squishy sofa in the middle of the common room when Laurence plopped himself down next to her. This was a public declaration of friendship; everyone could see them sitting together. She looked over at Robert sitting at a desk in the eves, and he looked back at her wide-eyed and mouthed, "Oh my jingle bells!"

"Hi," said Laurence. "You all right?"

"Yes, thanks. Are you?"

"I want to pick your brains. Are you busy?"

"Nope," she lied. She was not about to pass up the opportunity of sharing the sofa with Laurence; Shakespeare could wait. "My brains are yours for the picking." *Did that sound weird? It was a bit Hannibal Lector.*

"Thanks," said Laurence. "I think. I've been looking into what I can send Jamie for Christmas. It's pretty strict, but he can receive books and photographs and letters. I was wondering if you could help me choose some books to send him?"

"Sure," Milly said, trying to keep her voice even. "What genres is he into?"

"That's the problem. He wasn't really a big reader until he went to prison." Laurence was keeping his voice to a whisper and Milly was following suit. She was getting a thrill out of the closeness and she was sure he must be able to hear her heart knocking against her ribcage.

"We should probably rule out crime novels," Milly suggested.

Laurence laughed. "You see my point. I don't want to buy him anything that will remind him of where he is, if that makes sense?"

"Perfect sense." Milly thought for a moment. "How does

he feel about Neil Gaiman's books?" She spent the next several minutes happily lost in a conversation about books with Laurence, pausing only to wonder at how amazing it was that it was actually happening.

A shadow fell across the sofa and they looked up. Cassia was looming over them. Milly turned her phone over.

"Are you still going to help me with decorating the hall?" Cassia asked Laurence, completely blanking Milly.

"Er, yeah, sure. I said I would."

"Only I haven't seen anything of you and the clock is ticking."

"I've been a bit busy. Sorry, Cass. I'll try and get along later."

"Milky Parker helping you with an assignment, is she?"

It really was quite incredible, thought Milly. *I am right here!* But of course, she said nothing.

"Actually, *Milly* and I were just chatting about books," said Laurence.

Cassia reared back as though Laurence had just offered her a poo in the palm of his hand. "I didn't know you were into *books*!" She said the word "books" like it was heroin.

"I guess you don't know all my secrets," Laurence replied.

At this Cassia clearly thought they were back in flirting territory and she smiled. "I like a guy with hidden depths."

Milly suspected this was absolutely not true.

"Give me a call, yeah," Cassia said. "Try and rope in some extra muscle too." She leaned over Laurence, her satchel swinging off her shoulder and smacking Milly in the face. "Oops!" she said, "Sorry."

"Cass! For god's sake!" Laurence exclaimed.

"What? I said sorry!"

"You are unbelievable," Laurence sighed.

"Thanks, babe." She smiled, clearly not getting that this was *not* a compliment. She leaned in closer still, and ran her finger down Laurence's cheek.

Milly could swear she saw Laurence wince.

"I'll be needing you at my beck and call," Cassia said in a breathy voice, which was meant to be sexy, but which Milly thought came off like she was asthmatic. Then she snapped back upright, flung her satchel over her shoulder and wiggled through to the next common room, mean-minions tittering in tow.

"I'm sorry about her," said Laurence.

"Why are you always apologizing for her?"

Laurence shook his head as if he himself was bemused by the phenomena. "I don't know," he answered. "Habit, I guess? She wasn't always like this, you know."

"She's been like it for as long as I've known her," Milly retorted. And then she frowned. "Actually, that's not true.

Cassia and Robert went to the same primary school, and they were quite good friends. And I don't remember her being quite so mean in the lower years."

"She wasn't," said Laurence quickly. "She's had a pretty rough time of it."

"Lots of people have a pretty rough time of it but it doesn't make them act like a Krampus."

"A Krampus?"

"It's a Christmas thing," said Milly by way of explanation. "Are you and Cassia going to the ball together?" The words were out before Milly could stop them. *Oh, my giddy Santa! Check you and your audacity out!*

"No!" said Laurence.

"Are you sure?"

Laurence laughed. "What do you mean? Of course, I'm sure!"

"Does she know that?"

"I would have thought so. I mean, I haven't asked her."

"I'm no psychologist," said Milly. "But I don't think she got that memo."

"You think Cassia thinks she's my date for the ball?" he asked incredulously.

"I think everyone, including Cassia, thinks she's your date for the ball."

"I don't think that's true," he laughed.

"Ask anyone," she challenged.

Laurence called over to Tom, who was discussing the finer points of Minecraft with Robert (another product of the strange new world they were living in).

"Hey! Tommo, if someone asked you who I was taking to the ball, what would you say?"

"Cassia," said Tom without missing a beat.

"But why?" asked Laurence.

Tom shrugged. "Just the way it is, isn't it? It's always been you and Cassia."

"But we haven't been together for months!"

"Tell *her* that," said Tom and turned back to study a Minecraft diagram Robert was painstakingly drawing on the back of his chemistry homework.

"You see!" said Milly. "She's not my favourite person in the world, but if she thinks you're her date for the ball, you ought to put her straight so she can find someone else to go with."

"But surely she must have wondered why I hadn't asked her yet?"

Milly shrugged. "Maybe she thinks you're biding your time. If you want my advice, and you really don't intend to be her date, I'd tell her asap."

Laurence put his head in hands. "Oh god, do I have to?"

"I'm afraid so," Milly laughed. "Be brave!"

Laurence

Laurence had been trying to catch Cassia all afternoon, but she was in super-efficient mode, strutting from common room to common room, dishing out jobs to anyone in her line of sight, whether they wanted them or not, and crossing them off on her clipboard. Subsequently, there were a lot of slightly bedazzled students who one minute had been eating a hummus sandwich, or reading a book, and the next found themselves on the Christmas ball work rota.

He had been steeling himself earlier to ask Milly to be his date for the ball but had been sent spiralling off course by everyone's certainty that he and Cassia were a done deal. The knowledge had been pressing down on him ever since, like a timer ticking down to zero; he needed to sort this out now!

At four p.m. Laurence walked into the sixth form hall to the sounds of Leona Lewis declaring there was only "One More Sleep Till Christmas" and the sight of slightly terrified students frantically painting scenery and scrambling up and down ladders with silver garlands, which needed to be "*draped not stretched! Idiots!*"

"Having fun then?" Laurence asked, when Cassia took a breath from shouting orders at her minions.

"Lou, babe!" She flashed him a brilliant smile. "I just want it to look perfect. This is something we will remember for the rest of our lives. Our last ever Christmas at Millers Field."

"I'm not sure everyone's enjoyed school quite as much as you have."

"Well, that's really not my fault, I can't help being popular. Ooh, hold on one second, I'm going to do a quickie Insta video."

Cassia whipped out her phone and panned around the hall. "It's coming together, guys!" she trilled for her audience. "This will be the Christmas ball to end all Christmas balls!" She uploaded the video and turned back to Laurence. "Quick," she said, throwing her arm round his neck and thrusting her camera out in front of her. "Pout!" she demanded and snapped a selfie before Laurence had time to object or pout.

"Don't upload that," said Laurence.

"I have to, Lou. I've got to keep the likes coming in. I've been approached by a media company; they think I have potential as an influencer. This is the dream! Imagine the perks! Imagine the travel! Cocktails and cash, pretty boy."

"Don't call me that," said Laurence wincing.

"Why not? You are pretty and last time I looked, you were a boy."

Laurence shook his head. "Listen, Cass, can we talk?"

"Sure."

"Privately."

"Ooooh!" She smiled at him and winked.

Laurence grimaced. Oh god, this was going to be awful.

"Guys!" she shouted. "I'll be back in ten!" and she grabbed hold of Laurence's arm and pulled him into the sports store cupboard.

"So," she said pulling the door closed behind them. "What did you want to talk to me privately about? As if I couldn't guess! The ball is next week – you took your time asking, I almost considered going with Harvey."

Harvey was a guy Cassia had met at the auditions for *The Voice*. He'd gone through to Battle Rounds and had enjoyed a minor celebrity status ever since. He and Cassia had dated briefly and very publicly before he'd gone on a country-wide Butlin's tour with his band, D.A.M. – which stood for Deep And Meaningful, though Laurence was yet to find evidence of Harvey being either.

"Yeah, Cass, about that." Laurence rubbed his hand

through his hair and stared intently at a cluster of plastic hula hoops as though they might suddenly burst into life like the furniture in *Beauty and the Beast* and sing him a helpful song that would get him through this excruciating moment. "The thing is, Cassia, we haven't actually been together for a long time."

"Don't worry about it," she said, moving closer to him. "You've seen other people, I've seen other people, that's what helps to keep things fresh between us."

Laurence was backed up against a pommel horse and hemmed in either side by a stack of gym mats and a giant netted sack of basketballs. "Cass," his voice was strained as he leaned backwards into a limbo over the pommel horse, while Cassia continued to lean closer to him, eyes closed, her lips pouted in readiness for a snog. "I'm not asking you to the ball. I want to ask someone else."

Cassia stopped, mid pucker. She opened her eyes. "You what?"

"I didn't think you'd want to go to the ball with me anyway – we hardly even talk!" Laurence tried to sound like the voice of reason, but his voice was coming out higher than he'd like. He prided himself on being able to hold his own in high-stress situations, but now he was doubting himself. Cassia stood back and folded her arms.

"I'm sorry, Cass. I had no idea you'd think we were going

together. It was only when Milly said…"

"Say again?" she demanded.

Laurence swallowed. "Which part?" he stammered.

"The part where Milky Parker is suddenly your conscience."

"Don't call her Milky."

"Why not? Oh! Wait. Oh my god! You've got the hots for her, haven't you? Have you asked her to be your date to the ball?"

Laurence hesitated for a moment too long. He hadn't even asked Milly yet, she might say no. Did he really want to tell Cassia his plans and give her the power to crush them?

"Well?" Cassia asked. Her arms were crossed tightly across her chest, and she was tapping one foot. Her left – perfectly sculpted – eyebrow was arched in a way that suggested she was not to be messed with. If eyebrows could talk, hers would be telling him he was grounded with no puddings for a month.

"I haven't asked anyone yet," he said.

Cassia narrowed her eyes. "You'll regret this," she said, like she was making a promise.

"I'm sorry, Cass. I won't change my mind." Laurence walked tentatively towards the door and to his relief, Cassia didn't try to stop him. He opened the door and stepped back out into the noise of the hall. Ariana Grande was asking Santa to tell her if he was really there, and on the stage, Robert's band were setting up for a rehearsal.

"Don't come crying to me when you realize you've made a terrible mistake!" Cassia screeched. "You'll be sorry!"

As one, the Christmas ball minions turned to see who had made Cassia so violently angry. Laurence looked across to Robert, who was mid guitar tuning. Robert stopped to give him a thumbs up and goofy smile. Laurence gave him a wave and hurried out of the hall, and as the doors swung closed Cassia's voice echoed down the empty corridor: "WHAT A LOSER!!!"

Chapter 15

Friday 11th December

Robert

Robert held the paper bag above his open mouth and successfully tipped the last dusty bits into it.

"What was that?" Milly asked.

"Roasted chickpeas," Robert replied, taking a swig out of his bottle of water. "From that health food place on the corner."

"Who are you and what have you done with Robert?"

"What? Can't a man adopt a healthier lifestyle without abuse?"

Milly frowned at him.

"And look – " he waved the paper bag at Milly – "fully compostable packaging."

"Is this Miranda's influence?"

Robert shrugged. "She may have mentioned that my steak sizzler crisps were not good for my body or the environment," he said nonchalantly.

"Wow, you must really like her to have sacrificed your steak sizzlers."

Robert grimaced.

"What? It's cute!"

"Again with the cute!" Robert groaned comically.

"I'd allow it, it's obviously working for you."

Robert conceded the point. "Right," he said, smacking his lips together and dusting the crumbs off his jumper. "I'm going to extract a mean-minion from the hive."

"Good luck!" said Milly, looking up from her book. She had a bag for life at her feet with the first few sixth form donations for the food bank.

"With this jumper? I don't need luck, I've got the spirit of Christmas on my side! Where are you meeting Laurence?"

"Out the front of the school."

Robert gave her a thumbs up, grabbed his jacket and headed off to Miranda's common room. He was wearing a patterned knitted jumper with galloping stags in a repeating motif across the chest. He had borne the teasing and banter that came with wearing such a jumper to school with a kind of inverted pride.

"This is my primary school teacher at Christmas look," he'd told Sam earlier that day.

"As if you need an excuse to wear a Christmas jumper, Bertram," said Sam, planting a kiss on his shoulder.

Sam had left before lunch because the aircraft hangar was out of town. Robert fielded jibes of "Nice sweater!" and "Dweeb!" as he wandered through the common rooms with his signature good-humoured don't-give-a-crap attitude.

Miranda was looking rosy-cheeked in a black hoodie zipped up to the neck. Cassia was holding court while she delicately popped sushi rolls into her mouth with a pair of wooden chopsticks.

"He just got back the other day and he's been tied up with publicity and all that shiz," Cassia was saying to a rapt audience. "So we didn't get to hook up until last night."

"Are you, like, back together?" asked Trinity.

Cassia looked faux coy. "Who knows! We're just keeping it casual. We've both got super hectic lives at the moment; he's touring and my career's about to take off. But the chemistry between us is just *too* much! He's my date for the ball, so I guess that says it all really..."

"Oh my god oh my god oh my god! Harvey Tyne is your date for the ball?" Trinity was fan-girling so hard she was in danger of hyperventilating.

Cassia looked up from pretending she didn't like the attention as Robert approached and narrowed her eyes. Miranda jumped up and grabbed her coat and bag. She smiled at Robert as though she had been hoping to see him all day. Robert felt like he was in some sort of dream reality; to have a girl smile at him like that was the stuff of fantasy.

"Have you been going through the Salvation Army clothes bins again?" Cassia asked, eyeing his jumper with distaste.

"Nah, your mum knitted this for me!"

A couple of the mean-minions tittered before being quieted by a glare.

"You ready?" Robert asked Miranda.

"Ready!" said Miranda, smiling so hard her cheeks almost covered her eyes. "Bye, guys!" she called sweetly. Cassia let her eyes roam lazily over the two of them with a look of distaste as she dismissed them.

"I'm so excited," said Miranda as they made their way down the stairs to the exit.

"Have you got the stuff?"

"Ten tubes of biodegradable glitter, two rolls of cotton wool and a bag of googly eyes," replied Miranda. "How about you?"

"Twelve toilet rolls, two giant bottles of red poster paint and five folded cereal boxes present and correct."

"I only managed to get two toilet rolls."

"That's because you haven't got thirteen people in your house. We get through a lot of toilet rolls. We get through a lot of everything. We had to get extra recycling bins from the council to cope with the volume."

"I'd love to meet your family," said Miranda. "They sound hilarious."

"Really?" asked Robert, and then, changing the subject, "I trust there's a fully festive jumper under that hoodie?"

"Oh my god! I've been sweating all day; I couldn't let Cassia see it." Miranda unzipped her hoodie to reveal a sweatshirt with brightly coloured fabric baubles, stars and Christmas presents sewn all over it; it would have made Mrs Claus feel dowdy.

"I think that might be the best Christmas jumper I've ever seen!"

Miranda's smile was almost too big for her face. "Do you really think so? Thank you! My dad made it for me; he's a huge fan of *The Great British Sewing Bee*."

216

"I think you've been hiding your geekdom under a bushel."

"You have no idea!" said Miranda mysteriously.

Milly

Milly and Laurence were decorating a large Christmas tree in the corner of the food bank. Sarah had set them the task of making the shabby space look festive. They had found the tree in a tattered old box in the storeroom. The tree came in several pieces and it had taken them forty-five minutes just to assemble it. Now they were winding tinsel in and out of the branches, a large cardboard box of gaudy decorations lying in wait on the floor.

"Listen," said Laurence. "My dad's throwing a kind of party on Wednesday evening for his cronies. It's going to be pretty soulless and full of snobs, but I'm allowed to bring a guest and I wondered if you'd like to be my plus-one?"

Milly almost floated up to the top of the Christmas tree and knocked the angel off its perch. *Was this for real?* Laurence was asking *her* to be his plus-one at a family party?! She pushed down the party poppers going off in her stomach and tried to act casual. "Wow, you've really sold it to me. You're inviting me to a soulless party with your dad's cronies!"

"Ha, yeah, I realize I didn't make that sound very appealing. But it wouldn't be soulless if you were there. I'd really like you come. My mum's hired the best caterer, and it's worth coming for the canapés alone!"

He thinks my presence will make a party less soulless? This is a first! And canapés? I thought only Nigella ate canapés at parties! "Oh well, why didn't you say so sooner?" laughed Milly. "I never turn down an invitation to a dull party with canapés!"

"Great! That's sorted then. I'll tell my mum to add you to the guest list."

Guest list? Holy Santa sleighs, I'm going to a party with a guest list.

Laurence smiled at her and she was astounded to see that he looked relieved.

"I was a bit nervous about asking you," said Laurence.

"Why?"

"It's kind of short notice. And you know, it's not exactly an exciting date is it."

"This is a date?" the words were out before Milly could engage her brain to shut them down.

Laurence laughed nervously. "Um, I'd like it to be. If that's OK with you?"

Is it OK with me? Jumping gingerbread men! "It's ... it's very OK with me. I'd like that a lot."

"That's settled then," said Laurence, handing Milly one end of a piece of tinsel as he draped the rest around the back of the tree. "You know, I don't think you see yourself like other people do," he went on.

Milly shrugged her shoulders and studied a fake fir tree branch really closely.

"I like you, Milly," Laurence said.

At that she looked up, and her breath caught in her throat. "I like you too," she managed to squeak.

"Come on, you two!" came Sarah's voice from across the room. "We've got to get the paper chains strung yet!"

Milly and Laurence looked at one another, his eyes not leaving hers until the intensity became too much for Milly and she looked away smiling, feeling her cheeks colouring up and her heart beating like a herd of stampeding reindeer. When she chanced a glance back up at him, he was still looking at her, smiling. They carried on dressing the tree, neither of them quite able to squash their grins. Milly felt like they'd discovered a secret, just for them. Suddenly Milly's Christmas was starting to look a whole lot brighter.

Robert

Free play was in full swing when Robert and Miranda arrived at the community centre. The play leaders had set aside two tables for the Christmas craft activity and Robert and Miranda began to set up their equipment at once.

"So, you know how sometimes someone thinks they know you, but they don't really know you at all?" said Miranda.

"I guess," said Robert, standing a toilet roll tube at each place setting.

"And you think they might like the real you better than the you they think they already know, but you're worried that if you show them the real you, they might like you less because then they'll think the you they thought they knew was all fake, when really that's not true because the other you is still you, it's just an extension of you, because at the end of the day we're all multi-faceted, aren't we?"

Robert stared at Miranda, a tub of red biodegradable glitter in his hand and a confused expression on his face. "I literally don't know what you just said."

Miranda was gently placing small pots of PVA glue and spatulas along the middle of the table. She was biting her lip. "No, fair point. I'm not expressing myself very well here, huh! OK, how's this; it's like my jumper," she said. "This is

220

a part of me – I like a cheesy Christmas sweater, and I like being here with kids. I like art and painting and movies with subtitles, but then sometimes I really love hanging out with the girls and talking about make-up; there's lots of parts of me that make up me and not everybody sees every part of me all the time. So if there's something you didn't know, it doesn't make me a liar."

She looked up at him, tiny spatula in hand, her big eyes imploring him to understand. Robert was honest to god trying, but she wasn't making it easy and he kept being distracted by how cute she looked when she was concentrating.

"You like movies with subtitles?"

"Are you understanding anything I'm saying at all?" Miranda asked, her voice carried more than a hint of desperation. Her forehead was creased in consternation, a little dimple forming between her eyebrows where they knitted together. It seemed to Robert like she was trying to tell him something big without actually telling it, like she wanted him to guess. The trouble was, he'd never been that good at cryptic clues, that was Milly's department.

"If I'm being honest," said Robert, "not really. I think you're trying to tell me that there's more to you than just being in Cassia's entourage? But I already know that, and I like you anyway."

"But what if there was something else about me. Something that Cassia or you don't know about?"

"Are you a spy?"

"Be serious!" she chided. "I want to tell you something about me because I really like you, but I'm worried you might think I've been a liar."

"You're starting to worry me. Are you part of an alien task force sent to earth to check out the humanoids?"

"Wow, there really is no end to your geekdom." She smiled. "You know what, screw it, *show don't tell*, isn't that what they keep telling us in English class?" she said almost to herself. "Actions speak louder than words!"

"OK, you're just randomly spouting well-known phrases now; do you have a reset button anywhere I can press? I think your hard drive is overheating."

Miranda laughed. "I have a surprise for you," she said, still smiling. "I just hope you think it's a good one." Her smile faltered and Robert could see she was nervous.

"Well, the last surprise I had was when my little sister took a dump in my trainer during potty training, so I count any surprise that isn't *that* as a good surprise."

Miranda laughed again but it sounded forced.

The trikes and building blocks had been put away and the children had settled down for storytime with the play leaders. After that, Robert and Miranda would teach them the delicate art of making a Father Christmas out of a toilet roll tube.

"I'm going to the toilet, I'll be back in ten," said Miranda, grabbing up her rucksack and hurrying out of the double doors.

Ten minutes? Robert thought to himself. *Maybe she's constipated.*

Robert finished setting up the activity and went and sat cross-legged with the kids for the last half of *The Very Hungry Caterpillar.* As a kid, he used to envy that caterpillar for its access to so much tasty food.

When storytime was over, Miranda still wasn't back, so Robert herded the children over to the table and with no small difficulty managed to get them all seated and prevent any of them from eating the materials.

He had just picked up a toilet roll tube to demonstrate how to paint Father Christmas's coat when what must surely have been a mirage entered the room and began to walk towards him.

Mrs Grinch. *Miranda* dressed as Mrs Grinch, green face, red Mrs Santa outfit and a face full of drawn-on whiskers. It was a face he'd seen looking out at him from his phone a thousand times. The most beautiful, elusive, talented artist he had ever come across, the girl of his dreams: @secretgeek.

Miranda Grinch smiled up at Robert, while unravelling a roll of cotton wool – for Father Christmas's beard – and said tentatively, "Surprise?" which Robert decided was the understatement of the year. It took him a moment to regain the power of speech.

"I have literally never been more surprised in my life. Fact."

"So you don't hate me?" she asked. "Even though I've kept a secret identity from you?" She was looking at him again with those pleading eyes. If only she knew that he'd been crushing over her secret identity for over a year. But no, *try and play it at least a little bit cool, Bertram.* Robert tried to gather himself.

"Let's just say," he began, trying to give Miranda his most reassuring smile without creeping her out, "that of all the secret identities you could have had, this is the most perfect ever. And in answer to your question: no, I don't hate you. Never. I'm actually super honoured that you chose me to tell."

Miranda smiled at him then and it felt like the whole room lit up. Miranda-mean-minion was @secretgeek, aka Mrs Grinch, aka the biggest crush of Robert Barlow's life. Robert looked out of the window and mouthed, *Thank you, Santa!*

Sam

At 4.45 p.m. Sam and Tula were clearing down the decks to finish for the day. The wooden shed in the hangar was close to full of brightly wrapped boxes full of gifts. Next week they would be picked up and delivered to refugee children in desperate need of some Christmas joy.

There was a knock on the door and Tula went to answer it. "It's for you," she called across to Sam, who was locking the shed door.

Sam looked over and saw Nadia standing in the doorway.

"I brought some more boxes," she said.

"I've just locked up," said Sam defiantly. *Jeez! You give the girl an inch and she thinks everything's OK.*

"It won't take you a moment to unlock again," said Tula with a smile. "We never turn down a donation."

Sam huffed and undid the padlock on the shed.

"I've got some paperwork to do before we leave," said Tula. "You can handle this," and she disappeared into the makeshift office. Sam thought she detected a smirk on her face. Sam sighed; Tula and Libby had clearly been swapping notes about her.

"Do you need help bringing the stuff in?" she asked Nadia.

"Yeah, please."

Sam nodded resignedly and headed out to Nadia's dad's car. It was freezing out, especially here on the old airfield where there was nothing to shelter you from the relentless wind that swept across the open spaces. Sam shivered.

"Cold, huh?" said Nadia. "My dad says it's threatening more snow."

"I wish it would get on and stop being so half arsed about it. If it's going to snow, just snow already and settle and let us have a white Christmas; not all this, snow, not snow, sleet, stupid dusty snow that blows in your eyes..."

Nadia laughed. "I'd forgotten how much I enjoy your forceful opinions on absolutely everything!"

"Well!" Sam exclaimed, desperately trying to suppress a smile and failing dismally. "It just needs to make its mind up."

They lugged the boxes inside and stacked them neatly in the hangar.

"There's so many!" exclaimed Nadia.

"And still not enough to go around," said Sam. And then, thinking that she sounded like a moody ungrateful cow, she asked, "How's it going at the soup kitchen?"

"It's brilliant! I absolutely love it. They've let me fully loose on the soup now. The local greengrocer and supermarket drop off their unsold stock and people donate bread and stuff. We're doing evenings from this week, to make sure that people without housing get a hot meal."

"Sounds great," said Sam.

"I'll be there tomorrow night."

Sam wasn't sure what Nadia wanted her to do with this information. Was she inviting her to drop in? Or was she looking for congratulations on her do-gooding?

"Right," she said. She saw the hopeful look on Nadia's face and couldn't help but give her a smile. Why was she making it so hard for Sam to hate her? Didn't Nadia realize Sam's bitterness was the only thing protecting her from heartache? She had tried every which way to convince her heart that Nadia was no good, but it wouldn't listen. The only way to keep herself from getting hurt was to build a wall of "don't care" around her, perhaps she needed to start working on a moat too.

Tula came out from the office with her coat on. "You ladies finished?" she asked.

"All done," said Sam.

"Would you like a lift home?" Nadia asked. "It's no hassle. It's on my way."

Nadia lived above her parents' shop, two streets away from Sam's house.

"Thanks, but I'm getting a lift with Tula."

Nadia's face fell. Sam's heart squeezed. *Don't go there!* she warned herself.

"Oh, sorry, Sam, I'm going to have to renege on the lift offer," said Tula. "I've just remembered it's my turn to pick the dogs up from doggy day care."

Tula smiled at Sam, and Sam narrowed her eyes at her; she knew Tula was lying through her teeth.

"But Nadia here has offered you a lift, so it's all good!" Tula chirruped.

Aargh! Could you be any more obvious? Sam grimaced.

"Fabulous!" she said.

It was an awkward drive. Nadia put on some music to cover the silences not filled by polite conversation. When they pulled up outside Sam's house, Nadia said: "When you're ready to talk..."

"I'm not," said Sam quickly.

"I just want to explain."

"There's nothing to explain."

"I don't want to leave things like this."

"You made it like this," said Sam.

"You think that you're the only person with stuff happening in their life, Sam. Well, guess what, you're not."

It was the first time Nadia had been anything but

contrite since they'd split up, and her vehemence took Sam by surprise.

"What you saw isn't the whole story, but you would rather go on hating me than listen to what I have to say," Nadia continued. "And do you know why? I'll tell you: because you were always looking for a way out. Right from the word go. You were afraid to let someone get close to you, and I gave you the perfect excuse to draw back without having to confront your own issues. I screwed up, Sam, and I regret it every single day. But I can't keep hoping for your forgiveness for ever. If we are truly done, then fine, I have to accept that. But I'd like the opportunity to give you my side of the story."

Nadia stopped talking. She didn't look at Sam, she just kept her eyes on the road ahead. Sam was stunned. This was... This was... What was this? She was the victim here, wasn't she? For the first time, Sam felt like she might actually lose Nadia for good, and the notion caught her up short. The engine was still running.

"I've got to get back," said Nadia.

"OK," said Sam meekly, unfastening her seat belt and pushing open the door. "I'll see you."

"Yep," said Nadia. "See you around."

See you around? What does that mean? Sam walked into the house; every room spangled like a Christmas card, but it didn't warm her heart. Her mum called her into the kitchen. Sam had expected to find Bill happily chopping vegetables while her mum took charge of the pans, but the kitchen was markedly Bill-less.

"Hey, Mum," she said. "What's this?" She picked a bouquet of flowers – still in their expensive wrappings – out of the wastepaper bin and waved them quizzically. Beneath them were papers torn in two. Sam glanced at them; they were house details from an estate agents.

"Bill thinks he can bribe me into looking at properties, with flowers," said her mum, not turning around from the stove.

"Is that what he was doing?" asked Sam. "Maybe he just wanted to look at properties with you and buy you flowers?"

"Yeah, well, I won't be pushed into something I'm not ready for."

"You've never been pushed into anything in your life, Mum."

Her mum turned, hand resting on her hip, an apron which read "One Hot Mama" covered her body-con dress. "Exactly, babes," she said. "And I've no intention of starting now."

Sam let the flowers drop back into the bin. Something snapped inside her. "Why are you like this?" she shouted.

Her mum was shocked. Sam was shocked too – she didn't know where the anger had come from, but suddenly she was raging.

"Like what?"

"Closed off! You shut everyone out. You're going to ruin everything with Bill because you're so guarded all the time. I don't want to be like you! I don't want to freeze out the people I love! I don't understand you!" She hadn't realized she was crying until she tasted her salty tears on her lips. She rushed out of the kitchen and up to her room.

There was a knock on the door. Sam didn't give her mum permission to enter, but she came in anyway.

"You quite finished?" her mum asked calmly.

Sam's sobs made her breath ragged.

"Do you want to talk about it?"

"No," Sam stuttered. She heard her mum sigh.

"If I seem hard, it's because I've had to be," said her mum. "And I know I've got my issues, but I will never be closed off to you. So when you're ready to talk, I'll be downstairs."

She stroked Sam's hair for a moment and then left the room. Sam's sobs had subsided. Who was she angry with? She couldn't tell any more. Was it her mum, Nadia or herself? What if Nadia moved on without her? She'd been feeling pretty safe up there on her moral high ground; she was the one who'd been wronged, not Nadia. Nadia didn't get to call the shots, that's not how it worked. In all these months it had never occurred to Sam that Nadia might give up. And if she did, where did that leave Sam? Suddenly the moral high ground seemed more like a desert island.

Robert

By the time they were walking home – Miranda having managed to remove most of the green paint from her face – Robert was more or less over the shock of discovering Miranda's secret identity.

"You're @secretgeek," he repeated for the twentieth time.

Miranda smiled shyly. "Yeah."

"I've been following you for ages. I mean, we've had online banter – I've PMed you!"

"I know. Funny, huh?" Miranda gave a nervous laugh as though she still wasn't quite sure how her revelation was going down. If she could only have seen inside Robert's head, she would have known it had gone down very well indeed. "I didn't realize @oneinten was you at first," Miranda went on. "And then when I did, I didn't know how

232

to approach you in the real world. I mean, we were cyber friends; I wasn't sure how that translated in real life. And I was worried that..."

"That what?"

"I was worried that you wouldn't like me in real life. Because what I am isn't really me. I mean, it is me, but it's not me. Does that make sense? What you see at school, with Cassia and the others, isn't me."

"I guess in a funny way I always kind of knew that. You never quite fitted in; you weren't mean enough."

"I was grateful that Cassia took me under her wing. I still am. But I had this whole persona I had to live up to and then I was stuck. I know what you think of me, of us. I know you call us the mean-minions, so how could I come out to you?"

Robert was quiet for a moment. "I guess we've always felt kinda morally righteous because we thought Cassia and you guys were the mean, judgy ones; it never occurred to me that we might be making judgments of our own. I'm sorry."

"Don't be," said Miranda, looping her arm through his. "High school is like swimming with sharks: we're all just trying not to get eaten alive."

"Mouldy mince pies! That's a dark analogy of secondary school life."

Miranda laughed and squeezed his arm. Robert could

smell the perfume in her hair; dark berries and cinnamon. "If it's any consolation," she said, looking up at him, "it just got a whole lot brighter." She stopped, turning to face him, and then she reached up on tiptoes and kissed him. It was a good kiss. The kind of kiss that scrambles your brain and makes you forget where you are.

Robert: News!!!!!!

Sam: I'm all ears. Well, eyes. Shoot.

Milly: Spill.

Robert: I snogged Miranda. Rather, she snogged me first and I joined in.

Sam: Whaaaaaaaaaaaaat! You snogged a mean-minion? You just sold your soul to Beelzebub, my friend 😼

Milly: Ignore her, she's just BITTER cos she hasn't snogged anyone in a million years. EEEEEEEEEEKKK! Bertram!! This is so exciting!

Sam: Bitter my baubles, can you imagine what Cassia's gonna say?

Robert: I don't care what Cassia says. Miranda likes me and there's nothing you can say to bring me down 🦄

Sam: Fair play.

Robert: And there's more...

Milly: Do we want to hear about this?

Robert: Mind out of the gutter please, Milly. Turns out Miranda is @secretgeek.

Sam: No fricking way!

Milly: Wait. Miranda is Mrs Grinch?

Robert: Yup 😊

Milly: Hahaha what are the chances? That's too weird! I mean you've liked her for how long?

Robert: I know, right.

Milly: Of all the schools in all the world...

Sam: So you've fallen for a mean-minion?

Robert: Yeah. I think I have.

Milly: 🐱

Milly: So, I've got some news too...

Sam: I'm not sure I can cope with any more revelations. You didn't snog Cassia, did you?

Robert: 😨

Milly: Laurence asked me to go as his plus-one to some party his dad's hosting.

Sam: Shut the front door!!

Robert: Well, bless my baubles!

Milly: He asked me at the food bank.

Sam: Details. . .

Milly: We were decorating the tree and he asked me. It was well lush.

Robert: I thought that stuff only happened in the movies.

Sam: Food banks too apparently. Oh my god! This is so exciting. Just me left to fall in love for Christmas then 😫 Major falling out with Ms Chowdhury this evening.

Milly: OOOPS! What happened?

Sam: I lost my tinsel, big time. Mum's blowing it with Bill and I'm going to end up like Miss Haversham.

Robert: Dramatic much?

Sam: It's all right for you, you've got a love life and a normal family.

Robert: Have you met my family?

Sam: Fair play.

Milly: Did you sort it out with your mum?

Sam: Yeah, it's all fine. We pretended it didn't happen and went on as normal. It's the Chowdhury way 😬

Robert: Disfunction at its finest 😜 You know where I am if you need to talk it over.

Milly: Ditto.

Sam: Thanks, dorks. Love ya 🥰🥰

Chapter 16

Saturday 12th December

Milly

The main road through the town had been closed off for the Christmas market. The air was filled with the scent of roasted chestnuts and mulled wine. Strings of lights in the shapes of stars and holly leaves criss-crossed above the heads of eager shoppers dressed in their winter warmest. Christmas music blasted out from many unseen quarters to meet somewhere in the melee in a kind of festive compilation.

Milly finished her shift at the Old Windmill at 4.30 p.m. and met Robert and Sam by a stall selling roasted honey and cinnamon nuts. It was already dark, but the street teemed with activity. Robert handed her a bag of hot nuts and they began to walk down the road.

"How was work?" asked Sam.

"Busy," said Milly, wrapping her stripy scarf twice around her neck. "How about you guys?" Sam and Robert worked in a garden centre.

"Insane," said Sam.

"We sold out of trees by lunchtime," said Robert, throwing a hot nut into the air and catching it in his open mouth.

"You'll get more in, though?" said Milly.

"If the K.O.C. comes out of retirement, I promise we'll get you a tree, if we have to cut one down ourselves," said Robert.

"I think you can get arrested for that," said Sam.

"Not if you go under cover of darkness," said Robert, tapping the side of his nose.

"He's never been this late," said Milly. "Usually, he can't wait to get out there and start stapling lights to every inch of the house front. One of the neighbours actually asked if he was ill the other day! I hate to say it, but I think the King of Christmas has handed in his resignation."

Sam put an arm round Milly and squeezed. At the same moment, Miranda bounced up in front of them, making them stop abruptly.

"Hi!" she said, beaming. "This is great, isn't it? I heard it might actually snow for real! I miss the snow; we quite often had white Christmases in Canada. Mind if I steal your buddy for a bit?" she asked, indicating to Robert, who was grinning like Cindy-Lou Who on Christmas morning.

"Take him," said Sam. "But don't give him too much sugar or he'll never sleep tonight."

"Eat tinsel, bauble brain!" said Robert.

"Kiss my holly berries!" Sam returned.

"Nice comeback!" Robert conceded.

Miranda laughed and took Robert by the arm. He turned back to poke his tongue at Sam and Milly.

"I'd say he's smitten," said Milly.

"She'd better not hurt him, or she'll find herself facing my wrath," said Sam.

"Holy sugar plums!" laughed Milly.

Robert

"What did you want me for?" asked Robert as they wended their way through the bustling market. "Not that I'm complaining! But you know, was there something specific. . ."

Miranda stopped and stepped in front of him. She looked up in a way that made him feel hot under his skin, then she kissed him softly on the lips and all the blood rushed away from his head.

"Just that," she said. "Is that specific enough?"

Robert's head spun. He expected his ribs to explode outwards any minute, to shower the market with cartoon love hearts. "Yeah," he squeaked out and cleared his throat. "Ahem, yeah," he continued in a much deeper voice. "That's good and specific. To the point."

Robert and Miranda headed for the hook a holly wreath stall. The person overseeing the stall was dressed as one of Santa's elves in what Robert decided was a massive piece of miscasting. He would have been better off playing the ghost of Christmas present, with his long dark flowing hair and shoulders so wide he had trouble turning in the tiny, round hut.

In an effort to pull off a super manly vibe, Robert paid his money and set about trying to hook one of the holly wreaths, which revolved on a turntable in the centre, in the hopes of winning a cuddly Santa for Miranda. It was harder than it looked.

"I can't do it with you laughing at me!"

"I'm sorry," Miranda giggled. "You're doing really well, honest. Does poking your tongue out the side of your mouth help with concentration?"

Robert sniggered. "All right, smarty-pants, you have a go."

"I'll help you," she said, sidling up close to him.

Miranda clasped her hands around his and together they tried to aim the hook at the end of the rod into a holly wreath, giggling all the while. Her hands were cold on his, but her proximity was making him decidedly warm. Finally, they hooked a wreath and shouted in jubilation.

"Technically you cheated," said the giant elf.

"Oh, come on," said Robert pleadingly.

Miranda clasped her hands in front of her and together they said: "Pleeeaaasssee!"

The elf relented with a hearty chuckle. "All right then, as it's Christmas," he said. "You can pick any Santa off the top row."

Robert turned to Miranda. "Which Santa takes your fancy, my lady?" he asked but he was talking to air. He looked down to find Miranda crouched on the floor, her back pressed against the base of the stall.

"What are you doing?" he asked.

"Cassia!" Miranda whisper-hissed back.

Robert looked round to see Cassia hanging off a tall guy with a confident swagger, with Trinity and three other mean-minions in tow, wiggle-strutting towards them.

"Is that the famous Harvey?" Robert asked.

"Just shhh. Pretend I'm not here!"

Robert looked back up and Cassia made eye contact. He waved and shouted, "All right!"

Cassia narrowed her eyes. "Loser!" she said as she passed and the mean-minions giggled. Trinity blew him a kiss, which made them all erupt into gales of laughter. Harvey nodded in Robert's direction and gave a languid salute. And then they were gone, wiggle-strutting off in the direction of the churros bar.

Miranda stood up, brushing down her jeans.

"What was all that about?" asked Robert.

"Oh, nothing really. I told Cassia I'd promised to come to the market with my parents and that was why I couldn't hang with her. She was cool about it."

"Why didn't you just tell her you were going to hang with me tonight? Then you wouldn't have to hit the deck every time you see her."

"It's just easier this way," she said, taking his hand. "My parents are around here somewhere, so if she sees them, she'll assume I'm not far behind. She won't argue with a family commitment." She smiled really hard like this would make him understand her logic.

"But she'll argue if you've made a commitment to spend the evening with me?" Robert asked. He was trying to ignore it, but there was a nagging little voice in his head bleating out a warning.

"Relax," Miranda soothed, putting her arms round his neck and gently stroking the skin at the base of his hairline. "It's fine. And besides, sneaking around is kinda sexy, isn't it?" She reached up on tiptoe and kissed him long and slow, scrambling his brain and turning his knees to jelly. "Come on," she said brightly, pulling him in the opposite direction to Cassia. "Let's get some lebkuchen from the German stall."

Robert let himself be led, he loved the feeling of Miranda's small, cold hand in his and he definitely loved the way she kept kissing him, but something wasn't settling right in his stomach.

Laurence

Laurence had just bought a gingerbread hot chocolate from the hut of the self-proclaimed Hot Chocolate Emperor when he caught sight of Milly and Sam coming away from the chocolate pretzel stall. She had her hair in long plaits again; she must have been at work. The tip of her nose was pink with cold. She looked like a painting, laughing as she clutched a pretzel as big as her head in her mittened hands. Tonight was the night; he had to ask her to be his date to the ball.

"Come on," he said, nodding towards them. Tom and Ethan followed. "Listen, I need you to distract Sam for me."

"What?" asked Tom.

"Why?" asked Ethan at the same time.

"Because I want to ask Milly to be my date for the ball and I don't want an audience."

"You've changed, man," said Ethan mockingly.

"Shut up, Ethan," said Tom. "Don't worry, mate, we've got your back."

"Yeah, course we have," said Ethan, slapping him on the back. "You always were too deep for Cassia."

Laurence fielded his friends' good-natured ribbing and steeled himself for the task ahead. He didn't know why he was so nervous. He was never usually this shy around girls. But there was something about Milly Parker. He really wanted her to like him.

"Hey!" he said when they reached her. Milly looked momentarily startled. She looked around as though he might have been addressing someone else and then she smiled.

"Hi!" she said.

The smile she gave him felt exclusive and he couldn't help but feel a glow inside. Sam gave him a look that said: "mess with my friend and I'll break you". Laurence could believe it.

He turned his most disarming smile on her. "Hi, Sam," he said.

Sam gave him a flat sort of smile, but then Tom distracted her by asking about the refugee charity, and he felt himself relax away from her death stare.

"How was work?" he asked Milly.

She looked quizzically at him.

"I noticed you wear your hair in plaits for work."

"Ha, yes. People get well narky if they find hair in their sandwiches."

Laurence laughed. "Nice place to work, though. The Old Windmill, isn't it?"

"Yeah. It is a nice place. But my hair stinks of bacon and coffee by the time I leave."

"There are worse things to smell of," he said.

"True."

"There's a gig up there next week, isn't there?"

"Tuesday."

"Cool. Will you be going?"

"Probably," said Milly.

"Cool," Laurence said again. *Stop saying cool, you dork! Ask her!* So, um, can we, like, go over there for a minute?"

Milly looked over towards where he was pointing, and her brow crinkled. "To the fishing tackle shop?" she asked.

"Well, not the shop exactly, just away from here a bit."

Milly shrugged and cast a glance over at Sam, who was still deeply animated in a conversation with Tom. "Sure," she said, suddenly nervous. *Has he changed his mind about the party? Oh, holy Scrooge! This is going to be so humiliating. Maybe I can get in first, tell him I'm busy that night... Busy doing what? Homework? Squeezing blackheads? Being a loser dork?*

They wandered a little away, coming to a stop near where a group of carol singers were limbering up their voices before their performance. Milly's nerves were increasing by the millisecond. She was very close to being propelled skywards by the fear-farts building in her lower intestines.

"There's something I've been wanting to ask you," Laurence began. His throat had gone suddenly dry. Milly was looking at him like he was about to mow her down with a Santa sleigh. He tried to concentrate. "The Magical Snow Ball..." He saw Milly take in a quick breath, saw her eyes get suddenly wider, and it gave him the confidence to go on. "If you were to go, and I know you haven't been sure, and I don't want to put you under any pressure, but I was thinking that if you would like to go, then maybe you might like to go with me ... as my date?"

"*Hiccup!*" said Milly. *Whaaaaaat? Go to the ball with him?* She couldn't believe it. Was this actually happening?

Laurence smiled at her smiling back up at him through

her hiccups. *She looks happy,* he thought to himself. This was a good thing. She hadn't run screaming for the hills. He was feeling more and more like she was going to say yes.

Milly opened her mouth to speak before Laurence changed his mind about asking the intensely shy girl with weird bodily functions to be his date for the ball.

"*Hiccup!*" was all that came out.

"Is that a yes hiccup or a no hiccup?" Laurence asked laughing. "I'm not so well versed in the subtle language of hiccup yet." Her eyes were so wide now she looked like a cartoon. *Oh god! Could she get any cuter?*

Milly laughed through her hiccups. "It's a yes!" she squeaked. She was swooning so hard she wasn't sure her legs could hold her up. Just when she thought things couldn't possibly get any more romantic outside of a Netflix original movie, the carol singers began to sing "All I Want For Christmas is You". *Sweet Mary, Mother of Jesus!*

As they walked back over to the others, Laurence reached for Milly's hand and she took it without hesitation. Laurence saw Sam look at Milly quizzically, and then understanding broke over her face, and she opened her mouth in an "O" before breaking into a grin. He glanced down and saw Milly smiling back at her. *It must be nice to know each other so well you can communicate an entire conversation through a look*, he thought.

"Laurence!" Cassia's voice snapped through the air and burst the bubble he'd been floating in with Milly.

Milly looked down at the floor. How much of her time did she spend looking at the floor? he wondered. He felt her grip loosen on his hand but he kept his firm, not letting her hand drop. Laurence had already decided, after the last time he'd been caught between Milly and Cassia, that he wasn't going to make the same mistake twice, especially not now.

"Hey, Cass," he said when she reached them. "All right?"

"I leave you alone for five minutes and you're slumming it!" Cassia mock reprimanded him.

"Play nice, Cass, or go away," said Laurence. He meant it.

He saw Cassia wince and then clock him holding hands with Milly, and her expression turned into a sneer. Laurence held Milly's hand tighter.

"You remember Harvey, don't you?" Cassia asked.

Harvey, who had his arm casually draped round Cassia's shoulders, gave a languid nod in Laurence's general direction. With his matted dirty-blond hair and vintage leather jacket over ripped jeans, he looked every inch a rock star.

"We're having a party at mine later," Cassia went on, her fingers fiddling idly with a button on Harvey's shirt. "Come if you like." She waved her arm towards Sam and Milly.

"Dweebs are not invited."

Cassia's mum must be away for the weekend. Laurence knew she was away a lot; she partied pretty hard. And even when she was at home, she wasn't what you'd call present. Cassia made a big show of being allowed to host wild parties and having a socialite mum, but the closest thing she had to actual parental influence was the cleaning lady.

"I would rather stick pins in my eyes than come to one of your skank vomit parties," said Sam.

"Then it's for the best that you will *never* be invited to one of my parties," said Cassia.

Sam looked like she was getting ready for a war of words, which was the last thing Laurence wanted. He had enough of that at home, so he put himself in between them and said: "Sorry, Cassia, I was planning on hanging out with Milly and Sam this evening. But you enjoy your party. Good to meet you again, Harvey."

Cassia narrowed her eyes and was about to speak, but then she seemed to remember the would-be pop star hanging on her like an uber-cool cape.

"What-evs," she said, steering Harvey away. "Laters, losers," she called over her shoulder as they disappeared into the crowd of Christmas shoppers.

Sam

"Where are you going?" asked Milly.

They were queuing up at the churros stall. Sam could tell Milly was fully loving being out in public with Laurence. They'd been hanging around the market with him since losing Tom and Ethan to the noodle hut, where they were flirting wildly with two girls from the grammar school in the next town. The art of flirting had always mystified Sam. All that giggling and showing off – it reminded Sam of peacocks preening.

"I saw a handmade jewellery stall back there," Sam lied. "I thought I'd have a look, for my mum."

Milly looked at her quizzically. "OK," she said slowly. "We'll come with you."

"No, don't worry, stay in the queue. I'll meet back up with you in like forty minutes by the Ferris wheel."

"OK then," said Milly.

Sam could tell her friend was reluctant to leave her, but she was about to do something she didn't want an audience for. She waved to Milly and Laurence, then walked back down the hill.

The soup kitchen where Nadia was working was just off the high street, and it was here that Sam was headed. Sam hadn't intended on dropping in to see Nadia. In fact, all of last night and most of today she had been resolutely against going to the soup kitchen. And yet, here she was, compelled – by stupidity? Or the Christmas spirit? – to go and wave at Nadia through the window. Was she going soft?

The building was old, sandwiched between one building with boarded-up windows and a skip outside, and another that had partially collapsed and been cordoned off with orange tape. The windows to the soup kitchen were steamed up and running with condensation. Sam spent a moment standing outside, watching people go in and out, wondering what she hoped to achieve by coming here. Sometimes it seemed as though there were two sides of her, and they weren't necessarily working together.

A man emerged from the building and, assuming that she was waiting to go in, held the door open for her. Sam went in. The room was set out like a plain but functional café. Almost every table was occupied, and the air was filled with the genial hum of many satisfied voices.

Sam spotted Nadia immediately behind a cloud of steam emanating from a giant stainless-steel saucepan. Her shoulder-length wavy hair had bounced up into dark spirals in the humidity and her cheeks were shiny from the heat. She looked so pretty it made Sam's breath catch in her throat.

"You came!" Nadia smiled between ladling steaming soup into bowls and pointing customers towards the basket of bread rolls.

"I was passing," said Sam. "So I thought I'd pop in."

"I'm glad you did. Soup? I'm due for my break; we could sit together."

Sam stood, thoughts racing through her head. If she did this, she was signalling a ceasefire. Was she ready for that? It troubled Sam that she had found it so easy to hate Nadia. Worse than that, she'd found it easy to believe that Nadia would betray her in some way. The whole time they'd been together, Sam had been worrying that it was too good to be true, waiting for something to happen that would cause all her tentative bridges to come tumbling down. When they had, Sam wasn't surprised; that's what you got for letting people in.

"Sam?" said Nadia.

"Sure," said Sam, coming back to her senses. "Let's sit. But don't get any ideas."

Nadia smiled and blew a corkscrew curl out of her eye. "This will be an idea-free zone, I promise," she said.

Sam and Nadia sat at a table by the window, the lights outside a Monet blur through the condensation. They talked about everything and nothing, but not about them. It was good to talk with Nadia again.

Afterwards, when Nadia went back to work and Sam headed back out into the cold night to find her friends, it felt like she had left some of the weight she'd been carrying around in her heart behind on the bench in the soup kitchen.

Milly

It was late Saturday night. Milly and her mum were sitting on Milly's bed, looking online at second-hand prom dresses that had made it into the semi-finals. Her mum had squeaked, then cried, then bounced for joy and hugged Milly repeatedly for a full five minutes when Milly had told her that she would be going to the ball. Then she had pressed her for all the details of how and where Laurence had asked her, which Milly had been only too happy to relay.

"I can't decide," said Milly, trying and failing to imagine herself in anything so chic. "Which one do you think?"

"I think the green," said her mum, enlarging an image of a sleeveless Art Deco style evening dress with a V-neck and tiny silver beads sewn in a repeating chevron pattern down to the waist. "It'll be really flattering against your colouring. I've got a cream pashmina you can wear with it to keep out the cold."

"A pashmina, Mum? Really?" Milly laughed. "I'll be fine. I'm not going to go outside."

"No, but the hall will probably be draughty."

Milly rolled her eyes. "OK," she said. "Let's go with the green." She tried to sound casual, but she felt a thrill of excitement at the idea of Laurence seeing her all dressed up.

Before they hit "purchase" they checked with the seller that the dress would be posted straight away, in case any adjustments needed to be made ahead of the ball. The seller assured them she would send it on next-day delivery to arrive Tuesday. Another click and Milly had herself a ballgown.

"Thanks, Mum," said Milly, giving her mum a hug. Though the dress was alarmingly cheap, it was still a luxury that she knew they could hardly afford, and it was all the more special for it.

"You're welcome, sweetheart. It's not every day you get to go to a Christmas ball with the man of your dreams."

"Mu-umm!"

"Oh, what, like Laurence isn't your dream date?"

Milly snort-giggled. "I guess he is kind of dreamy. It feels a bit too good to be true. I keep waiting for something to go wrong."

"Why would anything go wrong? You deserve good

things, Milly, and this is a good thing. Don't spoil it for yourself by worrying about things that might not happen."

"What about the things that *are* happening?" Milly asked, tracing the pattern on her duvet cover.

"What do you mean?"

Milly took a deep breath. "Is Dad going to leave us?"

"What?"

"He's never out of his study and when he is it feels like he doesn't want to be."

"Oh, sweetheart!" Mum put her arm around Milly, squeezing her in close.

"Your dad's been going through a hard time," said Mum.

"So have you! But you haven't pressed the ejector seat and left your family."

"He hasn't left us, love. And he's not going to. He's just going through some stuff that he needs to deal with."

"But he's not dealing with it, is he? He's ignoring it and us!"

"Which is exactly why he's started seeing a counsellor."

"Has he?"

"Yes. Your dad realized he was becoming depressed with the strain of not being able to find work and he reached out for help. Sometimes things are bigger than we can handle, even as adults. But your dad is going to be fine."

"So you're not splitting up?"

"Of course not! Why would you think that?"

"Because of all the arguing." Milly looked down at the floor. "I can hear you, at night."

"Oh, my love. I'm sorry you've been worrying about this. I should have talked to you. It seems like neither me *or* your dad have been very good in the communications department recently. I know it must sound like we're always fighting but we're not. Well, they're not *all* arguments anyway; some of them are mutual moans. Your dad knows how stressful it is for me being the only one working and that makes him feel even more stressed. And then before you know it, we're having a who's the most stressed competition, which is stupid and pointless of course, but when you're worried about things you turn to your best friend for a moan, only in our case, we are each other's best friends, so we just end up moaning at each other. They aren't splitting-up moans. We love each other and we love all of you. We're just trying to figure it out the best way we can."

"What will happen if Dad doesn't get another job?"

"Something will turn up, love. Don't you worry."

"But what if it doesn't?"

"Well, then there are options we can look into."

"Like?"

Milly could tell her mum didn't want to be having this conversation. But she needed to hear about the *options* for her own peace of mind.

"Well, for a start, we could move house – downsize. But that is all a long way off. We aren't ready to throw in the towel yet."

"You sure Dad's with you on that one? It feels a lot like he's thrown in his towel already."

"You let me worry about your dad," said Mum. "All you need to worry about is not horror-hiccupping your way around the dance floor on Friday."

Milly laughed. "That is a genuine worry!"

"There is something that I've been wanting to talk to you and your brother about."

"Yeah?"

"You know, one of your dad's biggest joys is making Christmas wonderful for you guys. But the King of Christmas is having a little trouble finding his festive joy this year. So, I thought, how about us elves bring Christmas to the King of Christmas instead? What do you think?"

"I think sign me up!"

Mum cupped Milly's face in her hands and squeezed her cheeks, which Milly hated, but since it seemed to be making her mum happy, on this occasion she let it go. "I knew I could count on you." Mum smiled. "We're going to need some extra muscle, so maybe book Sam and Robert in for an evening next week. How about next Saturday? What's that now?" Mum mentally calculated the date. "That's the nineteenth of December, the day after your Christmas ball."

"Done," said Milly. "They'll be well up for it. And Mum?"

"Yes, Milly-moo?"

"Can you stop squeezing my cheeks now?"

Chapter 17

Sunday 13th December

Sam

Sam pressed the video button on WhatsApp and waited. It was eight-thirty on a Sunday morning. For Sam to be calling at eight-thirty on a Sunday morning, her friends must realize she was having an emergency. The first to respond was Robert.

"Yello!" he said breezily.

"Are you in the toilet?"

"Yes. I'm not actually on the toilet, but this is the only quiet place in the house. Talk fast before someone finds me."

"I'm conflicted."

"I'm gonna need more than that, Sam. Is this a Mum

thing, a Bill thing, a Mum and Bill thing, or a Nadia thing?"

"A Nadia thing."

"Oops, wait, looks like Mills is joining."

The screen split into three and Milly's face appeared, sleep-crumpled with sheet lines embedded in her cheek. "Do you know what time it is?" she asked blearily.

"Sam's having a Nadia crisis," said Robert.

Milly pulled herself up to sitting and leaned against her pillows. Sam loved how her friends were there for her, no matter what time of day it was. "OK, I'm ready. Hit me with your crisis," she said.

"So, you know I met Nadia last night."

"When you *accidentally* walked into the soup kitchen," said Robert.

Sam ignored this and carried on. "Do you think I was too hard on Nadia?"

"Well, she did snog someone else," said Milly. "And that's not OK."

"Yeah, but if it was you, would you have forgiven her by now?" Sam asked.

"I don't know," said Milly.

"Bertram?"

"Here!" said Robert.

"What do you think? I mean, you and Josie broke up and

you're still friends."

"Yeah, but me and Josie were together in like year eight. It's different when you're thirteen; you go out and break up and it's like done and dusted, swipe left, move on to the next girl," he said with a wink.

A laugh exploded out of Sam. "Move on to the next girl! I'm sorry, Robert, but you are the least likely player in the world," she said.

"Genuinely," agreed Milly. "Batman you ain't!"

Robert raised his eyebrows and nodded in reluctant agreement. "A boy can dream, can't he?" he said.

"I just don't want to end up like my mum," said Sam.

"What do you mean?" asked Milly.

"I guess my understanding of relationships has always been that if someone hurts you, that's it, they're gone. No second chances, no forgiveness. But I'm starting to wonder if that's right? Is it really that black and white? Because if it is, then I'm doing it wrong, because I'm not over Nadia. She really hurt me, and I still care."

"Sam," said Robert. "I don't know how to put this without it sounding like I'm dissing your mum, which I'm absolutely not. You know Mama Chowdhury is very special to me."

"Only cos she feeds you," said Sam.

"That helps for sure," agreed Robert. "But maybe

she's put her views on relationships on to you. Not on purpose, but you know, it's understandable. Your dad was a wrong-un."

"That's an understatement," said Sam.

"And he hurt your mum and it changed her outlook, and she may have unwittingly passed it on to you."

"So are you saying I should forgive Nadia?"

"I think what Robert means is, those are your mum's issues, not yours," said Milly. "You have to decide what's best for you. If you feel like you want to forgive Nadia, then do it. You and your mum are allowed to have different points of view on stuff. The right choice for her might not be the right one for you."

There was a banging on the door and a screeching child's voice began to sing: "Bertie, Bertie, Bertie, what are you doing?"

"For example," said Robert, leaning against the door to keep it shut. "I will choose not to have ten children when I'm older."

Sam laughed. The banging got louder.

"I mean," Sam carried on, "I'm not saying I want to get back with her or anything. But would you think less of me if we maybe started to hang out again?"

"Why would we think less of you?" asked Milly.

"Cos of all that stuff I said about no second chances and how I hated her and all that."

"Oh, we knew that was all fluff," said Milly.

"What?"

"We've known you too long to be fooled," added Robert. "You can't pull the wool over Bertram Barlow's eyes."

"Oh for..." Sam covered her face with her hands. "Fine then! I'm a soft touch."

"You're not a soft touch," said Milly. "You're just human. You change your mind sometimes, and that's OK. Nadia broke your heart, and you were gutted. And now maybe you're over it."

"But that's just it," said Sam. "I'm not over it. I'm still gutted!"

"Then there's your answer," said Robert. "If you didn't still like her then you wouldn't still be gutted. Give her a chance and see what happens. If it doesn't work out, you haven't lost anything."

"Apart from my self-respect."

"Overrated," said Robert.

"He would know," agreed Milly. "He's got none at all."

The cries from outside the door became a howl of: "I need a weeeee!"

"I've got to go," said Robert and the screen split back

into two again.

"Will you be OK?" asked Milly.

"Yeah," said Sam. "I'll work it out. Are you meeting Laurence again today?"

Milly grinned. "Yeah."

"I guess you two are like an item now, huh?"

Milly shrugged. "I think, maybe? I really like him."

"Enough to tell him about the food bank?"

"I'll tell him!" said Milly. "God, stop busting my baubles about it!"

Sam blew a kiss at the screen and clicked *end call.* She sighed and went down to breakfast. Her mum was making kedgeree and the welcoming scent of smoked fish and warm spices beckoned her to the kitchen.

Robert

Miranda was waiting for him on the wooden bridge. The water beneath was almost completely frozen over now. It had started to snow, and the flakes settled in her ebony hair. She smiled when she saw him and threw her arms round him.

"Sorry I'm a bit late," Robert said into her hair. Jeez, she smelled good, like frosty air and vanilla plum cake. "We had a Sam crisis."

"All OK now?"

"It will be."

"I love how close you three are."

They walked through the woods, the snowflakes falling down through the gaps in the branches. Miranda linked her arm through his and rested her head on Robert's shoulder. He liked this. He liked Miranda, he REALLY liked her.

"So how come you moved to England?" Robert asked.

"My mum wanted to come back; she's got family over here. She'd gone to Canada to study; it was never meant to be permanent, but then she met my dad and she stayed over there, although we moved all over Canada with my parents' jobs. We talked it over as a family first before deciding to move here. My brother wasn't really into it, but I didn't get on so well at my last school, so for me it wasn't such a big deal."

"And how does your brother like it now?"

"He's still miserable." Miranda laughed. "But he's made some new friends. You'd probably get on well, he's into music too. He hates the weather here!"

"Can't blame him."

"He liked snowboarding, so he's kind of bummed out about that."

"I can only apologize for our country's pathetic attempts at snow. And have you enjoyed getting to know your relatives in Britain?" Robert asked.

"It's been good. We live with my sobo, so our house is family meet-up-central."

"Sobo?"

"Oh, that's what we call my grandma. She's amazing, my brother calls her wrinkled lightning." Miranda laughed. "Because she's so fast on her feet for someone so old."

Robert laughed too. "I don't think anyone would describe my nan as wrinkled lightning. More like crinkled calm."

"I'd like to meet her one day," said Miranda. "She sounds lovely. You're the only other person I know who lives with their grandparent."

Robert was just trying to think of a time he could sneak Miranda in to meet his nan without her having to face his entire family, when Miranda's phone rang.

"Hi, Cassia! Nothing much, just out for a walk."

Robert tried not to let it sting.

"By myself, yeah, just listening to some music."

OK, now *that* stung.

"Sure, yeah, I'll be over after dinner. Bye!"

Miranda put her phone back in her pocket.

"Cassia?" Robert asked.

"You guessed it." Miranda hugged his arm and leaned up to kiss his neck. "Listen, would you mind if we kept us on the down-low at school?"

"Um, OK, sure," Robert agreed. "I don't mind, but why?"

"You know what it's like there. I just don't want us to be gossip fodder. You understand, don't you?"

Robert was about to say "not really" but then Miranda kissed him, and his brain melted, so all that was left was nerve endings and warm lips and he forgot about Cassia and keeping things on the down-low ... yeah, he forgot about everything.

Milly

Milly and Laurence were sitting on a bench in the park as the weather had another go at snowing. It had rained last night and then the temperature had dropped, so that the wet pavements and paths became instant ice rinks. Milly's mum had tried to insist on Milly wearing her brother's wellington boots but Milly had strongly revolted.

"Mum! I am not meeting Laurence wearing Jasper's Avengers wellies!"

"They're the only ones in the house that fit you. It's black ice out there, young lady," said her mum. "If Laurence likes you, he won't be put off by your footwear. You're going for a walk, not to a fashion show!"

"Seriously, Mum, were you ever seventeen? I cannot be seen in Avengers wellies!"

"You get him to come and call for you and I'll ask him if he minds what kind of shoes you've got on."

"Yeah, like that's gonna happen!"

"In fact, I'll bet you he's wearing wellington boots too! If you only knew how many broken legs we have to treat each winter..." This is what you got for having a mother who worked in A&E.

Eventually, Milly managed to win her mum round by promising to wear her most grippy-soled trainers. She really should have worn the Avengers wellies. From the moment she left the house, she had to inch her way along the pavement, clinging to walls, hedges, fences, and at one point a passer-by who looked less than thrilled at being used as a human skating aid.

Laurence found her clinging to a low-hanging tree branch just inside the park gates, her legs slipping in different directions every time she tried to put weight on them, and heroically came to rescue her; he was wearing a pair of green wellington boots. It was not Milly's finest moment.

"Hang on to me," he laughed. "You'll be all right when you get on the grass."

They made their way slowly – Milly slipping like she was walking on a bed of banana skins – to the grassy area, and finally Milly could stand unaided, although she had enjoyed being held so tightly by Laurence.

There was a frozen mud track that meandered through a small, wooded area and they walked together, spotting squirrels and laughing and talking as they passed ferns and fir trees silvered with ice. It was nice; Milly felt like she was in a movie montage. Beyond, in the park proper, was a wooden shack that sold freshly cooked doughnuts and the aroma carried on the cold air. Milly was feeling seven kinds of dreamy; it was too romantic. She couldn't cope with this level of heavenly. She imagined the top of her head flipping up to let the steam out. When Laurence reached for her hand, she hiccupped uncontrollably for a full two minutes. Laurence seemed to take this as the greatest compliment he'd ever been paid.

Presently they came to a bench, surrounded by an overgrown holly bush, set back from the path, and they sat down.

"I'm sorry I never got to know you sooner," said Laurence.

Milly shrugged, her coat making a swishing sound as she moved. "I didn't get to know you either. I guess we take faces we see every day for granted. We assume we know them, but we don't really. Do you know what's really sad? There are people I have passed in the corridor every day for like six years and I couldn't tell you the colour of their eyes. It's like we look but we don't see."

"Whoa, that's deep," said Laurence.

Oh, double bums and jingle bells! Milly berated herself. *This is the kind of stuff you should just keep in your head, Milly! What a dork.* "Sorry." She laughed self-consciously. "Sometimes I forget to filter."

"Why are you apologizing? You're right. That's exactly what we do."

Milly flushed.

"My perspective has had a serious reboot since Jamie went to prison," Laurence continued. "I didn't really think much past my own little bubble, but having to hide what was happening with Jamie made me question what other people were hiding. How many other people were struggling behind the smiles?"

Milly felt her blood freeze. Did he know about the food bank? How could he? On the other hand, what better time than now to come clean, while they were talking about people hiding stuff? *Do it! Do it now!* She took a deep breath and opened her mouth to say the words when Laurence gave a loud sniff.

Milly looked at him and found he was crying. Or at least he was trying not to cry but doing a really bad job of it. She rummaged around in her bag and found a clean tissue and handed it to him. He looked embarrassed but it didn't stop the tears. He sniffed again.

"God, I'm such a wuss!" he croaked.

"No, you're not," she said. "It's OK to cry. Crying isn't wussy, everybody does it."

"Yeah, but I'm a guy."

Milly laughed and rubbed his arm. "That's so stupid, being a guy doesn't mean you don't have feelings."

"I feel so bad, for Jamie I mean. When we first found out I was so angry with him, not just for doing it, but for putting my parents through all the stress and breaking our family apart. I was properly mean to him. And then when I saw him, before we went into court, and he was so frightened..."

Laurence lost his battle against the tears. Milly turned on the bench and put her arms around him.

"He's my big brother, you know? I'd never seen him scared before, not really scared. And I just keep seeing his expression, so frightened and pleading, and there was nothing

I could do..."

"You supported him," soothed Milly. "You still are supporting him. Think how happy he'll be when he gets his care package. He knows how much you love him."

The sobs began to subside, and Milly let go of him. Laurence blew his nose and wiped his eyes. "Thanks, Milly," he said, looking at her with red-rimmed eyes. "You're a really good listener." Milly smiled and shrugged again. "I can't talk to anyone about it. My mum is sad enough without me blubbing at her. And my dad acts like he doesn't care."

"I'm sure he does," said Milly, though of course she wasn't sure at all; it was just one of those things you said to people when they needed to hear it. She thought of her own dad, so different from the dad he was this time last year.

"I'm a real fun date, huh!" Laurence managed a chuckle.

"Well, maybe not so much today," she agreed, laughing. He was still hanging his head. Milly bent to look up at him. "But I'm glad to be spending time with you, and happy to be getting to know you."

"You really are one of the nicest people I've ever known," said Laurence. "And you're beautiful too."

Milly nudged him, laughing. "I am not, don't tease me."

Laurence cupped her face in his hands and kissed her. Milly forgot to breathe. All there was in the world was his lips warm against hers and the tickle of excitement, which ran through her. When he broke the kiss, Milly's eyes were still closed.

"Breathe, Milly," said Laurence, laughing quietly as he gave her a little shake.

Milly opened her eyes and took a sharp intake of breath as though she'd been underwater. She blushed instantly.

"Oh god! I'm such a dork!" she exclaimed.

"I've never had anyone stop breathing when I kissed them before," said Laurence, smiling down at her.

"I'm not good at multitasking."

Laurence pulled her up off the bench and she stumbled slightly, still light-headed from that kiss. "I can see I'm going to have to kiss you a lot more so that you can get used to it."

Wow! Swoon! Breathe, Milly! "That would probably be wise," she said. *Heavenly holly berries!*

Laurence draped his arm round her shoulder. "Come on," he said. "Let's get you some hot doughnuts to raise your blood sugar.

Chapter 18

Monday 14th December

Robert

The band finished practice, with only two complaints from the cleaning team to turn that bleeding racket down. Robert had told them that you can't actually turn live music down, but the tiny woman wielding a bucket had deftly turned down the volume on the mixing deck and silently gave Robert the sign that she had her eye on him.

The Magical Snow Ball prep team however had been most appreciative, especially of their rock rendition of "Let it Go". Miranda had cheered and whooped at the end of every song like their very own groupie.

Robert jumped down from the stage with his guitar case,

feeling pretty much like he might have to put his teaching career on hold because the Indigo Tigers would surely get signed for a multi-million-pound record deal any day now. Miranda rushed to greet him.

"OMG OMG! You were awesome!"

"Thanks," said Robert. He could feel his cheeks getting hot. He wanted to keep having Miranda look at him that way, with her warm eyes, which seemed to angle upwards at their edges when she smiled, and oh that smile; everything else in the room was a blur when Miranda smiled at him.

"Miranda!" Cassia snapped from across the hall. "I need you on snowflake duty."

"Sorry, Cassia." Miranda jumped to attention.

"Why do you let her boss you around like that?" asked Robert.

"She's my friend," said Miranda, her sweet smile faltered.

"Is she?"

"Robert, we've talked about this. I don't grill you about being friends with Milly and Sam."

"That's because they're not Ebenezer Scrooges."

"I've got to go," said Miranda. "I'll call you later." She threw a hopeful look in his direction and turned to meet Cassia.

Robert had a sinking feeling in his stomach. As he

made his way out of the hall, he heard Cassia hiss: "Why do you keep hanging around with that loser? If he asks you to the ball, you'd better say no. I do not want Robert Barlow bringing down the group average. Besides, I've earmarked Ethan for you; he'll probably ask you tomorrow."

Robert lingered by the door but Miranda didn't say anything at all, either in her defence or his. She just picked up the scissors and went back to cutting out paper snowflakes.

Frost was glistening on the tops of cars as Robert walked home, his mind a fug of conflicting emotions. He'd never felt embarrassed about who he was, until now. Miranda, the person who made him feel like a lottery winner when he was with her, had made him feel insignificant by her silence.

Milly

@off-centre-oddity

When I was a kid I felt like my parents knew everything. They were in charge, and there was nothing they couldn't handle. There was safety in knowing that whatever happened, the grown-ups had it under control. I realize that makes me very lucky. Not everyone has that.

Then, when I got older, sometimes my parents felt so removed from me, so incredibly unreasonable, that it was almost as if they were another species. But still, I was safe in the knowledge that though they seemed clueless in so many ways and their rules often felt arbitrary and unfair, ultimately, they had it under control; they knew the score.

The realization that my parents are fallible is terrifying. I'm a teenager, I'm supposed to not have a clue what the hell is going on. It's my job to feel unsure and make mistakes and feel afraid of the future. But they're adults! Their job is to be able to cope with anything!

I'm not an egomaniac, I promise. It's just that my understanding of the human life cycle was that one day everything would make sense and I would no longer feel this crushing sense of inferiority and confusion and uncertainty.

But if my parents, the most conventional, together adults I know, are floundering, that means the magical transformation from child to all-knowing adult is a myth. I won't, as I had assumed as a kid, reach an age where

I have all the answers. I won't be free of angst. I won't automatically know what to do in any given situation. If that's not terrifying, I don't know what is.

When adults condescendingly tell children that one day we'll realize that our school days were the best days of our lives, perhaps they don't mean actual school at all but rather those blissful moments in time when they didn't yet know that they would grow up and still not have a damn clue what the hell was going on.

Milly was lying on her bed, having just uploaded another blog and was now scrolling through Instagram stories. She clicked on @cassiakeepsitreal. There was a clip of Cassia and the Glee Club singing "Santa's Coming For Us" in a nursing home. Across the top was written *Love these guys so much!* #oldpeoplerock #fightinglonliness #givingback. Next was a close-up of Cassia singing, followed by a snap of the audience in the nursing home clapping, and then a series of selfies of Cassia beside various Christmas displays in town, looking impossibly cute in a red bobble hat with the title, *Santa Baby!* #dreamingofawhitechristmas #cutechristmas #girlnextdoor #influencerswanted.

Milly felt a niggle of annoyance at Cassia's two-facedness. She clicked on @oneinten's latest story and jumped at the high-pitched screeching emanating from her phone. The video was of Robert's lounge and the screeching was coming from what looked like a nursery-school riot. As well as Robert's younger siblings, Milly recognized his nieces and nephews in the room, bouncing off sofas, walls and chairs. The Christmas tree was being shaken violently from behind and the knitted stockings had been plucked from their hooks along the fireplace and were being worn as hats. His nan was sat in her armchair laughing delightedly at the mayhem. The video panned around the room and then Robert pulled the phone close to his face and said in his best Blair Witch impression: "I am so scared right now ... the elves have gone crazy! Send help!"

Milly laughed out loud and reacted with a laughing emoji. There was a knock at the door.

"Enter."

It was her mum.

"Did my dress arrive?" Milly asked hopefully. "I didn't hear the bell."

"No, love, sorry. I've sent an email to the sender to make sure it's definitely been posted."

"And?"

"They've not got back to me."

Milly felt her heart sink.

"Listen, love, um, are you busy?"

"Not unless you count freaking out over my prom dress."

"Your dad's not feeling so good, and I was wondering if you'd come to the food bank with me?"

"Again?" She realized instantly how petulant she sounded and regretted it.

It didn't need two of them to go to the food bank, but Milly knew her mum felt uncomfortable going by herself; like having someone else there vindicated her need to seek help.

"Sweetheart, your dad..."

"Yeah, I know, *he's going through some stuff.*"

Her mum looked stung.

"Sorry. I'm just being a brat," said Milly. "Ignore me. Hey, after we've done the food bank maybe we could break into the post office and see if we can find my prom dress?"

Mum laughed. "Righto, I'll bring the crowbar. It's probably in transit."

"I hope that isn't code for it's sitting in the back of their car!"

They pulled up at the food bank just after 7.30 p.m. It was quieter then. Sarah was on the front desk and greeted them both brightly. This evening some of the main lights were turned off to show off the twinkly Christmas tree which she and Laurence had decorated together on Friday; memories of that day made her stomach leap.

"Hi, Milly and Milly's mum! How are you?"

"Good, thanks," said Milly's mum.

"Milly's been so helpful," said Sarah.

Milly felt herself blushing.

"Oh, that's nice to hear, but I'm not surprised, although obviously I'm biased!"

The two women laughed, and Mum handed over their voucher.

"It's great when someone comes in with a fresh eye," Sarah went on, taking the voucher without comment. "Milly and Laurence have been batting around some ideas for our Festive Friday evening. I'll be back in a moment. I should be getting you to do this! You know your way around now," Sarah called over her shoulder to Milly.

"Day off," said Milly.

"That's what they all say!" came Sarah's disembodied voice.

In a few moments, she came back with the bags of shopping and Mum said far too many thank yous as she always did: like, *a ridiculous* amount of thank yous. Milly knew it was her mum's way of getting over the awkwardness of having to accept charity. The first few times they had visited, her mum insisted on telling the whole sorry tale of why they needed help, as if she felt the assistants were judging her. She had stopped that at least. Since working at the food bank, Milly had been able to assure her mum that there was definitely no judging.

As they walked out of the doors, her mum was still calling out thank yous, just in case they'd missed her first seventy-five. On the opposite side of the road was a corner shop, and a neon sign in the window flashed the word "OPEN" in pink. There was hardly any traffic and the *meepmop* sound the shop door made when it opened, carried across the street. Milly looked over, while her mum was wrestling her handbag on to her shoulder, so she could carry the food bags. Milly's heart stopped. Cassia was looking back at her, a slow smile spreading across her face. There was absolutely no way that Milly and her mum could not have just been picking up food at the food bank. She was caught, red-handed. Of all the people to have seen her, it *had* to be Cassia. Trinity tripped out of the shop behind Cassia and followed her gaze.

"Is that Milly Parker?" asked Trinity, squinting across the road.

Cassia didn't answer, she just continued to smile at Milly in a way that was anything but friendly.

"Right!" said Mum, finally having organized herself.

"Let's get this lot home. Hot chocolates all round, I think!"

Mum began to walk towards the car, but Milly's feet seemed to have planted themselves in the concrete. She was locked in a dreadful kind of stare-off with Cassia; Cassia smiling, Milly just mortified. She wondered if the horror showed in her expression and tried to manoeuvre her face into something that resembled defiance. She heard the *pip-pip* of the car unlocking.

"Come on, Mills!" called her mum, climbing into the car.

Cassia smiled wider. She made a shooing motion with her hands. "Run along, Mills," she shouted across the street. "Mummy's calling!"

The car started up and Mum revved the engine. Milly tried to think of something to say, some passing shot before she left, but she had nothing. As usual, her brain had frozen, and as she climbed into the car and pulled the door shut behind her, the last thing she heard was Cassia's peal of laughter ringing out into the night.

Sam

When Sam's phone buzzed with a message from Nadia, her first instinct was to wait a while before reading it. She didn't want to come across as keen. But when a second message came through hot on its heels, she decided to sneak a peek at the first line without actually opening the text. It read: *Don't ignore the first message.*

Sam smiled. Another message came through: *I know what you're like.*

Now Sam's interest was piqued. She clicked on the first message.

Look out of your bedroom window.

Sam turned her bedroom lamp off, to be able to see outside better. She pulled back the curtains and looked out. The street lamps were on and the street was quiet. Beyond the street was the park, completely shrouded in darkness, only the spindly silhouettes of trees at its perimeter giving any indication that it was more than just a gaping black hole in the landscape.

Something caught Sam's eye over by the railings. She peered down and saw Nadia, stood by the park gates. Her hat was wrapped in fairy lights, which flashed green and red. Nadia used her phone torch to illuminate an A2-sized piece of card, leaned up against the railings. The words read:

It's Christmas, and at Christmas anything is possible.
If you will open your ears to me, I will open my heart to you.
All I'm asking for is a chance.

Nadia took the card and placed it behind another:

If you still can't forgive me, I'll understand.
I won't bother you any more.
But I will always be a friend when you need one.

She switched the card for another:

This offer lasts until Christmas.
After that I'm taking my heart back.
But for now, because it's Christmas, and at Christmas
anything is possible,
I'll let you keep it.

Nadia gathered up her cards and stood, looking up at Sam's window for just a moment, before clicking off the lights on her hat and walking away into the darkness. Sam was breathless. She didn't care that Nadia had just basically ripped off *Love Actually* – secretly her favourite Christmas movie ever – she cared that Nadia had bothered to rip off *Love Actually* for *her*. Nadia had broken her heart, but if she let this last chance to sort things out slip past her because of her own stubbornness, she would be breaking her own heart.

Her mum came in. "Why are you standing in the dark?"

Sam shrugged. "Just watching the frost sparkle on the pavements," she said.

"Mmmm, *very romantic!*"

Sam ignored her mum's sarcasm. "Can we have Christmas at Bill's place this year?" she asked as her mum flicked the lamp back on and rearranged the cushions on her bed.

"Maybe," said Mum. "I don't want to give him the wrong idea."

"What, that you actually like him?"

"It's complicated, babes," said Mum, leaning over to kiss her forehead before going out and pulling the bedroom door shut behind her.

Sam flopped down on to the freshly plumped cushions on her bed and closed her eyes. She replayed Nadia's grand gesture over in her mind: the flashing hat, the notes on the boards, Nadia's expression as she turned her face up to meet hers. She didn't know how she was supposed to react to such a grand gesture. How was a WhatsApp message ever going to match up? Of one thing though she was sure; the feelings that felt like they would explode out of her chest any moment weren't those of heartache or anger – they were love, pure and simple.

Chapter 19

Tuesday 15th December

Laurence

Laurence was not having a good day. He had found out this morning that his dad couldn't make it to the pre-Christmas prison visit that Laurence and his mum had booked, and now it was too late to change it. Jamie was counting on their dad being there, Laurence knew that.

"Can't you change it?" Laurence had asked.

"I can't just alter court dates to suit my social life, Laurence. These things are booked weeks in advance."

"So was this!"

"I'm sorry, Lou, I know it means a lot to you..."

"It means a lot to Jamie! He's the one who's going to be stuck in prison away from his family."

"And whose fault is that?" snapped his dad and then immediately thought better of it. "I'm sorry, son. That was uncalled for. Jamie is paying his debt to society; playing the blame game is unproductive."

"Can't you get someone else in the firm to cover? Just for that day?"

"I can't let my client down."

"But you *can* let your son down."

His dad squeezed the bridge of his nose. "Do you have even the slightest idea what it's like to try and maintain credibility as a barrister when your son is serving a sentence for embezzlement? This lifestyle comes from having clients who will pay a great deal of money to ensure they don't end up like Jamie. It doesn't look good that I couldn't even keep my own son out of prison! I am trying my best, Laurence. I just ... I don't know when I became your enemy."

Laurence didn't reply; he couldn't because he didn't know either.

Laurence had always been very much the younger brother. He had happily fitted into that mould, knowing that whatever mischief the two of them got into, Jamie would take the bulk of the flack because he was the oldest. Jamie was the kind of big brother who used to tell him stories during thunderstorms to stop him being scared.

Now it was his time to step up. His big brother needed him to be the strong one, needed Laurence to fix things, and Laurence felt like he was doing a terrible job.

Usually, school would have been his haven: the place where nobody knew his problems and he could pretend he was still the Laurence Bashir of last year. But it wasn't enough any more, and he found himself counting the hours until he and Milly could disappear off to the food bank together.

Robert

Robert had just emerged from an hour of English literature, head down, eyes intent on his phone screen, as he shared Milly's latest blog with Flory, who would post it on her social media. Then he quickly pocketed his phone before any eagle-eyed teachers caught him, and was making his way along the corridor when he was grabbed and yanked behind a bank of lockers by Miranda.

"Hello!" she said brightly. She kissed him full on the lips and Robert's heart sped up in spite of himself. "I've been waiting for you. Let's sneak off to the far field for lunch."

"Where's Cassia?"

"Oh, she's just left for an orthodontist appointment, so she won't be back until the afternoon."

She looked so pretty, gazing up at him, the glitter shadow on her eyelids twinkling in the half-light behind the lockers. The roar of hundreds of students rumbled down the corridor unseen from their secluded spot. He almost backed out of what he needed to do. Maybe it wasn't so bad, hiding with Miranda. He really didn't have the heart to burst her bubble. But one of them had to be honest.

"Are you ashamed of me?" he asked.

Her smile slipped. "No, of course not."

"Then why do you pretend to Cassia that we aren't together?"

"I don't."

"Miranda, you literally threw yourself behind the hook a holly wreath stall on Saturday."

Miranda looked away, unable to meet his eyes. "It isn't you. You know what Cass is like, she's tricky. I will tell her, I just need a bit more time."

"I don't want to be one of those dirtbags who makes you choose between your friends or your relationship, but come on, Miranda, the least you can do is acknowledge my existence."

"I know. I will, I promise. But can we just go on like this for a little while longer? I just need a bit more time."

"And what about the ball?"

"What about the ball?" she asked.

"You *know* what, Miranda! Are you going to have to ignore me at the ball in case Cassia disapproves?"

"I thought you understood."

"Understood what?"

"Cassia was the only person who took me in when I started here, the only one!" said Miranda. "Look, I don't want to fight with you, but we both know Cassia's got a mean streak a mile wide and I don't want to spend my last year of high school being afraid. I've done that all my school life. You said you didn't want to be one of those guys, but that's exactly what you are being. Why are you making this so hard for me?"

"Me, making it hard for you?" Robert exclaimed. "I really like you, Miranda. I would shout it from the rooftops. I don't care who knows."

"I really like you too! But I'm not like you. And your friends aren't like mine. I'm not saying it's right, it's just how it is."

Robert felt as though he'd been winded. He'd never been made to feel more like garbage than he did right now. Was this what love was like? Even unrequited love hadn't hurt this much.

"I get it," said Robert. "You're embarrassed by me."

"No! No, that's not it, I think you're amazing! It's just it's complicated with Cassia. I don't know if I'm ready to take that step yet."

"Will you be my date for the ball?" Robert asked. "I want us to go together. I want to be able to hold your hand and dance with you."

Miranda didn't meet his eyes. She looked at her shoes and wrung her hands.

"That's what I thought," said Robert. "I'll see you around."

"Don't be like that," Miranda begged, her eyes suddenly filled with tears. "I don't have a choice."

"Sure, you do. You just made it."

Robert walked quickly. His chest ached. Maybe he just wasn't cut out for love. One thing was sure; working at the community centre this afternoon was going to be one big pile of reindeer dung.

Milly

"I wish you could be in two places at once so that you could come here on Friday too," said Sarah. "I think it'll be a really fun night, and you've worked so hard on making the place look special. But of course it won't be half so much fun as your Magical Snow Ball! Gosh, I bet you'll look wonderful all dressed up; I want lots of photos of you both, please! Oh, to be young and beautiful again!" she said dreamily and sashayed out of the storeroom.

Milly's stomach squeezed. Where was her dress for the ball? Lost somewhere in a sorting office? Or maybe it had fallen out of the back of the delivery van? She'd texted her mum at least twenty times already asking for updates. At this rate she'd be wearing her onesie.

"What's up?" Laurence asked when Sarah had gone out front, leaving them in charge of packing up the food bags.

"My dress still hasn't arrived."

"You've got a few days yet."

"What if doesn't come at all?"

"I don't care what you're wearing as long as you're my date." He smiled at her and Milly melted. A hiccup escaped her, and Laurence laughed.

"I thought you only got hiccups when you were nervous," he said.

"Apparently, I get them when I'm excited too," she laughed and hiccupped again.

"I'm really looking forward to it. I hate to say it but

Cassia has done a fantastic job of doing up the hall. If there's one thing she's good at, it's organizing."

Milly thought of seeing Cassia last night at the food bank and immediately needed a terror-tinkle. "Back in a mo," she said brightly and ran to the toilet.

She sat on the toilet worrying about what Cassia's next move might be. Would she tell everyone? Or would she hold it over Milly like a weapon? Should Milly tell Laurence now before Cassia got the chance? Oh god! What should she do? She'd left it too late and she was too deep into the deception now to just casually drop it into conversation.

"Oh god, Milly!" she said to her reflection in the mirror as she washed her hands. "What have you got yourself into? Why didn't you just tell him when you could?"

The toilet flushed in the next cubicle and Sarah came out. "Couldn't help overhearing you talking to yourself," she said, rubbing soap into her hands. Milly flushed. "Laurence doesn't know you have to use the food bank, does he?"

Milly pursed her lips. "I wanted to tell him," she said.

"If you want my advice, the truth is always best, no matter when it comes out. Come clean now and it'll just be an awkward conversation, but if you leave it too much longer ... well, what do I know?" Sarah smiled into the mirror at Milly. "I'm sure you'll make the right decision."

Laurence was pulling tins of beans off a high shelf when Milly came back. "Oh, there you are, shirker!" he grinned.

OK, Milly, tell him now. Just come right out with it.

"There's something playing on my mind, and I really need to talk to you about it," Milly began.

"I'm all ears," said Laurence.

"The thing is, for the last few months. . ."

"Laurence and Milly!" came Magda's voice from the office, "I'm putting the kettle on, tea or coffee?"

They called back their orders and Laurence looked at Milly and smiled. "You were saying?"

But Milly's nerve had left her once again. "Doesn't matter," she said.

Laurence held up two packets of biscuits. "If this was your food parcel, which biscuits would you want?"

Why didn't I just tell him!

"The Hobnobs," she said.

"Me too," and he popped the Hobnobs in the bag and the custard creams back on the shelf. "You're still on for tomorrow night at mine, aren't you?" He looked nervous. Milly didn't know why; it was in *his* house after all. Just the thought of it made her stomach gurgle alarmingly.

"Sure," she said. "When you say smart, what does that actually mean?"

Laurence rubbed the back of his neck. "I'll be wearing a suit, by order of my dad. But you can wear whatever you like, although maybe not jeans, or shorts, or scuba gear."

Milly laughed. "OK, that gives me something to work with."

"I'm so pleased you're going to come. It'll be a lot more fun with you there."

"It must be a really dull party if my presence is going to make it fun!" Milly said, laughing.

"Why do you always do that? Laurence asked.

"Do what?"

"Put yourself down like that?"

Milly shrugged. "I don't know really. Habit? I guess I like to get in quick before anyone else does it for me."

"I think that's a habit we should work on breaking," said Laurence. He was smiling at her, and Milly thought she might faint. "So, the gig at the Old Windmill tonight – we can go together if you'd like? I could pick you up from yours at about half six? We can grab something to eat up there."

"Sure," said Milly, trying to sound casual. "I would like. Thank you."

As they moved on to other topics of conversation, Milly realized that she'd missed her opportunity to tell him about her using the food bank *again*. She resolved to tell him later at the gig. She felt better at the thought that in another four hours or so, she would be free of the secret which had been following her around like Jacob Marley's chains ever since their first afternoon at the food bank.

Sam

Sam climbed the stairs, avoiding Toast and Spider as they shot past her on a giant teddy bear being used as a sledge. There seemed to be noise coming from every room in the house. No wonder Robert spent so much time hiding in the downstairs toilet.

She knocked on the door and waited. No response. She knocked again. Nothing. Nemo walked past in nothing but boxer shorts and socks. "Hey, Saaaaaam," he drawled. "How you doin'?"

Sam felt strongly that even if she wasn't gay, she would never be impressed by Nemo's *charms*.

"Robert won't open the door," said Sam.

"He can't hear you," said Nemo, leaning up against the

door frame. "He's listening to sad songs with his headphones on."

Sam rolled her eyes. "That's what I was afraid of," she said.

"Go on in. Maybe you can cheer him up. Nothing I've tried has worked."

"What did you try?"

Nemo listed his efforts off on his fingers. "Plenty more fish in the sea, plenty more pebbles on the beach, plenty more stars in the sky, oh, and plenty more chips in the fryer."

"And none of those pearls of wisdom worked? Wow, he must really be depressed!" said Sam. She pushed the door and closed it on Nemo just as he began flexing his pectoral muscles.

Robert was sat on his mattress in the room he was temporarily sharing with his brothers, Dot and Curly. He looked up at her, his eyes red-rimmed. Sam sat down next to him and plucked one of his earbuds out, placing it in her own ear; "It'll Be Lonely This Christmas" was playing. She took his phone and scrolled through his playlist: "Please Come Home for Christmas", "Blue Christmas", "Last Christmas", "I'll Be Home for Christmas"...

"What are you doing?" she asked.

"Feeling sorry for myself," said Robert.

"I see that. How was it at the community centre?"

Robert gave a long, exaggerated sigh. "Awkward. I avoided her as much as I could and then she asked if she could go because she had a headache."

"Lightweight," said Sam.

"She seemed really upset. I don't know what I'm supposed to do. She's making me feel like I'm asking her to choose between me and her friends. I don't want to be that guy."

"You're not that guy," soothed Sam. "She wants you to be her closet boyfriend; that's not fair."

"Am I really so embarrassing that she can't be seen with me?"

"Trust me, it's not you. The problem is with her. She's got stuff she needs to work out."

"It feels like it's my problem."

"That's because it's easier for her to push her crap on to you than step up and deal with her own issues."

Robert sniffed loudly. "When did you get so wise?"

"I've been where you are now and I know how much it sucks."

"That wasn't the same," Robert said, sulkily.

Sam gave him her best teacher look. "Being hung up on girls who haven't come out yet and having to hide in the shadows to save girls from trouble is basically the same."

"All right," Robert conceded, sniffing. "Point taken. What

should I do about it?"

"You know I'm always on your side, Bertie."

"I feel a but coming."

Sam smiled and squeezed his shoulder. "But I also know that those girls who had to keep me a secret were doing it because they couldn't see any other way around their situation, and carrying around that kind of worry must have been just as miserable for them."

"Are you giving me the benefit of your hindsight, oh wise one?" Robert asked, managing a weak Yoda impression and a hint of a smile.

"Yes, so you'd better listen up. I charge by the minute for these pearls of wisdom." Sam gave him a friendly nudge. "It's not unreasonable to expect your girlfriend to acknowledge your existence, and you have every right to feel the way you do. For what it's worth, I think Miranda is making a huge mistake if she lets you go. But from what you've told me about her past, I can understand why she might be struggling with the idea of being out of the group. Would you want to be Cassia's number one target?"

"I guess not."

"Give her a bit of time. She might surprise you!"

"Why do I always fall for impossible girls?"

Sam put her arm round him. "If I wasn't gay, you

would've been my type."

Robert looked at her, horror-stricken. "You knew?"

"It was hard not to."

"You never said."

"Would you have wanted me to?" asked Sam.

"I guess not. Unrequited love sucks. Maybe I should become a poet. They're full of repressed anguish."

"You're not exactly repressing it, Bertram."

"Do you think I'm an idiot? You know, for being in love with you and all that?"

"No, Robert, I think you are the most awesome guy I have ever known. And if I could have chosen any guy in the whole universe to love me, it would always be you."

"Thanks," said Robert, flushing scarlet.

"That is why I feel I am in the perfect position to tell you, that if Miranda throws you over for Cassia, then she is a massive idiot, and she doesn't deserve someone as amazing as you."

Robert sighed the sigh of the sorrowful. "I've never bought into that whole *cool/not cool* thing," he said.

"I know. It's one of the many and varied things I love about you," said Sam.

"But I get it now. For the first time I really get what Milly is always going on about; having someone I like feeling ashamed to be seen with me, because I'm not cool enough ...

I dunno, it made me feel ... less than everyone else. I don't want to feel *less*."

"You are not less than anyone!" Sam said, swallowing hard. "You are the best damn Who that Whoville has ever had!"

Robert managed a weak smile and Sam knew they were through the worst of it. "My poor Bertie," she said, giving him a friendly nudge. "You know what you need?"

Robert sniffed. "What?"

"You need to stop listening to songs of Christmas heartbreak and come watch a gig with me at the Old Windmill."

He looked at her with his big doe eyes and Sam felt all kinds of maternal towards him.

"You're right," he said.

"Of course I am."

"Thanks for coming over."

"Are you kidding me? *Bake Off*'s on. I left my mum shouting obscenities at Paul Hollywood, and you know how she feels about the Hollywood; I'm safer here than at mine right now. Now blow your nose and get your coat, we're leaving!"

Sam

The Old Windmill was heaving. The art had been removed from the gallery to make way for the band and crowd, while the café downstairs was full of people cooling off with cold drinks. They had seriously gone to town with the Christmas decor; the place was dripping with tinsel and the café alone had three Christmas trees shoehorned in the oddly shaped space. Sam and Robert grabbed a Coke each and headed upstairs to find Milly. Robert knew the band; the Indigo Tigers had supported them at the Summer Fair in the park last August.

Now they pushed towards the front and found Laurence by himself. A swift glance around revealed Tom going at his girlfriend's neck like a vampire by the fire exit and Ethan sucking Trinity's face off next to the gent's toilet. The band was, as expected, ear-splittingly loud in the relatively small, circular room, and they had to yell to be heard.

"Where's Milly?" asked Robert.

"I had a text from her about an hour ago," said Laurence. "Said she couldn't come; some sort of family drama. She's got to go with her mum to her sister's school play."

"That sucks! She'll be gutted."

"Not as gutted as I am," said Laurence.

Sam saw Nadia over by one of the windows talking to a

girl and she felt a twinge of jealousy spike in her stomach. She had done this; she had brought this on herself. Nadia had begged to be heard, she had pleaded for forgiveness and Sam had turned her away, week after week. How could Sam possibly blame her for moving on? Sure Nadia hadn't given the impression she was looking for anyone else, far from it, in fact, but since when was jealousy a rational emotion? Sam was consumed with the sensation that she'd screwed up royally.

At that moment Nadia turned and looked right at Sam. Sam felt like she was held in a tractor beam; she didn't want to look but she couldn't look away either. Nadia waved, completely oblivious to the tumult in Sam's brain and the hollow feeling in her chest. She waved back weakly and tried to force a don't-care smile. She felt as though her face would crack like a porcelain vase.

The girl Nadia had been speaking to turned, and Sam recognized her as one of Nadia's many cousins. The relief she felt was dizzying. Sam grabbed a hold of Robert to steady herself. Robert automatically put his arms round her to hold her.

"Hey!" he shouted. "Are you OK?"

"I'm fine," she said, though her voice was wobbling. "I think I've just had what people call an epiphany."

"Jingling mistletoe!" Robert exclaimed. "Do you need to

get some air?"

Sam nodded.

Robert led Sam out of one of the doors and on to the balcony, which wrapped around the first floor of the Windmill. Laurence followed them out. It was bitingly cold, and Sam was grateful for it; she needed to clear the fuzz in her head.

"What happened?" asked Laurence, concern etched on his face.

"It's just a bit loud," Sam lied.

"Now tell us the truth," said Robert.

Sam didn't really want to divulge her personal business in front of Laurence, but Robert was unlikely to let her off the hook until he was satisfied with her answer. "I saw Nadia in there and I thought she was with another girl. I mean she *was* with another girl, but she wasn't *with* her if you know what I mean."

Robert nodded. "Got a little reality check, huh?" he said knowingly.

"Something like that," Sam smiled.

"You know she's super into you, right?" said Laurence.

Sam and Robert looked at him quizzically. Laurence shrugged.

"We sit together in politics," he said by way of explanation.

"I know way more about Nadia's broken heart than I do about the Russian Revolution. It's a pity *Nadia and Sam's break-up* won't be on the exam papers!"

Sam laughed half-heartedly. "I'm such a candy-cane brain!" she exclaimed, taking a deep lug of the frigid air.

"You too with the Christmas swearing," said Laurence.

"It's a tradition," said Robert proudly.

"I was talking with Ethan earlier. Trinity told him you and Miranda have had some sort of bust-up?"

"Let's just say, I didn't quite make the grade," said Robert.

Laurence raised his eyebrows but didn't ask any more questions. "She's a nice girl," he said. "She's different to the rest of them."

"Yeah, that's what I thought," said Robert.

Sam reached out and squeezed Robert's hand. "So, you're taking Milly to a fancy party at your place tomorrow night?" she said, steering the subject neatly away from Nadia and Miranda.

Laurence smiled as though he had no control over it. "Yeah, I mean, it won't be *that* fancy!"

"Black tie, according to Mills," said Robert.

"Well." Laurence's cheeks had gone shiny with heat, despite the cold. "Yeah, I mean, you know, it's kind of smart."

"Mate, in *our* social circle, black tie is *fancy*," said Robert.

Laurence conceded the point.

"You ready to go back in?" Robert asked Sam.

"Yeah," Sam replied.

There was a sound of footsteps and they turned to see Cassia and Harvey swaggering up behind them; Harvey had his arm draped over Cassia's shoulder, and they both had the telltale unsteadiness that followed too much alcohol.

"Losers!" she said by way of greeting.

"Oh, hey, *Cassia*!" Sam managed to make her name sound like an expletive.

Laurence held out his hand to Harvey. "All right, mate," he said. "How was the tour?"

"The tour was awesome, mate," Harvey slurred. "Just back for Christmas and then we're off to Bulgaria to kick off the European tour."

"Cool," said Robert.

Harvey looked at Robert as though seeing him for the first time and held out his hand.

"Harvey," he said, shaking Robert's hand. "Good to meet you, dude."

"Robert," said Robert. "And this is Sam."

"Robert's in a band too," said Sam.

"Did I hear right back then, Laurence?" Cassia interrupted. "You're taking Milky to one of your dad's parties?

309

I hope you've warned her not to dress like a total peasant."

"Give over, Cass," said Laurence exasperatedly. "Your incessant meanness is just boring."

"Don't mind me," she said, raising her hands in surrender. "I'm just worried about how the poor girl is going to fit in with all your dad's cronies. Still, I'm sure you'll look after her. Come on, Harvey."

She yanked the door open and hot air and noise blasted over them. Harvey looked back sheepishly. "Good to meet you," he said, giving a general nod in their direction.

"He doesn't seem like a total dirtbag," said Robert. "He seemed way more arrogant on TV."

"Hmmm," said Laurence, sounding unconvinced. "He was giving off serious rock star wannabe vibes the other night at the market."

"Just like his girlfriend," Sam added.

"Shall we?" asked Robert, motioning to the door.

Sam saw Nadia here and there throughout the evening, but she was always too far away at the other end of the crowd for her to get near, and it was too loud to hold any sort of conversation even if she had. But Sam made sure, every time their eyes met, to give Nadia a smile, in which she tried to convey all her warmest feelings.

Chapter 20

Wednesday 16th December

Milly

Milly looked out of the window for the fiftieth time. She was wearing a pink skater dress with a sweetheart neckline and her hair up in a messy bun, with bits hanging down, which her mum had curled for her.

"You're going to wear the curtain out," said her mum. It was such a mum thing to say.

"I don't want him to be hanging around waiting for me."

"Surely he'll text you when he's outside? Speaking of which, you haven't given me his address yet; I want to know where this party is."

Milly rolled her eyes but got out her phone and texted

the address to her mum, and she heard the ping across the room as it reached her mum's phone.

"Is he your boyfriend?" asked Tara.

"No. He's a boy that is a friend." Milly wasn't completely sure if they were in boyfriend/girlfriend territory yet. For the moment they were placement buddies who kissed and that was good enough for her.

"Is he handsome?" Tara continued in her line of questioning.

"He's ... yeah ... he's ... you know, all right."

"Teagan says that her sister does snogging with her boyfriend. Do you do snogging?"

Milly felt her cheeks redden. She lifted the curtain again – risking wearing it out – so that her face was in shadow, and was grateful for the cold coming off the glass.

"I won't be snogging anyone at this rate," she murmured.

Dad came in cleaning his glasses and squinting at the television. "Who won't be snogging who?" he asked.

Milly caught Mum smiling wryly, but she was saved from further comment by Laurence's car pulling up in the street. "OK, bye!" she called, letting the curtain drop and swishing the baby-blue blanket scarf around her shoulders.

"Home by ten!" Mum called after her.

"And no snogging!" shouted Dad. He was smiling and

shaking his fist as Milly pulled the front door closed behind her and hoped that Laurence hadn't heard. But her heart had leaped at seeing a snippet of her *old* dad shine through. She turned to the street, smiling to herself, and then stopped as all coherent thoughts left her head.

Laurence was standing by the passenger door and HE LOOKED HOT! Milly's stomach leaped up and high-fived her tonsils. Her throat guinea pig was so excited she wasn't sure she could contain its squeak. She wondered if he'd notice if she quickly buried her face in the hydrangeas to let it out. He was wearing a skinny black suit with a white shirt and bow tie, and his normally unruly hair had been swept back off his face in dark shining waves. He waved at her and she began to make her way down the garden path, saying to herself *don't fart don't squeak, don't fart don't squeak* as she went.

"Hi," said Laurence, and Milly noticed he looked nervous, which annoyingly only made him look even more hot. "You look ... good. I mean, really good, I mean, like, stunning!"

In the glow of the street lights, he looked like a movie star.

"You look amazingly good," said Milly dreamily.

"I can't hold a candle to you," said Laurence and then he seemed to remember himself. "Sorry," he said, looking around as if checking to see if anyone else had heard him.

"Man, that's so corny. I can't believe I just said that."

Milly was smiling so hard it was a wonder her mouth didn't swallow her whole head.

Laurence pulled the car door open for her and as Milly moved to get in their eyes met. "You do look beautiful, though," he said.

"Thanks," said Milly, her voice, for some mortifying reason, coming out hoarse, like she hadn't had a drink for three days. As he pushed the door closed and made his way around to the driver's side, she cleared her throat several times. The smell of his cologne filled the car and she breathed it in deeply. *Damn, even his smell is hot! Is that a thing? Be cool, Milly,* she mentally slapped herself and added another self-imposed rule to the mantra: *Don't fart don't squeak don't sniff him!* The list was beginning to feel exhaustive; she was going to have to exert extreme self-control, or the pressure was going to become too much, and she might spontaneously combust – she could already feel a terror-tinkle brewing.

Laurence started the car and pulled out of her street. "Thanks for agreeing to be my date tonight," he said. "I almost feel bad making you come. But I figured if I'm going to be bored, I'd rather be bored with you." He darted her a quick smile before switching his eyes back on to the road. "I mean, I don't mean I'll be bored with you because you're boring, I mean like we'll be bored together. God, what's wrong with me? I can't seem to string a coherent sentence together this evening!"

Milly laughed. "I knew what you meant," she said. "And if it's any consolation, I'm glad you chose me to be bored with."

A car passed by on the other side of the road, the headlamps illuminating Laurence's face: dark skin, long eyelashes and a chiselled jawline which Milly just couldn't tear her eyes away from. Her stomach did a somersault to see that he was smiling to himself. She felt like she had just reached the top of the climb on a roller coaster and was about to drop.

They pulled on to a gravel drive and parked outside a large, Georgian property, which could easily have passed for a boutique hotel, with marble columns by the front door, and at least fourteen windows, to the front. The house was lit up by spotlights sunk into a large mound of grass, which also acted as a turning circle. Laurence switched off the engine and turned to face Milly.

Milly gulped. "You live here?"

Laurence looked uncomfortable. "Yeah."

"Holy Mother of Christmas trees! I don't think I can go in." Every muscle in Milly's body had stiffened. She felt like the Tin Man in a dress.

Laurence smiled. "You'll be fine," he said soothingly. "I won't leave your side. Unless you need to use the toilet, and even then, I can stand outside and wait for you."

Milly took a deep breath. "OK," she said.

"Right, some things you need to know about my family. My dad is a snob and so are all his guests. My mum is going to fuss around you and, if you let her, she will feed you until you're sick."

He must have seen the utter horror in Milly's expression because he continued. "Don't worry. We are only there to look the part for my dad. He will introduce us to his cronies and tell them all that I've got a place at Cambridge University and then he'll leave us alone."

"He must be really proud of you," said Milly.

Laurence smiled but didn't look convinced. "You ready?" he asked.

"Can I tell you something, before we go in?" asked Milly.

"Of course." Laurence turned and looked at her expectantly. But she'd left this far too late; it would have been so much easier to tell him when he was still a beautiful enigma, when her feelings for him were still only surface deep. Now she really knew him, really liked him, she had so much more to lose. She took a deep breath and began.

"It's about the food bank. I gave you the impression that

I'd never been there before..."

"Laurence! There you are! Come in, come in, don't keep the poor girl standing out in the cold!"

"Sorry, Mum!"

Laurence gave Milly a "sorry about this" look.

"Shall we finish this conversation inside?" he asked.

Milly nodded. What choice did she have? As they walked hand in hand up the gravel drive, Milly had never felt more like Cinderella in her life.

Sam

"Sam, babes." Mum poked her head into Sam's bedroom. "There's *someone* at the door for you." Her mum winked, several times in quick succession, which just made her look like she had a twitch. She had never learned the art of subtlety.

Sam was taking yet another virtual tour around the Nottingham University campus. She'd looked at it so much she half expected Nottingham Uni to serve her with an anti-stalking notice. She had to get over it. She had to accept that her mum would need her here. She sighed and closed the lid of her laptop. She knew who was at the door. So much of her destiny felt out of her control at the moment but this was one thing she had the power to change for the better.

Nadia was standing in the hallway, cheeks red from the cold, her hair covered by a striped knitted bobble hat and a matching scarf covering her chin. Ordinarily, her mum would never have left a guest unattended – or unfed – but the *Real Housewives of New York* Christmas special was on TV, so the normal rules of etiquette didn't apply.

"Hi," said Sam.

"Hi," replied Nadia. "I got your message. Here I am!"

Sam looked at Nadia for a long moment. She liked her just as much now as she had all those months ago. So, where exactly was all this stubbornness getting her? And besides, this was a Christmas-only offer; if she passed it up now, she'd never know what had really happened.

"Mum! I'm going out for a while."

"Righto, babes, keep your phone handy! Home by half ten," came Mum's voice from the lounge.

They wandered up the high street, the shop windows twinkled prettily and swags of Christmas lights above their heads zigzagged all the way up to the top of the hill, where the Old Windmill was dappled with falling snowflakes from a projector at its base. The trickling of the stream behind the shops on the left-hand side was noisy now that the shops were closed for the night, but Sam judged by the sudden drop in temperature that the stream would be frozen silent by the morning.

It seemed like each of them was waiting for the other to speak. Sam was usually the one to jump in first, but she was trying to channel patience: a new experience for her. "Why don't you go first?" she said.

Nadia took in a deep breath and then let her words out in a rush. "I'm not like you, Sam," she blurted without preamble. "You're so sure of who you are. So confident in what you want out of life."

"Is that the impression I give?" said Sam. This was a genuine question; Sam felt neither sure nor confident of herself lately.

"You made it all look so easy and I just felt like I was floundering around trying to make sense of things."

"And you don't think I was too?"

"It didn't seem that way."

"Well, I can confirm that things aren't always what they seem."

"The only thing I did know was that I really, really liked you," said Nadia.

"You had a funny way of showing it."

"Can you let me talk?"

"Fine!" Sam put her hands up in surrender. "You talk, I'll listen. But you can't stop me pulling faces."

"That's fair." Nadia smiled. She took a deep breath and began. "You told me once that you'd known you were gay since you were ten. But you know that it didn't happen like that for me. I've struggled with my sexuality and how I settle those elements of myself with the other parts of my life. I have to balance the choices I make with what they mean for the people around me as well as myself. I'm not saying it's easy for you, but you're so sure of yourself. If I'm having trouble accepting myself as bisexual, how am I supposed to expect other people to accept me? I know this sounds silly and clichéd but I'm not brave like you."

"You think I'm brave?"

"Don't you?"

"No! I'm just being me, there's nothing brave about it."

"Sam, you don't care what anyone else thinks. You stand up for what you believe in and stand up for everyone else as well. I'm much more of a fly under the radar person."

Sam was shocked into an uncharacteristic silence. She tried to think of something witty to say but nothing came. Nadia had frozen her brain.

"I really liked you, Sam, you know I did, I still do! All the things I said to you about how I felt were absolutely true. I felt so bad that I couldn't hold your hand when we were out, when I know how much you wanted us to be just like any other couple. But we weren't just like any other couple, Sam. People still stare when two girls hold hands, no matter how woke our social media feeds appear. I lived in fear that one of my mum's friends would catch us and report back."

"I understood that," said Sam. "I know it's complicated for you. You hadn't come out to your family. I never held that against you. Or if I did, I didn't mean to. Did you feel I pressured you?"

"No," said Nadia. "Not exactly. I felt pressure from myself. I wanted to make everyone happy. I wanted to be the girlfriend you deserved but I wanted to be the daughter my parents deserved too."

Sam couldn't imagine not feeling like the daughter her mum deserved. Sometimes her mum's adoration was a bit too much! But the flipside was that Sam never felt she wasn't enough. "And being bi didn't fit into that," she said gently.

"Not then. I couldn't see how it could."

"For what it's worth, I never minded that you were bi. I guess in a way I felt more special because I knew it would have been easier for you to be with a guy."

"You were special, Sam. I need you to understand that what you saw ... the way I behaved, was never a reflection of my feelings for you. It was to do with my feelings about me. Jake called me up and wanted to meet. I never intended for anything to happen; he promised me he just wanted to talk."

Sam was trying to push the image of Nadia very much not *just talking* with Jake out of her head. "So, what happened?" she asked, and then rephrased. "I mean, I know what happened. What I'm asking is, how did you end up kissing?"

Nadia was quiet for a moment and Sam knew she was trying to work out how to articulate what she wanted to say. Nadia was like that; she was measured, where Sam was reckless. It was one of the many things which had made them such a good couple, made their late-night conversations so intense; they came at one another from opposite ends of a subject and found balance where they met.

"The simple answer is, I chickened out," she said. "I knew that the more serious things got between you and me, the closer the time was coming when I would have to come out to my parents. Even having a boyfriend can be a contentious issue in my house! They're not as strict as my grandparents but they are still quite strict about that sort of thing."

Sam guessed she was pretty lucky she'd never had to factor other people's ideals into who she was; there were perks to having a mother who gave Beyoncé a run for her money in the fierce department. "Being with Jake would be a lot easier than being with me," she said gently.

"That's where my head was at that moment, yes."

"I get it. I don't like it, but I get it."

"But what you saw, what I need you to understand – " Nadia's voice was urgent – "is that I didn't take the easier path. That kiss made me realize I would be living a lie. I didn't want to spend my life in hiding."

Nadia looked at Sam, forcing Sam to look back. Sam couldn't doubt the sincerity in her eyes. "I told Jake I'd made a mistake and that I was sorry. And I went home, and I told my parents that I'm bi."

"Oh my god!" Sam was so shocked she forgot to festive swear. "How was it? Was it OK? Were they OK?"

Sam was suddenly worried that her presence in Nadia's life might be responsible for her becoming estranged from her family. Not everyone's parents were as easy-going as her mum. Family politics could be a minefield and that was before you brought religion into the equation.

Nadia smiled. "They were OK." She nodded at the memory. "I was a mess but they were actually really cool about it. I wish I'd told them sooner. I maybe didn't give them enough credit. Although a couple of my aunties were a bit shell-shocked."

Sam thought back to when she'd told her mum that she thought she was gay. She was twelve; she'd told her mum during their Saturday night ritual of Turkish takeaway, face packs and *Strictly*. "Course you are, babes," her mum had said. "I knew that year you made me watch *Tangled* with you, three hundred and fifty times!" It hadn't been all easy; just because her mum accepted her sexuality, didn't mean she hadn't come up against micro aggressions in her everyday life. There would always be someone who felt the need to push their insecurities on to her or attack her with their thinly – and sometimes not so thinly – veiled bigotry. But knowing she had her family's support made it easier to deflect the blows.

"The thing is," Nadia continued, pulling Sam back from her memories, "that kiss was monumental, not because of who I was kissing, but because it made me realize there was only one person I wanted to be kissing, and it wasn't him; it was the girl watching from her bedroom window, thinking I'd betrayed her."

Sam felt the last slivers of the ice block she'd built around her heart melt away. They had stopped walking. Sam turned to face Nadia. "Thank you, for telling me, for explaining. I'm sorry I didn't listen before. I was hurt and angry, and well, you know I'm stubborn at the best of times! I want you to know that my feelings for you never changed, Nadia," she said before adding wryly, "I may have added in a few extra feelings after I'd seen you with Jake." She saw Nadia's eyebrows rise, a small, knowing smile playing around her lips. "But I never stopped... How I feel about you, it's..." Sam was uncharacteristically lost for words. She took a breath, her heart beating hard and fast in her chest. "What I want to say is, it's always been you. Always. No one else has ever come close."

Sam tentatively moved closer to Nadia, and Nadia closed the space between them. They kissed to the sound of Wizzard belting out "I Wish It Could Be Christmas Every Day" from the jukebox in the Millers Arms pub. They parted breathless and smiling, and as the clock on the church tower chimed out that it was eight o'clock, Sam slipped her gloved hand into Nadia's and Nadia clasped it tightly in return.

Milly

The inside of Laurence's house was as intimidating as the outside. Laurence guided Milly through a formal dining room and into what Laurence referred to as the orangery. It was a large, low-lit room made entirely of glass. There were palm trees and oversized ferns, and giant, fronded plants, which cascaded down from the ceiling; if Milly had seen Tarzan swing past her, she wouldn't have blinked an eye. Glamorous people glided about quaffing champagne and making *mwarf*

mwarf mwarf sounds, which Milly took to be how posh people laughed. At the far end, a man in a tuxedo was playing a grand piano and being pointedly ignored by everyone; Milly assumed that these people were obviously used to having pianists playing in their conservatories.

Laurence was correct in his assessment of his parents. His mum seemed determined to fill Milly up with canapés, which as far as Milly could discern appeared to be meals which looked as though they had been shrunk with one of Willy Wonka's shrink rays: tiny Yorkshire puddings with slivers of beef, weeny eggs on toast and burgers fit for the Borrowers. She had lost count of how many of these morsels his mum had thrust at her.

"Laurence!" his dad called and beckoned them over. Milly fought the urge to vomit up a miniature Yorkshire pudding and followed Laurence's lead.

"Laurence is volunteering at the local food bank," said his dad, a suave man with a commanding voice. He was quite a bit older than her own dad, Milly thought, his silver hair bright against his dark skin. "A worthy cause, I'm sure you'll agree, Clive."

"I didn't know there was one," said Clive, a pompous-looking man wearing an expensive suit.

"Clive!" chided a woman in a green evening dress.

"You're so oblivious."

"I think there's probably one in every town given the way the economy's going," said a tall man with hair the texture of a doormat and introduced as David.

"People need help," said Laurence's mum, lifting a silver tray of the smallest pizzas Milly had ever seen up to Milly's face in a way that gave Milly no option but to take one. She smiled as Milly popped the morsel in her mouth.

"It's so sad," she continued. "It's not right that in this day and age, people should be going hungry."

"What I don't understand," said David doormat hair, "is why there's so much of it about?"

"What? Poverty?" asked Laurence's mum incredulously. "I don't think it's a new thing, David." There was a note of derision in her voice, which made Milly warm to her even more.

"Well, I mean, we've got a benefits system, haven't we? That should provide people with what they need."

"Clearly it doesn't," said Laurence.

Milly saw his dad look up sharply from where he looked to have been smirking at something in the bottom of his wine glass. She could feel herself getting hot. It didn't feel like they were talking about the food banks any more; Milly felt very much like they were talking about her family; about things they knew nothing about – with their teeny foods and invisible pianists. They were discussing things they couldn't possibly understand.

"Of course," chimed in pompous Clive, "a lot of them simply don't *want* to work!"

Milly dug her nails into the palms of her hands and tried to stop the anger that was burning in her stomach from boiling over.

"Or they spend the money the state gives them on cigarettes and alcohol," said David.

Milly began to feel dizzy with rage.

"Don't talk such crap!" said Laurence.

"Laurence!" his dad snapped.

"What? Two minutes ago, he didn't even know we had a food bank in the town and now he's an expert on poverty? I'm sorry but *he is* talking crap."

"Our guests are entitled to their opinions," his dad said frostily.

Milly wanted to leave. She wanted to be anywhere but here. She looked up to the glass ceiling and wondered where all the air in the room had gone.

"Maybe politics isn't the right topic for a party," said his mum, rubbing Laurence's arm.

"Sure, let's pretend it's not happening, we're good at that

in this family," said Laurence locking eyes with his dad.

His dad's stare could have frozen water, but it did nothing to cool Milly's rising temper. She was stuck in a nightmare and now Laurence and his dad were engaged in a stand-off, while she stood there like a spare part, full of stupid tiny party food.

"They could help themselves by not having children that they can't afford," said Clive, oblivious to the tension.

Milly was amazed that steam wasn't spouting from her ears; she felt as though she might erupt at any moment, and her head felt like the top of a volcano.

"Ah, but you'll notice they've all got the latest smartphones!" chuckled doormat hair.

That was it, it was as though she was a steam engine, and someone had just opened her valve. "That's such a stupid, ignorant thing to say!" Milly exploded. She was vaguely aware of the room turning her way, but the words were already bubbling out of her. "How much is a smartphone worth? So, they sell it, then what? They've got enough money to maybe pay a bill and buy a couple of bags of shopping. But next week they'll be in exactly the same situation, only now they're cut off from the world, completely isolated in their struggles! Why would anyone want to punish them more? How poor would you like people to be before they can earn your compassion?"

Milly stopped. She was wrung out and suddenly conscious of many pairs of eyes upon her. The heat in her cheeks changed from anger to mortification. She grabbed hold of Laurence's hand.

"Can we go somewhere quiet?" she asked him. "There's something I need to tell you, and I need to tell you now."

Laurence must have seen how grave her expression was because he bit back whatever comeback he was about to spit at doormat hair. "Sure," he said and began to lead Milly through the crowd that had gathered around them.

"Milly Parker. Well said!" came a familiar, unwelcome voice that made Milly's insides squirm. "I must say, I didn't have you down for public speaking, but bravo! That was quite a speech."

Milly looked over to see Cassia – her arm looped with a blond man with designer stubble – and felt her stomach drop. *No no no no, please no!*

"You should listen to Milly, she knows what she's talking about," said Cassia. "Her family are no strangers to the food bank..."

Milly felt Laurence looking at her.

"Oh, didn't she tell you?" Cassia said, smiling. "I am surprised, since you two seem to be so close. Milly gets her food from the food bank..."

Cassia was still speaking but Milly couldn't hear what she was saying over the rushing in her ears. She did the only thing her mortified brain would allow and bolted from the room as fast as her silly shoes would allow. She didn't stop to grab her scarf, she didn't stop when Laurence's mum called after her, she didn't stop until she was outside with the gravel beneath her feet and the cold night air scratching at her bare arms. Only then did she let her hot tears fall.

Milly began to walk, unsteadily, along the drive. She pulled out her phone and blinked several times to clear her vision enough to see her contacts. "Mum," she sobbed into her phone. "Can you come and get me?"

"What's the matter? What's happened?"

"I'm fine, Mum, I just need you to come and get me from Laurence's."

"I'll be there in ten," said her mum and rang off.

"Milly!" Laurence's voice cut through the dark.

She kept walking, but Laurence wasn't hobbled by ridiculous shoes and he caught up with her easily. He stood in front of her forcing her to stop.

"I don't want your pity," said Milly.

"Why didn't you tell me?"

"Because it's irrelevant."

"But we've been working at the food bank together, that

331

feels pretty relevant."

"Well, it's nobody else's business how my family gets their food!" She tried to sound defiant, but her voice was wobbling too much to pull it off.

"I thought we had something," said Laurence.

"We do!"

"Not if you don't trust me, we don't."

"It has nothing to do with trust."

"I think it has everything to do with trust. I've told you things I haven't told anybody. I told you about my brother. That's a hell of a lot bigger than whether your family visits a food bank..."

"Bigger to you maybe, but not to me! You don't get to belittle my problems just because you're a poor little rich boy!"

She pushed past him and stomped angrily through the gravel. He came up behind her and laid his jacket over her shoulders. She would have thrown it off, but she was absolutely freezing.

"I was just trying to say that it's not that bigger deal to me. I'm not bothered about where your family gets their food from. I'm bothered that you couldn't trust me with it."

"You have no idea what it's like to be worrying all the time about whether we'll have to move house, or whether we'll even have a Christmas this year!"

"You're right, I don't, not if you don't tell me. I'm not a mind-reader, Mills!"

"You want to know why I haven't publicized my trips to the food bank? People like Cassia." Milly laughed bitterly as angry tears prickled her eyes. "You have to give her points for knowing how to make an entrance!"

"I swear I didn't know she was going to be here."

"It doesn't matter," said Milly, waving her arm dismissively. "It just proves my point. Cassia and people like her are exactly why I didn't tell you."

"Fine. But I'm nothing like Cassia, you should have been able to confide in me."

"But I didn't know that at first, did I? I mean, you hang out with her all the time."

"Way to judge a person."

"Oh, like you don't judge us!"

"All right, so we both make judgments about people. But once you'd got to know me..."

"I wanted to tell you everything, I honestly did, it's all I've wanted to do, but I kept getting interrupted and then I'd lose my nerve. And the longer I left it, the more I knew it would have seemed like I..."

"Like you didn't trust me," said Laurence. "Which brings us back to where we started. You don't trust me. And I don't want to be with someone who lies."

"I didn't lie!"

"As good as."

"I tried to tell you."

"If you'd really wanted to tell me, you'd have found a way."

Milly's mum's car skidded into the drive, stopping just short of them. Milly opened the passenger door and handed Laurence's jacket back to him, and he took it without looking at her.

"I just wanted you to like me because I'm me and not because you felt sorry for me," said Milly pleadingly.

"I did," said Laurence. He turned away from her and walked back towards the house without looking back.

Milly thought her heart would crack clean in two. She climbed into the car, pulling the door closed, and Mum drove away in a shower of gravel hitting the paintwork.

It was a long time before Milly could stop crying long enough to form a coherent sentence. Her mum parked up in the garage and they sat together in the dark car. John Legend and Kelly Clarkson sang "Baby, It's Cold Outside" on the radio, and Milly poured out all her worries, while her mum listened, stroking her hair and handing over tissues, until Milly was all cried out.

"I guess now is as good a time as any to tell you, I got an email about the dress. It got sent back to the sender. I'm sorry, love."

"It doesn't matter," Milly sniffed. "I won't be going to the ball anyway."

"Well, if things change, I've asked Aunty Mel if you can borrow Cousin Bronwyn's prom dress. I think you're about the same size and Nan is on hand for last-minute seamstress duties. It won't be the dress you'd hoped for, but you'll still be the belle of the ball."

Milly did a snot-bubble laugh. "You always think I'm the belle of the ball."

"Of course I do! Sometimes I look at you and I can't believe I made something so utterly perfect."

"You would say that; you're my mum."

"If you decide to go to that ball, I will do everything in my power to make sure you go in there feeling like a million dollars. You don't need a guy by your side to make you feel special. You make your own special."

"Thanks, Mum."

They were quiet for a while.

"I wish you'd told me your worries," said Mum.

"I didn't want you to think I was ashamed of us. Because I'm not. It wasn't like that at all. I just missed my chances to tell him and then it got harder and harder to say anything."

"That's the trouble with secrets, even little ones; they burrow down like moles, making a maze of tunnels, until you can't find a way out."

"Do we have to tell Dad?"

"I think so," said Mum after a moment's contemplation. "He's going to ask why I ran out of the house like a bat out of hell and I don't want to lie to him."

"Because of the moles and the tunnels," said Milly.

Mum laughed quietly and pulled Milly across the steering rack and into a hug. "Exactly," she said. "It'll be all right, Milly-Moo, you'll see."

When at last they ventured out and made their way to the house, the night sky had taken on a curious golden glow and fat snowflakes fluttered down to balance on the frosty grass tips.

Chapter 21

Thursday 17th December

Milly

Milly, Robert and Sam all arrived purposely late the next morning so as to avoid registration and went straight to their study period, where they did absolutely no studying. It would mean a tardy note on their reports, but there were times when you just had to take a tardy for the team. They were hiding out in the furthest common room, a dark little side room where nobody ever went because the old water heater housed in the wall groaned like a restless spirit.

"I can't believe Cassia!" said Robert.

"Can't you?" asked Sam.

"You've got to admit, this is a new low, even for her," argued Robert.

"Yeah, well, there is the argument that if I'd have told him in the first place it wouldn't have been such a big deal," said Milly.

"Between you and Laurence maybe, but seriously, what right does she have to go around blurting out people's personal circs? That's not OK, Mills, no matter what spin you put on it," said Sam.

"You and Nadia, though!" said Milly.

Sam tried her best not to beam out of solidarity with her friend's pain, but it was impossible; the smile just wouldn't be quashed. "Yep. Me and Nadia. There comes a time when you just have to put all that other stuff to bed, you know? Plus, she's hot."

"She's a sugar plum for sure," said Robert.

"But I feel kind of bad feeling so happy when you're both having such a crappy time."

"Well, you shouldn't," said Milly.

"No way," said Robert. "It's great that you and Nadia are back together. What sort of friends would we be if we wanted you to feel miserable just because we do?"

"Will she be your date for the ball?" Milly asked.

Sam looked sheepish. "Yeah. But you can join us."

"Thanks, but I'm going to help out at the food bank; I already messaged them. It's their busiest night. I'd rather be there than trying to dodge Laurence and Cassia."

"Nadia said they were so frosty with each other you could practically feel the icicles at registration," said Sam.

"Well, anyway," said Milly. "It's nothing to do with me any more. I don't think Laurence will forgive me and I don't blame him."

"There's nothing to forgive!" said Sam, outraged. "And if he can't see that then he doesn't deserve you anyway."

"I hurt his feelings."

"Oh, boo hoo to him in his mansion!" said Sam.

"If we dismiss his feelings just because he's got money, then we're as judgy as Cassia," said Milly.

"I think he'll come round and realize that you were in a really difficult situation," said Robert. "I know this is an unpopular opinion right now, but Laurence is an all right guy."

Sam snorted but didn't comment.

"You're right," said Milly. "He is a nice guy. And I blew it. I should have known it was a bad omen when my dress didn't turn up. At least now Mum can get her money back."

"Do you want me to come with you to the food bank tomorrow night?" asked Sam. "I don't mind, it's only a stupid ball."

"I would skip it too, Mills, you know I would, but I can't let the band down," said Robert.

"Oh, Bertie," said Sam. "This sucks for you too, having to see Miranda there."

"Yeah, well, I'll just keep my mind on my strumming. Maybe I'll come and help out at the food bank once my set's over?"

"That would be great!" said Milly. "I think if I'm going to find my Christmas spirit anywhere, it'll be at the food bank."

She looked out of the tiny, leaded window at the fat snowflakes brushing against the glass on their way down. It had been snowing on and off since last night and the view from the attic room was like a Christmas card. She thought of kissing Laurence in the cold and let out a long sigh that steamed the window. She wanted to apologize to him so badly, but the stinging humiliation of last night at the party was still fresh in her memory. *It was nice while it lasted*, she thought to herself and tried to convince her heart that the ache would stop soon.

Laurence

Laurence had been steeling himself to see Milly at registration and found himself both relieved and deflated when she hadn't turned up. Robert and Sam were absent too and he wasn't surprised; that's the sort of friends they were – the rallying kind. Laurence couldn't help but feel a twinge of jealously. He supposed they saw him as the bad guy in all this. After all, it was Milly's family who were going through a poverty crisis, not his. He couldn't help feeling like a bit of a dirtbag showing off his fancy house when her family couldn't afford to eat. But that didn't make her an angel. She was a closed book, secretive like his dad; he didn't need another one of those in his life.

When Milly had left last night, Laurence had gone straight up to his room. He hadn't stopped to see Cassia. He didn't know if she had stayed at the party to gloat, or if she had left once her mission was accomplished. His mum had come up to see him. At first, he had ignored her knocking and soft cajoling voice asking to be let in, but eventually he had relented. He'd tried so hard not to burden his mum with any more weight than she was already carrying, but when she folded him into her arms, his words spilled out in a torrent.

"Your feelings are bruised right now. But of all people," said his mum softly, "we know how important it is to forgive someone when they're sorry."

Laurence wasn't ready to forgive Milly yet. The betrayal

was still too bitter in his stomach. He'd opened up to her, told her stuff he hadn't told anyone else, and she hadn't trusted him enough to do the same. He felt gutted and the worst part was, the one person he wanted to talk to was the person who had gutted him in the first place.

Cassia was unusually quiet in registration. He could tell that she was waiting to gauge his mood before she approached him. He'd let so many of her spiteful jibes at people go unchecked over the years, thinking that if he didn't join in, he was somehow innocent of the harm they caused. And now he saw that *not* speaking out against her meanness was as bad as agreeing with her. He'd enabled Cassia to behave appallingly by his own wish for an easy life.

He sat with his back to her and didn't make eye contact even when she hovered in front of him on the pretext of discussing last-minute ball details with Ethan. What did she expect? That he would be grateful to her for exposing Milly like that? Did she think that he would just fall back into line?

"I heard about you and Milly," said Tom quietly.

"What about me and Milly?" Laurence asked. He was suddenly cautious; despite it all, he felt protective of Milly. She didn't deserve to have her personal circumstances bandied about class. It was nobody else's business, just like Jamie being in prison was nobody else's business.

"Cass said you two split up last night. She said it was pretty explosive."

"Did she. Did she say why?"

"Something about Milly not being the good girl she makes herself out to be. Care to elaborate?"

"Not really," said Laurence. "But it's not about Milly being a good or bad person. She's a good person." He was relieved that Cassia hadn't divulged Milly's business to the class the way she'd done at the party; maybe she had some modicum of conscience after all.

"Fair enough," said Tom. "I'll tell you what, the atmos in this place is well depressing at the moment. Miranda's got a face like a wet weekend, you've got a cob on, and Cassia looks like she's sucking on a lime."

Laurence forced a smile. "Pre Magical Snow Ball blues?" he suggested.

"Either that or they've put something in the water. Are you going to skip the ball now it's all off with Milly?"

"I don't know," Laurence said. *Was it all off with Milly?* Sure, he had been angry, but his anger seemed to be fading like an old bruise: tender at first but lessening by degrees each hour. His mum was right; dammit! "Maybe I'll go by myself."

"I'll save you a slow dance," Tom said, winking.

"Cheers, mate." Laurence left for class, hoping he would

and would not bump into Milly in the corridor. He'd never felt this conflicted over a girl before. He was all over the place, for god's sake! The snow was falling in cotton-wool balls and Laurence wondered if Milly was somewhere in the school watching it too.

Sam

Sam pushed the key in the door and entered into a space where she had clearly interrupted a row. The atmosphere was muggy with it like the air before a thunderstorm, and the words which had been hurriedly bitten off as she walked in hung in invisible speech bubbles.

"Everything all right?" she asked. Bill and her mum looked guilty, like she'd just busted them breaking into a safe.

"Fine, babes," trilled her mum. "Good day at school?"

"It was all right."

"Your mum told me about you and Nadia," said Bill. "Great news! That should put a spring in your step."

"Yeah," said Sam. "It's good."

"Got a date to the ball now!" he added.

"Yup, guess so. Will you be over tomorrow night?" she

asked. It was daft but she wanted Bill there to see her go off to the ball.

She saw Bill dart a furtive glance at her mum and her mum raise her eyebrow in return in that way she did that meant *Do what you fricking want, it makes no odds to me!* Bill was in trouble again, and when she saw the small red velvet box discarded on the sofa, Sam guessed why. Her heart sank. Poor Bill. Only her mum would be affronted by a proposal of marriage.

"I'll be here, love," said Bill, smiling at her.

What was wrong with her mum? Did she have a self-destruct button or something? Sam knew her mum adored Bill; she'd never, in her seventeen and three quarters years on this planet, seen her mum so happy with another human. Was she worried to commit because she knew she was sick and didn't want to be a burden? That would be peak mum: so independent she'd probably volunteer to perform her own heart surgery!

Sam smiled at Bill and in that one smile she tried to convey all the things she couldn't say like: I'm sorry my mum is like this, she loves you I promise, don't leave us, please don't leave us. "Dinner smells good," she said for something to break the thick silence. Ordinarily, the smell of Bill's lamb hotpot would set her stomach gurgling with anticipation, but the bad feeling in the air seemed to have dulled her senses leaving an acrid scent in her nostrils. "Are you staying?"

Again, the almost missable glance between Bill and her mum. Her mum had gone full poker face now. Bill seemed to be considering whether it would be better to just make his excuses and leave. Maybe he saw the desperation in Sam's face because his jaw unclenched, and he said: "Yes, love, I'm staying. My old ma would never approve of leaving a lamb hotpot to go to waste."

"Good!" Sam's voice came out too enthusiastic and her mum gave her a betrayed look, which Sam ignored.

She went upstairs, leaving the "grown-ups" to continue their discussion.

Sam: I'm going to be living at home for ever!

Milly: Really?

Sam: Yup. I'd better start collecting cats, so me and Mum can be the weird cat women.

Milly: Do I need to bring you over a crochet blanket and some half-moon glasses?

Sam: Please.

Milly: What's happened?

Sam: Looks like Bill proposed to Mum and Mum went full jingle bells. And not in a good way.

Milly: 😳

Sam: It's weird downstairs right now.

Milly: I'll bet. You really to need to talk to your mum.

Sam: It's fine, I'll just cancel the rest of my life.

Milly: Good option.

Sam: How are you feeling?

Milly: Like I messed up really bad. Talk to your mum.

Sam: Maybe.

By dinner time an outsider would never have guessed there was an argument simmering beneath the table. Sam's mum was an expert at sweeping things under the rug. There were so many things under that rug now it was becoming a trip hazard. Sam didn't know how to fix things. If she could just make things right between her mum and Bill, that would be a start. But what she mostly felt at the moment was anger towards her mum. She was angry that her mum was hiding something as big as a heart condition, for cranberry sauce's sake! And she was angry that she was going to push Bill away, because seventeen years ago Sam's biological father had acted like a total Christmas turkey and her mum needed to punish all men because of it.

Milly

Milly sat with her laptop open, her finger hovering over the "Send" button. She had talked herself in and out of sending an email to Laurence for over half an hour. There were things she wanted to say but knew she would never be able to in real life. Real life wasn't her strong suit; she was better surrounded by words.

Her latest @off-centre-oddity blog was a call-out to the

universe and the explanation that she could never say to Laurence's face. She hadn't posted it yet. She wanted to send it to him first before she cast her words out into the ether, but she couldn't seem to make her finger press the "Send" button.

Jasper walked in without knocking to tell her that dinner was ready. "What are you staring at?" he asked. "You looked like you were in a trance."

"None of your business," said Milly.

Jasper took *none of your business* to mean *come on over and read my private correspondence.*

"Is that to Laurence?"

"No. Yes. Maybe, I haven't decided whether to send it or not."

"Having no money sucks."

"Yeah, it does."

"So, is he picking on you because our family is skint?"

"No!" Milly was shocked by how defensive she felt towards Laurence. "It's not like that at all."

Jasper shrugged. "Do you want to make it up with him?"

"It's not that simple."

"Want me to beat him up for you?"

Milly turned to see her scrawny younger brother down on one knee and flexing his muscles like a fairground strongman. She couldn't help but laugh. Jasper stopped gurning and grinned at her, then he kissed his non-existent biceps and got back to his feet.

"Thanks, Jazzy, I'll let you know if I need your services."

Jazzy was the pet name she'd had for her brother ever since he'd been born, but she hadn't used it in ages, mostly because they hadn't really spoken in ages.

"Remember when we used to play *Mario Kart* all the time?" said Jasper.

"Huh, yeah, I do."

"And I beat you like ninety per cent of the time..."

"I let you win."

"Why?"

"Cos that's what big sisters do. It's in the handbook."

"You know what younger brothers do?"

"They annoy big sisters?" Milly was half smiling, wondering where this conversation was going?

"Yep!" said Jasper, and he leaned right over her and pressed "Send" on her email to Laurence.

"Jasper!" Milly screeched, but Jasper was already up and running out of her room.

Milly leaned back against her pillow. *Well, I guess now it's in the lap of the Christmas gods.*

Laurence

Laurence had managed to avoid his dad since last night. To be honest it wasn't that hard in a house this big with a parent who is so consumed by work that he probably went several days at a time without remembering he even had children.

He hadn't called Milly, even though he wanted to.

"Laurence."

Urgh! It was his dad. Laurence stayed quiet. Maybe his dad would think he was getting an early night. Another knock.

"I just want to talk. I know you're not asleep. Please, Lou."

Laurence sighed. "Come in." He sat up, cross-legged on the bed, and prepared for battle. His dad sat down on the bed, smoothing the duvet out with his hand as he did so.

"I get things wrong," he said.

Well, that was unexpected! Laurence made no answer.

His dad continued. "When Jamie went to prison, I felt like I'd failed, on many levels. Even with all my years as a barrister behind me, I'd failed to keep my own son out of prison. I'd clearly failed as a parent if my son turned to embezzlement for a career! I threw myself into my work to try and deal with my grief that one of my children, one of my babies, was suffering in a prison cell and I couldn't help him. And in the process, I failed you too."

Laurence didn't know what to say. Tears pricked his eyes, threatening to spill. It had been so long since he'd talked with his dad. He hadn't realized how much he had missed him.

"I miss him," said his dad. "And I miss you."

That did it. Tears overflowing, lump in throat, constricting breath. Laurence wanted to say something, but if he opened his mouth, he'd start bawling for sure. There were a lot of things that infuriated him about his dad, but he was still his dad and he still loved him, even if he was the worst snob in the world and thought socks and sandals with corduroy slacks was trendy casual wear.

His dad reached over and pulled Laurence into a hug. "I love you, son. I love you both; you are my world. I get things wrong but that doesn't mean I don't love you. Never forget that. When Jamie comes out of prison, we'll go camping, just like the old days: try and rebuild some of those bridges that this mess burned down."

They pulled apart, both of them clearing their throats in the most manly way they could muster and dashing the tears from their eyes as though they were annoying mosquitos.

"I want to talk to you about your friend Milly."

Laurence felt a stab of regret in his chest. He hadn't realized how hard he had fallen for Milly until last night and now it was too late. He tried to visualize his heart being hard like a stone. This was something he had started doing when Jamie first went to prison. It made it easier to handle the hurt if your heart was stone.

"I don't think we're friends any more, Dad."

"I would really like you to rethink that."

"Why?"

"It took a lot of bravery for her to go up against a bunch of outspoken middle-aged men."

"Yeah, but she wasn't brave enough to speak to me about what was going on in her life. I guess she's more comfortable with strangers."

"Or you could look at it another way," said his dad.

Laurence raised his eyebrows incredulously and waited. *This ought to be good.*

"Sometimes it's harder to be honest with the people who mean the most to you because the stakes are so much higher with someone you care about; you've got more to lose. I talk for a living but look how hard it's been for us to communicate these past months. Perhaps Milly gave Clive and David what for because their good opinion means nothing to her. But your good opinion clearly means a great deal, and she was afraid of losing it."

Laurence hated to admit that his dad had a point, but his dad did have a point.

"Anyway," his dad said, getting up off the bed and leaning to kiss the top of Laurence's head. "I've given you my two pennies worth. The rest is up to you." He made his way to the door and then stopped. "I'm sorry Cassia was so rude to your friend. You were right, Lou; just because someone looks the part doesn't make them suitable company."

He smiled at Laurence and Laurence smiled back, and as the door closed, one of the knots that had taken up residence in Laurence's stomach for the last few months untied itself. He sighed and looked out of the window. It was snowing again; it had been snowing on and off all day. His laptop dinged with the sound of an email, and when he looked, he was surprised to find it was from Milly. He wasn't sure he was ready to converse with Milly just yet, he couldn't trust his own feelings at the moment, but equally his curiosity was piqued; why would she send an email and not a text like a normal person? There was an attachment entitled "blog" and the subject bar read: Explanation and Apology.

Dear Laurence,

I'm not good at explaining things in person. I get tongue-tied and say the wrong thing, sometimes I don't say anything at all. I'm sorry that I hurt your feelings, that was never my intention. I guess I got in a hole too deep to climb out of. I should have trusted you, I know that now.

I write a blog, it doesn't have many followers but it is a way that I can get my words out without stumbling over them. I am attaching my latest blog. It says all the things that I wanted to say but couldn't.

I hope you can forgive me. I'm sorry.

Milly

Laurence was torn. He was still angry at Milly and in some ways, it felt good to be angry; it made a change from feeling guilty and sad. But he knew that was unfair. He was pushing his crap on to Milly. But if he forgave her, he'd have to unfreeze his heart and risk having it broken. No, he told himself, Milly deserved better than to be ignored because he felt fragile. Milly had reached out to him, the least he could do was read what she had to say. He clicked on the attachment and began to read.

When does omission become a lie?

I didn't mean to not tell my friend. I certainly never meant to hurt him. It's just that once you begin by not telling a thing, it becomes harder and harder to tell it. I hid the thing in a box and pretended it wasn't mine.

I told myself that an omission wasn't a lie. To begin with, it was to protect myself. I didn't know him well enough to be sure I could trust him. And by the time I did know him well enough, I was in too deep.

It was easier to be the girl without the problems. But with each little denial, the mistruth wrapped itself more thickly around me. It seemed like every time I plucked up the courage to tell him, the universe threw something in my path to distract me and I lost my nerve; I let myself be distracted. I didn't want to risk breaking the fragile thing which was growing between us. I wanted to remain in the perfect snow globe world for just a little longer.

My omission became a monster, which fed on my denials, until it was so big that it barely fitted in its box any more. I didn't know how to deal with it, how to let the monster out of the box without hurting my friend.

Inevitably the monster freed itself and I hurt someone who means a lot to me, and I don't know how to fix it. I wish I could go back in time and blurt it all out to him, I wish I had been braver, I wish I hadn't hurt my friend.

If there is a message in this blog, I'm not sure what it is. Only the most corny, clichéd phrases spring to mind, but then perhaps the reason they've lasted so long is because there is truth in them; honesty is the best policy? You don't know what you've got till it's gone? Maybe it's just that I made a mistake and I really hope I get the chance to make it right.

Robert

The doorbell sounded while Robert and Spider were stacking the dishwasher after dinner. The Barlow family were getting ready for the annual viewing of *Elf*. Flory was going to watch it from her barracks, and Robert's dad had set up the laptop so that they could see Flory on Skype while she watched the movie with them on her iPad. Beany and Pod had come over with their partners and kids, and the sitting room resembled a departure lounge experiencing flight cancellations. Humans from nought to ninety were sat on sofas, armchairs, beanbags, dining chairs, garden chairs, cushions and each other. Robert's parents were buried beneath small children and his nan was sat in her rocking chair – children cross-legged at her slippered feet – smiling and nodding appreciatively at the chaos.

"Oi, Bertram!" Nemo's voice boomed through to the kitchen. "Door. Now!"

Robert left a disgruntled Spider to finish up the cleaning and headed to the front door. He had expected to see Sam, or Milly, but he had not expected to find a sobbing, slightly frozen Miranda on his doorstep. For a moment he just stood there looking at her in astonishment and then, as though someone had wound a key in his back, his brain began to work again.

"Hi! Hello! Are you OK? Come in. What's wrong? Do you need help? Are you hurt? Can I get you any of the emergency services?"

Despite her tears, Robert's awkwardness made her laugh through her sobs. "Thanks," she sniffed, stepping into the hallway.

OK, this is happening! Hopping holly berries! Nightmare before Christmas! thought Robert, closing the door behind her. *Actual nightmare.* With the whole Barlow clan waiting to start the movie, there was no way for him to slope off without being noticed. His family were a full-throttle experience for people who *did* know them; for people who didn't, it was like being hit by a human tidal wave. He couldn't subject Miranda to that. Especially not while she was upset.

Rescue came in the form of his eldest sister Pod, who walked into the hall and assessed the situation in less than three seconds. "Leave the rest, Spider," she called into the kitchen. And then beckoning to Robert and Miranda she said, "Make your friend a cup of tea and take it into the conservatory. I'll tell Ma and Pa to start the film without you."

"What about Nemo?" He knew Nemo would be champing at the bit to lob some brotherly embarrassment his way.

"I'll deal with Nemo." She winked. "Go on, off you pop!"

Robert led Miranda into the now empty kitchen. Every cupboard door bore a Christmas-themed picture drawn by one of the children, stuck on with sticky tape. In the centre of the huge, pine dining table, an advent candle was burning through number seventeen. The giant corkboard on the back wall was covered in a tapestry of half-opened advent calendars.

"This is nice and cosy," sniffed Miranda. Robert offered her a box of tissues. "Thanks," she said.

"Feeling better?" he asked.

"Yes," she said and immediately began to cry again.

"Cup of tea?"

"Yes, please."

"Is there anything I can do to make whatever this is better?" he asked.

Miranda smiled weakly at him. "You already are."

He wanted to hug Miranda, but felt weird about it. What was happening to him? If ever there was a girl who needed a friendly hug, it was Miranda, and yet here he was being all stumbling and bumbling. He patted her awkwardly on the shoulder and mentally smacked himself in the face with a frying pan.

Robert made tea, keeping up a steady stream of unconscious babble, while Miranda sniffed and the noise from the sitting room sounded like an indoor play centre. He carried their mugs out into the conservatory and closed the door. It was quiet in there, if a little cold, so Robert switched on the fake electric wood burner and they sat in wicker armchairs on either side of it.

"Do you want to talk about it?"

Miranda gave a shaking sigh and nodded. "I had a massive fall-out with Cassia. I'm out of the group."

"Oh, that's rough."

"She made me choose."

"Choose?" asked Robert.

"Between her and you."

Robert's heart began to beat quicker. "And you chose me?"

"Of course I did!"

"Me?"

"Yes!" Miranda was laughing now.

This was unprecedented. "And you're crying because you think you've made a mistake?" he asked.

She laughed again and then stopped suddenly. "No! Wait. Do *you* think I made a mistake?" she asked.

"No! God no. I mean that dynamic is seriously toxic. But if you aren't upset about being kicked out of the Cassia-cult then why are you upset?"

Miranda blew her nose. It was a good strong blow. "It was a pretty brutal break-up." She shuddered. "I'd given her my password once so she could use my phone when her battery ran out, and when we started to argue, she grabbed my phone and locked herself in the bathroom with it. She found my @secretgeek account and deleted it." Miranda's lip began to wobble. "All my pictures. All my followers. All the people I follow. Gone. I've spent the last two hours trying to get it back, but it's hopeless."

Robert's mind was running through the logistics of how he could deposit a few cooked prawns into Cassia's satchel without her noticing, when he remembered the iPad.

"Wait just a moment," he said, jumping up. "Actually, do you want a biscuit to go with your tea?"

"No, thanks."

"OK then, in that case, wait just a moment."

Robert left a confused Miranda while he grabbed the iPad, which was charging on the hall table. "Right," he said sitting back down and pulling up the Nan's Book file. "This isn't as weird as it seems. I told you my nan loves your paintings, right? So, for the last year I've been screen-shotting your pictures and putting them in a file for my nan, so she can look at them when I'm not around."

Miranda gasped as page after page of her pictures appeared before her.

"It's not all of them," said Robert. "And I'm afraid I can't help with the followers you've lost..."

Miranda's eyes filled again.

"Oh god," he said. "More crying. I was hoping to make you cry less."

Miranda laughed and threw her arms round him. "These are happy tears," she whispered, burying her head in his shoulder. "Thank you!"

Robert's mum chose that moment to come into the conservatory, with Widget resting on her hip. "Everything all right?" she asked, looking at Miranda's tear-stained face.

"Happy tears," said Robert.

"Smashing," said his mum. "Give me a hand with these, would you?" she asked, opening the door to the third fridge, which had to live in the conservatory, and motioning to six litre-cartons of chocolate milkshake. "Would you like to join us?" she asked Miranda. "We're having a Christmas movie night. With milkshake. You'd be very welcome."

Robert interjected. "Mum, I don't think Miranda is quite ready to meet all the Barlows at once."

"I'd love to," said Miranda, smiling broadly and taking three of the cartons out of the fridge. "Thank you."

Mum smiled. "It's lovely to meet you, Miranda. I was wondering when our Bertram was going to get around to bringing you home."

"Aaargh, Mum!" Robert groaned.

Widget held her chubby little arms out to Robert and he took her from his mum.

"Right! Come on," she said. "We've got three hundred milkshakes and two tons of gingerbread stars to dish out before there's a mutiny."

Miranda took the multiple greetings at sound-barrier-breaking levels of excitement in her stride, which only made Robert like her even more. She was introduced to Nan, who was delighted, if a little befuddled, and commented that

363

Miranda didn't look at all like a geek, secret or otherwise. Whatever hold Pod had over Nemo, it was effective enough to ensure he neither taunted Robert nor hit on Miranda, which was a win all round.

Milly

Milly was sitting at her desk, not doing her assignment. She was watching the snow flurry past the street lamps outside. It kept snowing and settling and melting and then snowing again. Why wouldn't it just make up its mind?

Her bedroom door was ajar, but her dad knocked anyway before he came in. "Homework?" he asked.

"Supposed to be."

"I'm sorry about your dress," he said.

"It's OK. I don't have anyone to go with anyway."

Her dad looked pained. "If he doesn't want to take you to the ball, then he's an idiot," he said.

"Thanks, Dad. I wish he was an idiot."

"Do you want to talk about it?"

"Not really."

"Do I need to go round there and have a word with this boy?"

"Jeez, Dad, no!" Milly laughed. Her dad was the least confrontational person she knew.

"I'm sorry I haven't been very present recently, love. I'm sorry for a lot of things, actually."

"You don't have to apologize." Milly turned and pretended to swish some invisible crumbs off her desk. "It's fine. You've got a lot of stuff on your mind. I get it."

She heard her dad sniff. "That's not a good enough reason, is it?" he said. "I think maybe I got lost for a while and couldn't find my way back."

"Do you feel better now?"

"I'm starting to. The counselling is helping. It's no good keeping it all locked up inside; it doesn't do you any good. I suppose I felt like I'd let you all down."

Milly turned around to face her dad. "But you didn't let us down! It's not your fault you lost your job, or that employers are too stupid to give you another one!"

Her dad smiled. "Well, thank you for your faith in me, perhaps I should take you to interviews with me." He leaned over and kissed the top of her head.

Milly breathed in the smell of her dad's jumper, a mixture of coffee, fabric softener and woody aftershave, and swallowed down the lump in her throat that threatened to become a sob.

"Speaking of interviews," said her dad. "I've got one on Saturday."

"Saturday?"

"Yes. I've already had a phone interview and an online meeting with them, and this is the final stage. I'm going up to their main office in London to meet them face to face. I don't want to jinx it, but I've got a good feeling about this one."

"That's brilliant, Dad! I'll keep all my fingers and toes crossed for you," said Milly.

"Thanks, love, all positive vibes gratefully received. What about you? Are you certain you don't want to go to the ball? Don't let an idiot boy stop you from doing something you want to do. You could go rebel and turn up in jeans. I'm sure Robert and Sam would be happy to see you there."

"I'm positive, Dad. Anyway, I've said I'd help out at the food bank; they're trying to make it a really special evening."

"I'm proud of you, you know. The way you've got involved."

"I didn't have much choice, Dad, it was my placement."

"Still. It's the perfect way to say thank you for all the help they've given us these last few months. I'd never given it too much thought before this; I suppose I thought it was the kind of thing that happened to *other* people. If we … *when* we get back on our feet, I'll never take for granted how lucky we are again."

"Me neither," said Milly.

Robert

Robert's sitting room was as quiet as it ever got – which is to say not very quiet at all. Nan sat in her rocker by the fire and Robert and Miranda sat cross-legged at her feet, watching with the rest of the Barlow family as Buddy the Elf tried to start Santa's sleigh in Central Park.

"Do you have a date for the Magical Snow Ball?" Miranda whispered.

"No," said Robert. His stomach fizzed with excitement. He didn't know if it was her close proximity or the warm tickle of her breath on his neck, but his internal organs seemed to have left their stations to start "Rockin' Around the Christmas Tree" inside his body.

"Would you like one?" Miranda asked. "A date, that is."

Robert had to push his body down into the carpet to stop himself whizzing off round the room like a Mentos in a Coke bottle. "It depends who's asking," he whispered, his attempts at being casual sabotaged by the grin on his face that would not quit.

"Oi!" hissed Curly. "Be quiet, will you? We're trying to watch the film."

"What's going on over there anyway?" asked Nemo, smirking.

"I believe that Paint Girl is asking Bertram to be her date to the Christmas ball," piped up Nan. "Is that right, dear?" She smiled down at Miranda.

Robert put his head in his hands. "Oh god, sorry about this, Miranda. Do you want to duck out?" he asked, feeling mortified on her behalf.

But to his delight, Miranda turned to the Barlow clan and said: "Yes, I was just asking Robert if he'd like to be my date to the ball." She swivelled on her knees back to face Robert. "Well?" she asked. "Will you be my date?"

Robert was smiling so hard he wasn't sure if his mouth would let him form words, but he managed a strangled, "Yes, please," at which his family exploded into whoops and cheers and popcorn confetti was thrown over them.

As the movie credits rolled and the light from the fire illuminated the faces of twenty-four of his closest family members, plus one on the laptop in an army barracks in Estonia, and Miranda smiling shyly by his side, Robert felt so contented, he thought he might actually purr.

Chapter 22

Friday 18th December

Sam

Sam came downstairs to find her mum making pancakes in her "Beware Sexy Mama Cookin'" apron.

"Good morning, bubsyboo! Big night tonight! Is Nadia calling for you? I want to get a pic of you two in your ball gowns! I've got corsages for you both."

Peak Mum, pretending nothing's happened, thought Sam. "Didn't Bill stay last night?" she asked, rubbing the sleep out of her eyes.

"No, babes. Pancake?"

Sam sat down heavily. She could go along with her mum and make both their lives easier or she could dig in and try to find some resolution. Sam opted for the latter. "Why don't you want to move in with Bill?"

"Why do you want to start a fight with me as soon as you wake up?"

"I asked you first."

"It's complicated."

"Do you love him?"

"Yes. But sometimes love isn't enough," said her mum, still busy at the stove.

"Why not?"

"Because you can love someone, and they can be wrong for you."

"Are you talking about my dad?"

"I suppose I am."

"But Bill is nothing like my dad." Sam didn't actually know this; she didn't know anything about her dad, other than that he didn't deserve the title.

"No, sweetheart, he isn't. But when you've been hurt by someone before it makes you more cautious. You build walls around you to protect yourself, so that you don't get hurt again. Does that make sense?"

It made perfect sense. It was exactly what Sam had done with Nadia. But she'd taken the walls down and let Nadia back in. Why couldn't her mum do the same for Bill?

"The thing is, Mum, your walls are keeping the wrong person out. If you love Bill, breaking up with him isn't going to protect you from heartbreak, it's just going to give you more. What's the point of walling yourself in and being lonely?"

"I won't be lonely, will I?" Mum said, plopping four steaming pancakes in front of Sam and pushing the maple syrup towards her. "I've got my baby. The Terrific Two for ever!"

"Oh my god, Mum!" The frustration that had been bubbling beneath the surface for weeks finally burst through. Sam stood up suddenly, causing the cutlery on the table to clink. "You can't wall me up with you, like some kind of Rapunzel!"

"I'm not!" Her mum was clearly taken aback. "I'm just saying I don't need anyone else."

"Mum! It's not fair, you can't put that on me! I feel stuck! I feel stuck in this town with you and I'm worried I'll never get out because we're the *Terrific Two!*"

Her mum took the pan off the heat and sat at the table. "Now wait just a moment here, babes. I think me and you have been talking at cross purposes. I don't need you to look after me. I'm the look-er after-er around here."

"You say that, but it doesn't feel like it! You keep going on about me staying here. I feel like I can't breathe!"

"I'm only teasing! Well, half teasing; obviously I'll miss my baby, but I'd never stop you following your dreams."

"But you are, Mum! How can I follow my dreams if I'm full of guilt about leaving you?"

"Where's all this coming from?" asked her mum. "I thought we were talking about Bill."

"We were. We are. It's all mixed up together. You lean on me, Mum, and I can't handle it any more. It's too much. And I have to sit here watching you mess things up with Bill when I know you really bloody love him. It's infuriating! If I can't fix you, I can't leave you!"

Her mum was quiet for a moment, as she smoothed out the tablecloth. "You don't need to *fix* me, Samantha," she said quietly. "I had no idea you were feeling like this."

"Well, I am!" said Sam, her instinct was to backtrack and try and leave without making a scene, but she was in too deep now to turn back.

"You should have told me," said her mum. "We don't keep secrets, not us two."

"But we do, Mum! We do keep secrets, great big secrets that we pretend aren't there. You pretend you don't love Bill and I pretend I don't want to go to Nottingham Uni. I feel guilty every time I look at the prospectus. And what about your heart condition, huh? That's a pretty massive secret. Does Bill even know?"

"What heart condition?"

"Come on, Mum, I know about it, so you might as well just get it out in the open."

"What heart condition?" her mum asked again.

"The one you have to take beta blockers for," said Sam.

"Beta ... Sam!" her mum exclaimed. "I haven't got a heart condition! Those are to control my migraines."

"But I looked them up..."

"They *can* be used for people with heart problems, but they are also very effective in the treatment of migraines. You silly arse!" Her mum laughed, leaning over and kissing her cheek. "There's nothing wrong with my heart! Aside from my reluctance to give it to Bill apparently," she added wryly.

Sam was stunned. Now she thought about it, her mum hadn't had a migraine for a couple of months; usually she would be knocked out by them a couple of times a week. She felt giddy with relief. Her mum didn't have a heart condition. *Hallelujah and Merry Christmas!*

"So, now you know I'm not hiding a major illness, let's talk about uni. I realize that sometimes, in the past, I've relied on you more like a friend than a daughter, and that's my bad. I shouldn't have done that."

"I like being your friend," said Sam.

"And I love being yours," said Mum. "But ultimately, I'm the parent and you shouldn't have to deal with my BS, especially where men are concerned. You don't ever have to feel responsible for me."

"But what about the Terrific Two?"

"Babes, we will always be the Terrific Two! No matter where you are in the world. That's what video calling's for. If you want to go to Nottingham Uni, then Nottingham it is. You don't need to worry about me, that's not how this parenting malarkey works."

"What about Bill?"

"We both know I've got hang-ups where men are concerned, but you need to let me worry about Bill. I've got a few things to get my head around and Bill knows that. God help him, he knows what he'd be getting into with me and he's still keen!"

"I was worried he might be breaking up with you,"

"He's giving me space, babes, because he's a good man. But that's not the point. It doesn't matter whether we split up or we move in together, you don't need to worry about me. I will be fine because I'll know my baby is out there kicking the world's arse and I gave her the power to do it."

"You are the best world-arse-kicking trainer," said Sam, trying to avoid her mum's lipstick kisses.

"You'd better believe it! Now eat your pancakes and get out there and get educated; it's going to take more than just that pretty face to get you into Nottingham University!"

Sam left for school feeling positive for the first time in a long while about her future. The clouds had lifted and finally Nottingham didn't seem like some unattainable dream.

Milly

Registration that morning was a strange mix of excitement and awkwardness. It was unrealistic for Milly to skip another registration – she would have to be in the same room as Laurence at some point, but she needn't have worried about there being a scene. Laurence sat at the opposite end of the room and didn't make eye contact; at least not when she was looking at him, which she tried to avoid doing. She wondered if he'd read her email.

To her surprise and relief, Cassia also ignored her; she was too busy regaling her remaining mean-minions and anyone else who would listen about how Harvey was going to see if he could get a film crew in to film the ball.

Milly was pinning all her hopes on being able to explain things better to Laurence when they were at the food bank together that afternoon, away from catty comments and prying eyes. She'd been building herself up for it ever since her talk with her dad last night. She didn't expect things to suddenly go back to the way they were, and she certainly didn't expect to have her invite as his date to the ball reinstated, but she hoped they could at least find some common ground from which they could start again.

Nadia and Miranda had joined Milly, Robert and Sam in "loser corner" and seemed delighted to be there. Miranda hung on Robert's every word, while Nadia argued against Sam's every word, which seemed to make Sam supremely happy.

"Someone really needs to teach Cassia a lesson," said Sam.

"Karma will catch up with her in the end," said Nadia.

"Don't be so sure," said Milly. "The normal rules of the universe don't seem to apply to the likes of Cassia. Somehow she always comes up smelling of Chanel Number Five."

Laurence pushed his chair out from the table – ignoring how Cassia's voice became even louder when he passed her – and came to stand beside the desk where Milly was sitting. Milly froze. All her anxiety-fuelled bodily functions conspired to try and let rip at the same time; she tried to focus on not turning inside out.

"Hi, Milly." He looked nervous.

"Hi." Milly's voice came out like a squeak. *Apologize again,* she thought. *Say you're sorry and keep saying it until he believes you.* She pulled her courage into a ball in her stomach. "Laurence, I..."

"I got your email. Thank you for sending it. You're an amazing writer, by the way. Anyway, I wanted to let you know that we're good." He smiled but Milly could tell he was distracted. Were they good? She couldn't read his face. "I won't be able to make it to the food bank this afternoon. Something's come up." He continued. Laurence was rubbing the back of his neck and looking around furtively like he didn't want anyone to overhear what he was saying. "I rang Magda this morning and explained that I couldn't make it. I'll pick up the last of the donations and drop them off there at lunchtime. So, anyway, I just thought I'd let you know that you don't need to worry, I know that you worry about stuff. It isn't because of you that I won't be there. It's ... other stuff. Honestly, please don't worry."

"OK," said Milly, unconvinced.

Laurence was hovering; he looked uncomfortable. *Here it comes,* Milly thought. *I'm about to get dumped.*

"About the ball..."

"I've said I'll help out at the food bank," Milly said too quickly. She'd had enough humiliation for one week, so she decided to get in first and save him the trouble. "I don't have a dress or anything, and it sounds like it'll be a really busy night for them."

"Oh," Laurence looked crestfallen.

Wait. Had she read the situation wrong? Too late now. He probably wanted to be the one to get in first and Milly had pipped him to the post. "Right," Laurence went on. "Well, good. I'm sure they'll appreciate the help. I've got to go. I'll see you soon, yeah?"

He walked back across the room, grabbed his coat and bag and left the room, leaving Milly confused. Had she just sabotaged things with Laurence again?

Milly

The food bank was busy. Sarah had rigged up the speakers and Christmas tunes were belting out into the centre. The donations which Laurence had dropped off had been bagged up ready for collection. In the last few days, the amount of food being donated by the local community had almost doubled, and the storeroom was looking fit to burst.

"I can't believe how much extra stuff has been brought in!" Milly had said when she arrived.

"Amazing, isn't it?," agreed Magda. "But sad too when

you think about how many people need the help." She smiled and rubbed Milly's arm. "But I don't need to tell you that, do I, love?"

Milly didn't say anything.

Magda wrapped her arms round Milly and squeezed. "Things will work out," she said. "If this place teaches us anything, it's that kindness is alive and kicking, and where kindness thrives, hope is never far behind."

People were starting to arrive. It felt surprisingly festive with the lights turned down low and the illuminated Christmas tree twinkling in the corner. Father Christmas – aka Sarah's husband – was sitting on an armchair that they had hastily covered with a red and green Sherpa blanket. He had a pile of presents around him and more around the tree, each one had a name tag and Milly had the list of children's names ready to cross off as they collected their gift.

A table was laid out with green cups and saucers and plates of biscuits, and behind it, Magda babysat a giant, stainless-steel hot-water urn for making teas and coffees. Geoff and Tricia, regular volunteers at the food bank, were handing out the bags of shopping and the Christmas extras.

A family came in with four excitable children and Milly took their names and helped Father Christmas locate their gifts. The children were delighted; even the ten-year-old who had come in looking grimly sceptical was now grinning and bopping along to "Merry Christmas Everyone". The jolly atmosphere was infectious.

Sam and Nadia had sent her a selfie of them in their ball gowns in Sam's front room. Milly had sent one back of her in her baggy jumper and ripped jeans next to the Christmas tree.

Sam: It's not too late to join us!

Milly: It's really busy here, they need the help. But thanks. Have a great time!

Sam: I'll save you a slow dance in case you change your mind 😊

Milly: 😊💙

Robert had offered her a backstage pass.

Robert: If I was you, I'd take me up on the offer, cos we'll probably be signed to a record label after tonight and then, you know, I'll be too cool to hang with you any more...

Milly: 😂😂😂 I'll bear it in mind. Break a leg, or whatever they say when you go on stage. You'll be amazing! You always are. Are you excited?

Robert: Ahh maaaaaan I can't wait to get up there, I love it! It's such a rush.

Milly: Rather you than me! Have fun. Sorry I can't be your groupie tonight.

Robert: Thanks! Don't worry, Miranda is taking over groupie duties in your absence.

Milly: How are things with her and Cassia?

Robert: 😱😫🙈

Milly: That bad huh.

Robert: Sam and Nadia are going to hang with her while I'm on stage, she'll be OK. How about you?

Milly: I'll be fine. Father Christmas is here, and Geoff and Tricia keep feeding me Christmas truffles, so I'm filling up on Christmas spirit.

Robert: Heard anything from Laurence?

Milly: Nope. Guess I really blew it.

Robert

Robert's band had set up at lunchtime before afternoon lessons and in Robert's case, placement. When they arrived back at half past six to do a final run-through before the ball began, they found their equipment carefully pushed to one side and another band warming up. Harvey was at the front of the stage, swaggering, or rather staggering as he screeched out a Nirvana medley into the microphone, a half-empty bottle of Jack Daniels at his feet. He threw his head forward with such force on the final chorus that his bandana flew off.

Robert texted Miranda to see if she knew what was going on.

Robert: Is Harvey's band playing the ball tonight?

Miranda: Not that I know of, why?

Robert: He's rehearsing as we speak. All our gear has been shifted.

Miranda: Oh my god! No, I had no idea. Cassia still hasn't spoken to me. I thought it was just the Indigo Tigers and the Glee Club for live stuff.

Robert: Yeah, me too.

Miranda: She wouldn't just scrap your set. Even Cassia has her limits.

Robert: Wouldn't she?

Miranda: She's blocked me on all her social media accounts so I can't snoop to find out either. I'm so sorry! This is royally crap.

Robert: It's not your fault. I'll see if I can find her.

Miranda: Do you think she's done it because of you and me?

Robert: Who knows what goes on in Cassia's head.

Miranda: I could try asking Trinity?

Robert: Don't worry about it. At least now I get to spend more time with my gorgeous date 😊

Robert didn't much feel like a smiley emoji at that moment, but it wasn't Miranda's fault. Anger wasn't an emotion Robert often felt. In a family as big as his, you had to learn to sort out differences or let them lie pretty quick. But he felt angry now, not just for him but for the rest of the band. They'd practised really hard, after all, and festive favourites weren't part of their usual repertoire; when else were they likely to have the need to sing ten Christmas hits?

It took him a while to find Cassia. In the end, he located her by following the sound of sobbing coming from behind the stage. Cassia had her back to him, her shoulders hunched over and shaking, her beautiful ball gown spilling down to the ground in layers of silk.

"I just wanted you to be there. I wanted you to help me

384

get ready and see me on my special night like all the other mums," Cassia sobbed into her mobile. "That's not the point, Mum! I didn't need a hair and make-up team, I just needed you! I'm not being ungrateful ... couldn't you have gone tomorrow instead?" Her voice suddenly went quieter. "No ... no, of course I don't want to ruin your night... Yep, I'll send you photos."

The call ended. Robert found the heat had gone right out of his anger. "Cassia," he said quietly.

She spun round, her silk dress whispering as she moved. Mascara stained her cheeks in two long dark lines, all the way to her jaw. "What do you want, loser!" she spat.

Robert walked slowly forwards. Cassia looked wild like a cornered animal. "Hey, Cass," he said softly, still walking towards her, even though she looked like she might pounce at any moment. He was standing right in front of her now. "Need a friend?"

Cassia dissolved into tears. Robert pulled her into a hug, and she let him. She put her arms round him and held on tightly as she sobbed into his shoulder. After a few minutes, the sobs receded to little involuntary shudders. Robert led her over to a set of wooden stairs which led up to the stage wings and they sat down.

"I just wanted her to put me first, just once," Cassia

managed to hiccup.

"Where is she?"

"Paris, she left this morning. Someone invited her over to a party, and she *simply couldn't say no!* The thing is, she can never say no to anything or anyone, except me."

"That sucks," said Robert.

"Yeah." Cassia sniffed and wiped her nose on her arm. "Do you know what she did for my seventeenth birthday?"

"You had a big party, didn't you? I seem to remember being very much not invited."

Cassia choked out a laugh and rested her head against Robert's shoulder. "She hired a party planner and caterers, and she left the morning of my birthday to catch a flight out to Morocco for a house party. She was gone before I even woke up. I opened my presents with the housekeeper. I don't know why she didn't just send me away to boarding school and forget about me."

"She tried that, remember? You flunked the entry test. Personally, I think you did it on purpose, so you could stay near me."

Cassia gave a snotty laugh-cry. "Yeah, that's the reason."

"Do you know what I did for my seventeenth birthday?" Robert asked.

"What?"

"Went out for pizza with my whole family. It was like a scene from World War Z with stringy cheese."

Cassia laughed. And then they were quiet for a time while they waited for her tears to subside.

"I cut your set short," said Cassia at last. There was no malice in her voice.

"I noticed."

"Harvey threw a strop; he said if he couldn't play, he'd go back to London. I couldn't face being dateless at the ball I'd spent so long organizing. You can still do half your set."

"Well that's something, I suppose."

"Sorry. It was a crappy thing to do."

"Don't worry about it. You know he's drunk, right?"

Cassia was sniffing, still hiccupping little sobs. "I know. He's an idiot. Thinks he's a cross between Harry Styles and Stormzy. I told him he could only do half a set. He wants the Indigo Tigers to go on first so he can headline."

"He wants to be the headline act at a school ball?"

"He's got a big ego."

Robert handed Cassia the bandana he'd caught from Harvey's earlier head-flinging. "Do you want to clean up a bit before you go back in and be belle of the ball?"

"I don't feel very belle," she sniffled.

"Well, you should. You organized it. No one else would

have done it as well as you. And for what it's worth, your mum's missing out."

Cassia smiled. Robert hadn't seen that smile in a long time, and for a moment she was the kid who used to sit and do colouring-in with him while they waited for their music lesson to start. "Thank you," she said. "I don't deserve it, but thanks. What is this, anyway?" she asked, wiping the mascara off her face. "It smells kind of funky."

"It's Harvey's bandana."

"He loves a bandana," she said and blew her nose on it.

Sam

Sam's mum had repeatedly tried to feed Nadia ever since she'd arrived.

"Honestly, Ms Chowdhury, thank you but I couldn't eat another thing. My mum already stuffed me full of food before I left."

"How about a couple of samosas then? Hmm? Or a little bhaji?"

"I don't think you're going to win this one, Nish," said Bill, laughing. "It looks like Nadia's mum got there first."

Sam's mum seemed unable to compute this information

and stood with her hands on her hips in her "I'm So Sexy It Hurts" apron, shaking her head.

Sam's dress was unapologetically feminine. A deep maroon, strapless, down-to-the-floor chiffon affair with a ruched sweetheart neckline. She was incredibly pleased with how her cleavage looked in it. Nadia's dress was an empire line, full-length satin gown, in electric blue. She was the most beautiful thing Sam had ever seen; she could hardly bear to take her eyes off her.

"Come on then, you two," said Bill. "Let's get some photos for the family album."

"Oh!" screeched her mum. "Yes, yes! Photos, lots of photos, wait, I'll get my phone." She disappeared and reappeared a moment later, minus the apron, waving her phone about.

What followed was tantamount to a *Vogue* fashion shoot. Sam and Nadia were placed in various poses around the small front room; in front of the sexy tree, by the wall, next to the door, on the sofa, on the armchair, some standing, some sitting, some with one of them standing and the other sitting. Then came the facial expressions: laughing, smiling, goofy, serious, faraway... "You know what I mean," said her mum. "Look wistfully into the distance like they do in the catalogues." Bill took shots of Sam and Nadia with her mum and some with just her mum, and then they swapped, so that Bill could have one with Sam too.

Sam was glad that Bill had come over. Things still didn't feel quite right between him and her mum, but it meant a lot to Sam that he wanted to be there on her big night. Not for the first time, Sam wondered if she could keep Bill as a stepdad even if he and her mum split up.

Laurence

The hall was transformed. Low lights lit up the snowy mountain backdrops and disco balls sparkled and picked up the many tons of silver glitter strewn across them. Paper snowflakes hung from invisible threads, and miles of paper chains looped in zigzags from the ceiling. Everyone was in their finery; it was tuxedos and ball gowns as far as the eye could see. On the stage, the Indigo Tigers were belting out Christmas hits and making them sound rockier and cooler than the original artists could have ever imagined. But neither the glitter nor the Christmas songs could lift Laurence's spirits.

He almost hadn't come. He'd considered ditching the ball and going to the food bank, but things were weird with him and Milly and he didn't know how to fix it. He'd lost count of how many times he'd picked up his phone to message her and then bottled it at the last minute. Instead, he had clung to a distant hope that she might change her mind and come to the ball after all. He should have tried harder this morning. Laurence spent the day going over and over ways in which he could have handled things better; ways which would have ended up with him here with Milly by his side, instead of alone and missing her intensely.

Laurence scanned the hall. No sign of Milly. His heart sank. At the front, near the stage, Sam, Nadia and Miranda were going full groupie, rocking out to the band in a whirl of satin and hair glitter – Robert beamed on stage and played to his audience. To the side of the stage, half-cut, wearing ripped jeans and a holey T-shirt, and clutching a bottle of Jack Daniels by the neck, Harvey swayed, jeering and heckling the band.

Cassia came over to stand beside him. "I didn't think you'd come," she said.

"Neither did I," said Laurence. "I was hoping Milly might have changed her mind."

Cassia didn't say anything.

"That was a really crappy thing you did to Milly at the party," Laurence went on.

"I know. If it's any consolation I feel awful about it."

"It isn't. And you should."

"Thanks."

"Your new boyfriend is behaving like a giant reindeer's arse," Laurence noted. He seemed to have picked up the festive swears bug.

"Yes," said Cassia. "I have a strong feeling that the evening is going to go downhill pretty fast once the Indigo Tigers have left the stage."

"You kind of had that coming," said Laurence.

Cassia was quiet again.

The Indigo Tigers began belting out "Santa Baby", and the crowd went wild. Harvey appeared to be having an argument with himself, kicking out and swearing at invisible perpetrators.

"You know my mum hired me six stretch limos for tonight, to take everyone back to mine for the after-party," said Cassia. "They're just sitting outside. Empty."

Laurence looked at Cassia and she looked back, nodding infinitesimally at his unasked question. Then he headed over to where Nadia, Sam and Miranda were moshing. The last song in the band's recently curtailed set ended to ecstatic cheers and whoops.

Robert leaned over to the lead singer's mic and drawled, "Ah, thank you very much," in his best Elvis voice.

Harvey's band flooded the stage before the Indigo Tigers

had even finished unplugging their amps. Harvey took the mic and began to shout in a slurring growl: "Now that bullshite is over with, you're gonna hear some real music!" He hurled the bottle he'd been clutching at the wall, where it smashed against a painted mountaintop and shattered.

Milly

It had just gone nine o'clock but the queue for food parcels still snaked around the room and out through the double doors into the car park. Milly could hardly believe how many people needed help this Christmas. The food bank was too small to cope with demand really, but the cramped quarters and long queue didn't dampen anyone's spirits.

The local chippie, Chinese restaurant and pizza parlour had all sent over trays of food as donations. Geoff hastily erected two more trestle tables and Magda and Tricia laid out the impromptu buffet to be distributed amongst the people waiting in line.

Milly purposefully hadn't checked her phone; she couldn't face the Insta posts of a ball she wasn't at. But the last half an hour had been so busy she wouldn't have had the time anyway.

It was when she handed over a slice of Napolitano pizza

to a woman with a fuzzy pink bobble hat, that she first heard it: the sound of guitars and people singing "Santa Claus Is Coming to Town" outside. A frisson of excitement ran through the queue. Sarah turned down the volume on the music inside and the sounds became clearer.

Milly listened. It sounded like... She squeezed out past the crowd and into the night.

On the patch of lawn outside the food bank stood the Glee Club and the lead singer of the Indigo Tigers – puffer jackets and winter coats pulled over ball gowns and tuxedos – belting out Christmas hits at the top of their lungs. And to the side of them, Robert and Ali on their guitars and Simon's hastily put together snare, bass and high-hat drum kit. Robert smiled when he saw Milly and gave her a wink.

For a moment all Milly could do was stare. And then a laugh of absolute joy burst out of her. The people in the queue were singing along and clapping in time. Suddenly it didn't feel cold any more.

"Boo!" said a voice in her ear.

Milly jumped and turned to see Sam grinning at her, Nadia and Miranda close behind, smiling like a pair of Christmas elves.

"I can't believe it!" she stammered. "What about the ball?

How did you...?"

"If our best girl can't make it to the ball, then the ball has to come to our best girl," said Sam.

"But ... but ... how?"

"We had help from a most unexpected quarter," said Sam. "And your boyfriend made the rest happen." She pointed over towards a row of stretch limos in the car park. More cars Milly recognized from the sixth form car park began to pull in beside them and her very glamorous sixth form peers began to climb out of the vehicles and make their way towards the food bank, holding bags of shopping which seemed incongruous beside their ball gowns and tuxedos.

As she looked, the crowd ahead of her seemed to part to reveal Laurence, looking absolutely smoking-hot in a black tuxedo.

The air whooshed out of Milly's lungs as though she'd been squeezed like a bottle of ketchup. *Is this happening? Is this actually happening??* Laurence began to walk towards her, and Milly felt her legs turn to jelly. She concentrated on breathing and trying not to faint. How could anyone stay upright with this much hotness coming in their direction?

"Hi," said Laurence when he reached her.

"*Hiccup!*" was all that came out of Milly's mouth.

Laurence laughed. "Are these horror-hiccups or

excitement hiccups?"

"*Hiccup!* These are new. *Hic!* These are surprise hiccups. *Hic!*"

"Good surprise or bad surprise?"

"Good. *Hic!* I think. *Hic!* I hope."

Laurence smiled at her.

"What about the ball?" she managed to say.

"The ball had to be abandoned."

"Really?"

"We received news that the hottest party in town was happening at the food bank."

Milly threw her head back and laughed. Three more cars pulled into the car park and more overdressed sixth formers, including Tom and Ethan, joined the throng.

"I've got something for you," Laurence said, and from his jacket pocket he pulled out a corsage of two cream rosebuds surrounded by red berries and dark green leaves.

Milly gasped. She couldn't help it. "It's beautiful," she whispered as Laurence reached forward and attached the corsage to her old chunky-knit jumper. "Thank you," she added, looking first down at it and then up at Laurence. "I guess it's not really meant to go with a baggy sweater."

"I think it looks perfect," said Laurence.

"I'm sorry I didn't tell you about the food bank."

"It doesn't matter. I understand. I'm sorry too. I handled things really badly. It was much more about me being an emotional idiot than it was about you; you just caught the brunt of it. I read your blog. Blogs," he corrected himself. "When I'd read your latest one, I went back and read your entire back catalogue. I know I said it before but you are an amazing writer, Milly. I don't think you have any idea how special you are."

"Where did you go this afternoon?" Milly asked, looking up at Laurence.

"Are you changing the subject because you can't take compliments?"

"A little bit," Milly confessed, laughing.

"We managed to get a last-minute family slot to visit Jamie. My dad put us on a list in case there was a cancellation, and one came up for this afternoon."

"That's great!"

"I'm sorry I so was weird with you this morning. I was having a bit of a meltdown about everything. This was the first time my dad had come with us to visit my brother and I was freaking out about he would handle it. I didn't want Jamie to end up feeling worse than he already does."

"How was Jamie?"

Laurence shrugged. "He was OK. I mean, you know, as OK as you can be spending Christmas in prison, but I think it meant a lot to him to have Dad there too. I'm glad I got to see him."

"And how did your dad handle it?"

"Better than I expected. I'm glad he came."

"And you can phone him? Your brother I mean, at Christmas?"

"Yeah, we've saved up our video call allowance too, so we can chat to him on Christmas Day. I'd been dreading Christmas, but now I think maybe it won't be so bad."

"Same."

"You could have trusted me you know."

"I know," said Milly.

Laurence put his arms round Milly and pulled her in close to him.

"How about we make each other a Christmas promise," said Laurence.

"And what would that be?"

"No more secrets," said Laurence.

"It's a deal," Milly agreed. "No more secrets."

And with that, Laurence Bashir, hottest boy in Miller's Field High and possibly the world, bent down and kissed Milly Parker softly on the lips. She couldn't be sure, but she thought her feet might have left the ground.

Sam

The night was a bigger success than anyone could have imagined. The glamorous ball-goers lent a sense of occasion to what was already a party atmosphere. The best-dressed volunteers the food bank had ever seen stationed themselves behind the counters and handed out Christmas supplies, while others dished out hot food and drinks. In no time at all everyone had been served, and the steam from many mugs of hot tea rolled up into the cold dark sky to meet the snowflakes on their way down.

Robert's band got to play the full set they'd practised for the ball and were encouraged by the lively crowd to play encore upon encore. Miranda, looking exquisite in a teal taffeta gown, bounced at the front of the audience on the lawn and could be heard to whoop the loudest at the close of every song.

"Someone's going to sleep well tonight," Sam laughed as Miranda screamed in delight, fists punching the air as the group played the opening chords to "Nine in the Afternoon" by Panic! at the Disco.

"She'll have no voice by tomorrow," said Nadia.

"I think this is much better than the actual ball," Sam said, laying her head on Nadia's shoulder.

"I think anywhere is better when I'm with you," said Nadia.

Sam looked up at her. "Did you actually just say that?"

"Yep."

Sam smiled. "I feel the same."

"What, you're not going to rib me for being hopelessly romantic?" Nadia asked, smiling back at her.

"No," said Sam. "I'm going to kiss you for being hopelessly romantic. And for not giving up on me."

"Any time." Nadia smiled.

Sam let herself be folded into Nadia's arms and kissed her. Nadia's lips were soft and slightly sweet with raspberry lip gloss. Sam let herself melt into her embrace, the feelings of hurt and anger of the past months flaked away and fluttered up into the night sky, passing fat white snowflakes floating lazily down to the world below.

Milly

Milly was helping Geoff tidy up in the storeroom; the sudden influx of donations, helpers and people in need had meant the food store currently resembled a looted supermarket. His wife Tricia was half buried beneath a pile of stock sheets as she heroically tried to make the numbers tally.

Milly heard the door open but continued with her task

until she heard a cautious little "ahem" from behind her. She turned to see Cassia standing there. Instinctively, Milly looked at the ground.

Cassia took everything in and then let her eyes fall on Milly. "I'm sorry," she said.

Milly's eyes flicked up to Cassia's and then looked away. She wasn't going to give Cassia ammunition by falling over her words if she tried to speak.

"What I did to you, at Laurence's house, that was unforgivable and I'm sorry. I don't know why I did it. It feels like I hate everyone a lot of the time for no good reason." She let out a nervous laugh. "I was jealous, I suppose."

"Jealous of me?" The words shot out of Milly's mouth.

"Laurence never looked at me the way he looks at you," she replied simply. "I wanted someone to look at me like that."

"Maybe Harvey..." Milly trailed off.

"Don't bother. I mean, thanks for trying to make me feel better, even though I've been a class-A cow-bag, but I think we both know the only love affair Harvey is having is with Harvey."

"Sam said he trashed your Magical Snow Ball," said Milly. "You didn't deserve that. You worked really hard to make it nice for everyone."

Cassia waved an arm dismissively. "Well, half the attendees

had already defected to the food bank by then anyway, and the rest followed when the police arrived." Cassia was studying her nails. "I'd say a night in the cells might knock some sense into him, but I think it'll feed perfectly into his bad boy of rock image, and I'm sure it'll play well in the papers. Anyway, I just wanted to say, I'm sorry. Laurence really likes you."

She turned and left the room before Milly had time to construct an answer.

Families left the food bank that evening with smiling faces and bulging bags; tonight wouldn't suddenly solve all their problems, but right at that moment everyone was feeling tinged with the Christmas spirit. The snow was coming hard and fast now, blanketing everything in white. Outside the food bank, fifty or more cold-cheeked revellers stood with their faces upturned, catching snowflakes on their tongues. Robert stood behind Miranda, his arms round her waist, his chin resting on her shoulder. Sam and Nadia had joined the impromptu choir on the white lawn and were singing "O Holy Night" while holding hands.

Milly was tucked in close to Laurence's side, his arms protecting her from the cold.

"Are you happy?" he asked.

"Very," she replied.

Chapter 23

Saturday 19th December

Milly

They couldn't get started until Milly's dad had left for his interview in London and they'd all been waiting impatiently for Milly to give them the OK. Finally the message they'd been waiting for came through.

> Milly: The target has left the building. Operation K.O.C. is go!

> Robert: Finally! Roger that.

Sam: Over and out!

Laurence: Message received.

Milly's dad wouldn't be back until six o'clock at the earliest, but it took them until two just to locate all the decorations and the tools they needed, and wrestle them from the back of the garage, on to the lawn. Then they had to sort everything out. The fairy lights, which would cover the fascias, had been wound into a ball the size of a space hopper, and between the light-up Father Christmases, reindeers and snowmen, there were enough wires to give even the most seasoned electrician cause for head-scratching.

Tara was set to work giving all the life-size figurines a good wipe down, and even Jasper ventured out of his musty pit to lend a hand buffing the sleigh. Dad had apparently been shopping in the January sales back before he lost his job and there were several new additions to the extravaganza still taped in their boxes. One of these was a set of hanging decorations – two strings of baubles the size of basketballs – which Mum suggested would look great either side of the front door, next to the light-up garland which Sam and Nadia were busily attaching to the door frame.

Miranda helped Robert to untangle the snarl of lights,

and then fed them slowly up to him as he balanced on a ladder, stapling them to the fascias. Milly and Laurence arranged the light-up figures around the front garden and laid lanterns with LED candles along the length of the drive. Mum rushed here and there supervising and fretting – especially when Robert was at the top of the ladder – and kept up a constant stream of hot chocolates and warm cookies. The grass was still white and crunchy with the remnants of last night's snowfall, but more was forecast for later.

At four-thirty Sam's mum and Bill pulled up and began to ferry covered silver foil serving platters into the open garage, which they laid out on Dad's wallpaper pasting table. The platters were filled with a bounty of hot finger foods; everything from Nish's famous pakoras, to chicken nuggets and potato smiley faces were present, and the workers fell upon them hungrily.

Milly's mum set up the projector, which would cast images of stars all over the walls of the house. Bill checked over the electrics and took charge of making sure everything could be plugged in and lit up safely without causing a town blackout. He emerged from the garage, giving a thumbs up, and Sam's mum handed him a steaming mug of tea.

It was dark already and the tops of the cars were thickly painted with ice, which glittered in the street lights. Bill and Sam's mum came over to where Milly and Sam were trying to stop Donna and Blitzen from toppling forwards and headbutting Dasher and Vixen's backsides. It was proving tricky.

"We've got something we want to run by you," said Sam's mum.

Sam stood up and Blitzen face planted Vixen's fibreglass bottom with a clunk.

"What's up?" asked Sam.

Bill and her mum exchanged glances. "It's like this, babes," her mum began. "Bill's asked me to marry him, and I've said yes. It won't be anything fancy, just two or three hundred of our closest family and friends."

Sam stood with her mouth open, looking from one to the other. Milly gently popped her hand beneath her chin and closed her mouth for her, but it dropped back open immediately.

"We've set a date for this time next year," said Bill. "And that gives us plenty of time to plan the wedding and buy a house."

Sam's mouth was working now, opening and closing but no words were coming out.

"Well?" said her mum. "Cat got your tongue?"

"Are you serious?" Sam stuttered.

"I never joke about matrimony," said her mum.

Sam smiled then. "This is the best news ever! I can't believe it."

"Believe it, babes! And believe this too: I may be getting a ring put on my finger, and I may be buying a house with my new fiancé, but rest assured I am now and will always be a VERY independent woman!"

Sam and Milly laughed as Bill swooped down and kissed Sam's mum on the lips. "I wouldn't want you any other way." He grinned.

"Ewww, get a room, you two!" laughed Sam.

"Oh, we intend to," said her mum. "Several. And a walk-in wardrobe too!"

Bill shook his head. "What have I got myself into," he chuckled.

Sam threw her arms round them. "I'm so happy for you both," she said. "This is the most awesome news!" and she rushed across the garden to where Nadia was helping Miranda to secure a blow-up snowman to the ground.

Milly's mum came out into the garden, laden with yet another tray of hot drinks. "I just had a text from the King of Christmas," she said. "He'll be home around half six. Bertram, I've called your mum, she's rallying the troops!"

Robert went to stock up on Ms Chowdhury's buffet before

his family arrived, leaving Laurence to continue trying to sort out the reindeers with Milly.

"Thanks for coming today," said Milly.

"I wouldn't have missed it." Laurence smiled.

"There were probably more glamorous things you could have been doing."

"I think coming to my house has given you the wrong impression of how my family live," he said. "It's not all fancy soirées and caviar, you know."

"How disappointing."

"Are you having second thoughts about us now?"

"Well, I was expecting afternoon jacuzzi parties with butler service at the very least," said Milly.

"I could probably rustle up a paddling pool and a cup of tea?"

Milly sighed exaggeratedly. "I suppose it'll have to do," she said.

"Do you think your dad will be pleased with all this?" asked Laurence, gesticulating to the winter wonderland that had sprung up in the front garden.

"I think he'll love it. I guess he's been the King of Christmas for so long, we took it for granted. I just kind of sat back and waited for Christmas to materialize around me. I never really thought about *how* it happened."

"I suppose even bona fide adults need a bit of a mojo reboot occasionally."

"Exactly. This year we're bringing Christmas to the King of Christmas."

"Do you think your dad will get the job?"

Milly shrugged and bit her lip. "I don't know. I hope so."

Two minivans pulled into the close and parked across the drive, one had an enormous Christmas tree strapped to the roof.

"I told you we'd make sure you had a Christmas tree," said Robert, beaming.

As soon as the doors on the vans were slid open, children of all ages spilled out, with Robert's parents and eldest siblings bringing up the rear, including his sister Flory, back from Estonia; she had small children hanging and clinging to her, clearly delighted to have their big sister and aunt home. Robert hugged his sister as best he could around the human limpets.

"Good to have you back, sis."

"Good to be back, little bro. You ready to join forces and mess with Nemo?"

"You bet your candy-canes I am. Let the pranks begin!"

Robert's nan was last to alight from the van, holding tightly on to Pod's arm. Robert and Miranda rushed over to greet her.

"Hello, Bertie my boy!" his nan trilled. "And Paint Girl is here too, how lovely. Are you two stepping out together officially now?"

Robert laughed. "Yes, Nan, we are officially stepping out together."

"How lovely. Make him take you to the local dance hall on Baker Street," she said to Miranda. "They have the best bands there. That's where I met Grandad, you know!"

Miranda smiled and nodded. The dance hall on Baker Street had been knocked down in 1963 to make way for a Co-op, but Nan didn't need to know that.

"You look so like your grandad, Bertie. He was a handsome devil too, a real looker!"

Miranda looked at Robert and he grimaced. He had loved his grandad but when he'd known him, he was no looker; a chain-smoker with Brylcreemed hair, no bottom teeth and a wheezing cough, like a tractor engine being started in a blizzard.

It took a while to get the Christmas tree off the roof of the van and situated in its new home, to the right of the path just before you reached the front door. Tara and all the Barlow children were let loose on the decorating. By the time Bill plugged in the lights and lit it up, the tree looked like a tinsel bomb had exploded all over it.

"It's like a migraine," said Robert.

"On steroids," added Sam.

"It certainly makes a statement," said Laurence.

"You're just jealous because none of you have got a tree adorned with every pigment on the colour wheel outside your house," said Milly.

Laurence grimaced, laughing, and said: "Aha, yeah, that's what it is!"

At 6.35 p.m. Jasper, who had been keeping watch from his bedroom window, announced that Dad was just rounding the corner into the cul-de-sac now. Bill slipped into the garage ready to flick the main switch. It would have been futile to try and make Robert's family be quiet, but the speakers hanging out of the front room window began to blast out "Mary's Boy Child" by Boney M, which helped to drown them out. Just as Dad came into view, Jasper shouted, "Now!" and Bill flicked the switch.

The effect was dazzling. The house and garden were awash with light. Projected stars danced over the walls and fairy lights twinkled from the fascias and in the trees and hedges, which had been liberally wound with lights by Tara and Nadia. The multiple jolly Santas dotting the lawn glowed red and white, while eight life-size reindeer – one with a red pulsing nose – stood proudly, their dark golden fur lit from within. The berry lights woven through the dark green leaves of the garland around the door frame flickered invitingly.

All eyes were fixed on Milly's dad. For his part, he stood on the street gazing up at the house, a bunch of flowers hanging limply in one hand, his woollen overcoat buttoned up over the suit, which hadn't seen much action in the last few months. On his face was a smile of the purest pleasure.

A hush had fallen over the scene, and even the Barlows were uncharacteristically quiet. Milly's mum made her way down the garden path to meet her husband, her cardigan pulled tightly around her. "Do you like it?" she asked tentatively.

Milly could see her dad's eyes glistening in the twinkling lights. "It's the best thing I've ever seen!" he said, pulling her into a hug and kissing her hair.

To Milly's astonishment, everyone erupted into a round of applause, including their neighbours, who had ventured over to check out the competition – which by the way, was pretty stiff! Mum stepped aside and Dad opened his arms wide. Milly, Tara and even Jasper rushed forward for a group hug. "I love you guys," he said.

"Do you think you got the job?" Jasper asked as Dad loosened his bear-like grip on them.

"I find out Monday," said Dad. "But I feel cautiously optimistic. Unlike this," he said, waving his arms about to encompass house and guests, and shouting, "About which I feel positively exuberant!"

Everyone cheered at that and Bill produced several bottles of Prosecco, which he and Sam's mum proceeded to open, while Milly's mum gathered all the glasses she could find from the kitchen. Robert's mum had brought fifteen large cartons of chocolate milkshake, which Robert and Miranda helped to distribute amongst the under eighteens.

Milly's dad wandered about the garden, nodding appreciatively at the handiwork and declaring loudly that the King of Christmas was back in town, and that everyone who had helped could be his Christmas elves.

The snow began to fall, thick and fast, quickly covering over the footprints of many trampling elves. Children in bobble hats and brightly coloured scarves ran wild about the garden, overexcited by the fat white flakes, which stuck to their mittens and noses, while the adults laughed and joked and drank too much Prosecco.

Laurence came up behind Milly and slipped his arms round her waist. "How is this Christmas working out for you so far?" he whispered.

Milly could feel the warmth of his breath and the soft brush of his lips against her neck. She shivered and not because of the cold.

"It's shaping up to be my Best Christmas Ever," she said, smiling.

@off-centre-oddity

What is magic?

I have always felt that Christmas brings its own magic. But this year I have discovered that Christmas magic is not some ethereal festive sorcery but rather human-made alchemy.

It's people who make the magic; I make it, you make it, we all make the magic.

Every kind word to a stranger or a friend, every extra tin put in the food bank collection, every toy given to someone who wouldn't otherwise get one, every hot drink handed to a person without a home, is a little bit of magic. All those small acts of kindness are accumulative, you can feel it in the air, the more kindness we push out into the world the bigger the magic grows.

The magic of Christmas is a self-fulfilling prophecy; the prospect of magic makes us behave with more kindness, and our kindness makes us feel the magic.

I was sceptical about the Christmas magic this year. I wasn't sure it would be visiting me at all. But the random – and often not so random – acts of kindness all around me, by friends and strangers, created more than enough magic to sweep me up when I wasn't feeling it.

What can I say? I'm a Christmas dweeb. I love it. And I'll count my blessings, every one.

Acknowledgements

When the marvellous Yasmin Morrissey from Scholastic and my super-agent Chloe Seager asked me if I'd like to write a YA Christmas rom-com, I couldn't get my YES PLEASE! out fast enough. Thank you, wonder-women, for giving me this chance and for your faith in me.

The thing about writing a book is that it is so much more than a person typing away at a laptop. A book doesn't become a book at all without a huge team of dedicated people working behind the scenes to make it happen. And with this book, everyone was working to a super-tight deadline. So, believe me when I say that the following 'thank you's come from the bottom of my heart.

Huge thanks to Ruth Bennett, my editor, who has supported me right the way through this process and helped me to grow my characters into three-dimensional personalities. Thank you for making this book better. And also for dealing with my panic-emails with warmheartedness and calm.

Tanya Byrne, I am forever grateful to you for being my sensitivity reader. Thank you for giving me so much of your time. I am more appreciative of your guidance than words can express. I have learned a lot from you.

Thank you to my copyeditor Susila Baybars for making sure everything made sense and for keeping my continuity in check. And to Pete Matthews for being an excellent and vigilant proof-reader – my excessive use of semi-colons knows no bounds!

My thanks go to Hannah Love, Harriet Dunlea and Rebecca Gillies for being publicity and marketing superstars and propelling this book out into the wide world. I cannot tell you how much I appreciate your kindness in guiding me through things that take me out of my comfort zone when I am being a complete nervous nelly!

Jamie Gregory and Liam Drane, thank you so much for designing the cover of this book – just to look at it is an explosion of Christmas joy! And to Lucy Page, Georgi Russell and Leanne Burke, thank you for enthusiasm and hard work in getting this book out there!

To my nieces, Lily and Amelia, thank you for being ever ready to answer my weird WhatsApp messages that always seemed to begin: "As a teenager, what would you say to this..." even when you are out with your friends! You are amazing, the world is so lucky to have you in it.

Thanks to my mum and my sister Linzi for being my first readers, and to my dad, who taught me from an early age that books are things to be revered. Thank you to my friends for putting up with me being completely unavailable while I've been hidden away writing.

To my husband Dom and my sons Jack and Will, thank you for your unending encouragement and for being proud of me even when I doubt myself – I couldn't do it without you.

Finally, thank you, dear reader, for picking up this book and taking the time to read it, you'll never how thankful I am for you.

About the Author

Jenni Jennings lives in a small seaside town in Kent with her husband, their children having left home for big adventures. She is obsessed with Christmas, candles, and flouncy dresses, and loves reading and walks along the beach. Jenni attended Canterbury Christ Church University as a mature student and graduated with a BA in Creative and Professional Writing. Throughout her many

~~the years – waitress, cruise consultant, auxiliary~~